# THE EAGLE'S FAVOUR

## Robert Vaughan

UK BookPublishing.com

Editing, design, typesetting and publishing by UK Book Publishing

www.ukbookpublishing.com

ISBN: 978-1-916572-73-7

# THE
# EAGLE'S
# FAVOUR

# AUTHOR BIO

Robert Vaughan is a native of Yorkshire, who has lived, visited, and worked in numerous countries around the world. These experiences have shaped his love for cultural diversity, open-mindedness, and for the dignity of all members of the human family. He has worked for many years as a human rights officer with the United Nations and these experiences have helped shape his perspectives and this book. He has a firm belief that with imagination, and political will, a better world is possible.

*The views expressed herein are those of the author and do not necessarily reflect the views of the United Nations.*

# CHAPTER

## 1

"Ah Werner, it's about time. We were wondering if you were ever going to make it," said Helmet. As Werner strode into the dimly lit, damp room, a thick smell of stale ale, cigarettes and day-old sweat hit his nostrils. A pungent smell, that was offensive to the nostrils, until you got used to it. The people milled around, shuffling around each other in a semi-dance like state, enough to be able to move but never to touch. A cheeky grin flashed onto his face as he saw the smiling, familiar, fat, red face of Helmet sitting in his rocking chair next to the stone fire. Helmet was always well dressed in a downtrodden way; it was obvious his clothes must have been expensive when he purchased them. His shoes were hanging off his feet, as he never put them on properly now due to his age and, as he called it, his gammy knees. His shirt looked like it hadn't seen an iron in years. Still, though, Werner thought, he did have an air of decadence to him, in the same way the old tramps had down the local park.

"Helmet, always a pleasure never a chore," Werner said.

"So, I was going to have my usual but as it's your turn, my boy, for being frightfully late again, I will have a double of the barkeeper's finest Scotch," Helmet spluttered.

It was clear to Werner that Helmet had already been 'enjoying a drop' for quite some time and was in the mood to 'have a few sherbets' as he so often remarked. Helmet was a fat, ageing, grey-haired man whom Werner had known for some good twenty years. Any other person probably would not have gotten a drink so easily, but there was something about Helmet that Werner instinctively warmed to. Like a stranger in the street who you automatically feel a connection to, but cannot for the life of you work out why, that was Helmet. Werner had pondered on his fondness for Helmet many times and concluded that it was his fatherly qualities or maybe just that he presented a person from a different time in history, one that seemed a lot simpler and more at ease with themselves. Sitting at the round wooden oak table were Helmet and Werner's regular drinking partners, Hans and Wolfgang. Hans was a thin, tall bean of a man, who didn't make much of an impression when Werner first met him many moons ago. Werner remembered that his initial impression of Hans was not great and even asked Helmet who the tall dullard in the corner was on his first meeting. Like a fine wine though, or eating olives, Hans grew on Werner – there was a certain upper-class quality that working and middle-class people just can't seem to hate about the high orders in society. He constantly referred to the 'commoners' with hateful glee, just itching to share his latest thoughts on the 'lower orders' of society. Wolfgang, on the other hand, was a different kettle of fish. He had an uneasy air to him like he was never comfortable in his own skin, the way his glasses slid down his overly pointed Roman nose used to always fill Werner with suspicion and a little dread. Werner couldn't even remember how Wolfgang came to join their merry gang in the first place – was he invited, or was he just another bar fly waiting to land on an adopted family?

"Okay, okay, I know the rules, you don't half know how to take the piss, don't you. What is everybody else having? Wolfgang, pint of vodka? Hans, what can I get you, a bottle of champagne?" Werner replied sarcastically.

"Come on, Helmet, have some consideration for the lad, it's not payday and times are hard right now. I tell you what, Werner, as I am feeling flush, I will shout you your round and you can sort me out on payday," offered Hans.

Werner listened to Hans's offer with no intention of accepting it. Hans would often offer to cover the rounds when he knew the others were hard up; it wasn't that he was trying to show off his wealth, he just had that generous nature that men have when they have no financial woes. He remembered a conversation he once overheard Hans having with a friend. The friend's boy had been asking his father for some more money so that he could have another strawberry jam crepe, and Hans's friend was getting frustrated with the boy. 'Listen, I've told you, you have had one already. I am not buying you anymore,' the man said. To this Werner remembered Hans saying, 'come on, it's only money, I will buy you another'. On hearing this Hans's friend got mad: 'Hans, you can't just keep buying him things, he needs to learn the value of money!' To this day, Werner would never forget Hans's reply: 'money has no value'. This, Werner thought, was profoundly Hans to the core and a message that maybe all humanity needed to learn; then again, it's easy to be philosophical about money when you have it.

"No, a deal is a deal, I know the rules of the house, the last one in gets the drinks in. I've been coming here long enough to know you mugs ain't going to let me off," Werner said.

"Right you are, then I will have a stein of Kaltenberg and I am sure Wolfgang will also join me in one," Hans noted.

It always made Werner chuckle that Hans would drink lager with the rest of the guys – he was more at home with a sherry or a gin and tonic, but for some reason, he felt the need to drink the commoner's brew when he was with the guys. Werner never knew if it was a need for acceptance or a need to just put the others at ease; either way, he thought, he shouldn't question it, it was a lot cheaper than buying from the top shelf.

"So, what's the word around the campfire? Please tell me someone got some action last weekend? My god, I am climbing the walls right now, I haven't had sex in weeks," Werner said.

"Werner, you need to get a grip, my boy, this obsession with sex is going to be the end of you! Honestly, you young lads, sometimes I think all you ever have on your brain are women. You know there are other wonders in the world, other beauties that just have a pulse. One day I will have an intelligent conversation in this stinking excuse for a pub, and I tell you when I finally do, I just hope you lot will be here to witness it," Hans said.

"Hans, for god's sake get a hold of yourself, what else is there to life?" Werner said.

"No comment!" said Hans.

"My point exactly. Now back to the matter at hand, so anyone?" said Werner.

On hearing how the conversation was going Werner could see, Klaus had a little wry smile, indicating to the group that he had had some kind of action over the weekend.

"Well, guys, much as I would like to kiss and tell, I don't think a German gentleman such as myself should be sharing details, especially when it involves a lady that is so close to all of our hearts," said Klaus.

"So, are you saying you have finally won the wager, or is this hot air we are hearing?" asked Hans.

"Yeah, Klaus, are we going to hear about how you almost got Margot into bed or are there actual results behind this story?" said Werner.

"All I will say, boys, is she has a smile on her face for a reason, make no mistake," said Klaus.

"You're full of shit, we all know she is after pretty boy Hans, touching his hand, offering him free drinks, dropping the old wink now and then, he's clearly her favourite," said Werner.

"Well, I couldn't exactly take a picture but if you don't believe me why don't you go to the bar and ask her yourself," said Klaus.

"Leave this to me, young men; in a delicate situation like this it requires a discreet yet classy touch," said Hans.

Werner's eyes followed Hans as he left for the bar. Just watching Margot's reaction to Hans's questions, Werner could see from her face Klaus was telling the truth; it was in her eyes. Werner could always remember his father saying that to read a woman you needed to look deep into her eyes as they were the secret passages to the soul.

"For fuck's sake, how the hell did you manage that? In fact, fuck it, I don't even want to know. Here are my ten marks," said Werner.

"What can I say, when it comes to the use of the beef bayonet you either have it or you don't, and you guys are not even close!" said Klaus.

"So, congratulations are in order then, I see from Margot's beaming glow she was extremely satisfied by a certain someone's performance," said Hans.

"Well, I wouldn't say *extremely satisfied*, but I didn't hear any complaints, that's for sure," said Klaus.

"Well, I am impressed, I always thought I was in the running, guess if you snooze you lose; anyway, I am a man of my word so here are your ten Marks, and don't spend it all at once," said Hans.

"You know, Hans, I am sure you could have scored with Margot had you only just made the effort, she was interested, I mean with your flashy suits, blond hair, and blue eyes you are just the picture of a German playboy," said Werner.

"Looks can be deceiving, Werner, I can be a shy lad when I want to be," said Hans.

"I don't feel too bad for you anyway, it's not like you need the money," said Werner.

"Look, can we just stop talking about this? I am fed up with hearing about Margot and how she jumped into bed with the worst welder who ever walked the Deutsche Arbeit factory floor," shouted Werner.

"Isn't someone a little bitter? Annoyed at wasting their hard-earned cash on cinema tickets? Yeah, that's right, Margot told me the whole story, and just to let you know the old yawn and drop the arm trick has been around since the dawn age," said Klaus.

"Oh, Werner, you didn't try that move, did you? You couldn't pull a dead weed out of the garden with that one!" said Hans.

"ALRIGHT, alright, can we just drop it now? I am sick of this whole conversation, Klaus wins okay, okay, yeah I lost! He's amazing, his dick's bigger, he's the real man, whatever! We have all paid, so can we for fuck's sake just stop talking about how wonderful he is! What were you guys talking about anyway?" said Werner.

"Whilst you three were boring everyone to death with your lowbrow conversation regarding our less than scrupulous barmaid, myself and Wolfgang were discussing something that is clearly not for you gents – the results of the local elections and how we voted. Wolfgang here was telling me that he voted for the National Socialist German Workers Party, while I being an old warhorse went for the local candidates from the Social Democratic Party of Germany," said Helmet.

"It's all in our history, you see, gentlemen, since being employed at the library I have had hours to read the latest scientific journals, books on our country's history and where we stand in the world, in terms of international relations and how other countries see us. If we are to be a truly great nation with an empire that can rival that of the British or the French, then we need to follow the latest science and use the superior brains that God has given us," said Wolfgang.

"Only yesterday I was reading some of the latest work by Professor Fritz Lenz and Professor Eugen Fischer. They argued that the Europeans' brain is far superior to that of the Africans' or the Asians' due to how we have evolved. Just look at what the white races have achieved as opposed to the others – we created the railways and all other modern means of transport, modern medicine, political theory, and philosophy. I mean, there isn't one area of human endeavour that hasn't been created or shaped by the Europeans. What the party is saying is that if we come together our nation can get back on its feet and be the global player it should be. Klaus, even your beloved Karl Marx would agree. I don't have any love for his teaching, but one can see based on the scientific data we have available today that only a European could come up with such radical thinking," said Wolfgang.

"Hang on a minute, Wolfgang. Karl Marx was a revolutionary, who wrote about a better kind of society that aimed to improve the lives of the working classes, and with respect to all of us, apart from dare I say it Hans, his teaching would create a better Germany that wouldn't lead to us always being told what to do by some rich, elitist group of society. Would my life get better if the fascists take power? I am guessing it wouldn't and all I would do is swap one dictator for another; whichever way you look at it, the government always seems to have its foot on the working man's throat," said Klaus.

"Exactly, that is what I am saying to you. If we all come together then we can achieve something for the greater good but in the right way. Who the hell wants some uneducated foreman running the country? Certain things need to be learned if you are to manage a country and an economy successfully. Also, think about what Herr Marx is suggesting: why would I work hard when others are not, just to share the profits of my labour with some lazy freeloader?" said Wolfgang.

"Wolfgang does have a point, Klaus – only tonight on the tram I was thinking to myself that things seem to be more efficient and well managed since the party started taking control of the local council," said Hans.

"Yeah, he might have a point and yes things like the railways and roads have improved under the party, but these things could have improved under any government if the political will had been there. Let's just think about what we are all giving up for these clean roads. Our right to vote for our own representative seems to keep getting smaller, more and more we see executive orders coming from the top, and not the people, and that's not to mention the policies the party has against certain groups of society like the Jews, homosexuals, or the Gypsies," said Klaus.

"Well, the Jews and Gypsies have always been a menace to our society, all the Jews care about is making money, taking jobs and companies that could be owned by real Germans, and swindling the poor like us out of our wages. Do you know how the Jews came to be so rich? I bet you don't. It's because years ago the Church told all Christians that making money from lending was wrong, so who decided to profit from this – yes, you got it, folks, the Jews, who else? As for the Gypsies, don't get me started on them, they turn up with their caravans, looking for easy ways to steal and con people rather than working like the rest of us. A group of them passed through my village once, within a day all the hanging gardens and flowers were stolen. A friend also told me that they went to the local park and stole all the ducks and geese. As for the homosexuals, I think we can all agree that their immoral behaviour needs to be stamped out at every turn, they are morally corrupt and should be punished for their choice of lifestyle," said Wolfgang.

"Well, as a man who enjoys the good life, I am not sure I have much of an opinion on the Jews and the Gypsies as I do not come across them all that much, but I have to agree with Wolfgang when it comes to the homosexuals. There is often talk of their foul behaviour at some of the more glamorous parties I have been to, and indeed, I have heard that even some of the government ministers tend to play for the wrong team. Of course, a gentleman such as myself would never mention any names, that is just crass, but the quicker these parasites in our society are dealt with, the quicker we will all live in a more peaceful, moral country the way the good Lord intended," said Hans.

"Well, I think we are all in agreement with you there, Hans, that's for sure," said Wolfgang.

"We all can see who Wolfgang voted for, but I am interested to hear from our old self-proclaimed warhorse, so come on, Helmet, who did you vote for?" said Klaus.

"Boys, I can still remember that hell I was sent to in France, and I can tell you that if the country keeps on its current course, we will be at war, a place I would not like to see any of you. Trust me, fellas, it cannot be described; all I will say is things like seeing your friend's head blown off or the smell of rotting corpses doesn't leave you, following you like a millstone around your neck," said Helmet.

"You ask your father, Werner, he could tell you all about it being the great hero that he is. As for the Jews, Gypsies, and homosexuals, well when you get to my age things become much simpler. Who cares if the Jews are making money? If the German working class wasn't so lazy, they could open their own companies and compete with the Jews. After all, isn't that what the free market is all about, voting with your feet or pocketbooks. And the homosexuals, what difference does it make to me? What happens in the privacy of someone's home is none of my business," said Helmet.

"The Gypsies, well maybe you have a point there, but I know they are not all bad, what about Jacob Anhalt, the bloke who comes in here? He's a nice enough man, always happy to shout a round, apart from him being a little darker and having a Polish name, he could be like any other German sipping on a stein and the rest of us would never know; in fact, there he is now. Let's invite him over and see what he thinks of the election results," said Helmet.

"No, no, don't bring him over here, Helmet, I hate having to make small talk," said Klaus.

"It's not small talk, it's a valid opinion for our debate. Anyway, I thought you were a man of the people, well he is the people, so let's get him over here. Jacob, Jacob, come here, lad, we would like your insightful opinion on something we are discussing," said Helmet.

On hearing Helmet's words, a well-built man emerged from the corner of the bar, near the tradesman entrance. At first, Werner couldn't make out his face as the shadows were hiding it – the dimly lit candles provided no assistance either as they were almost burnt down to the plates they were resting on. Like a tiger emerging from the jungle, all of a sudden Werner saw a face appear from behind a pack of men huddled together. Jacob was smiling as he walked over, his face not quite as white as a city resident, but like a German who had picked up a suntan on holiday, Werner thought. He was a good-looking man, with symmetrical features, apart from a small scar he had across his chin. For a moment Werner started to ponder where this scar could have come from, maybe he had it since birth, maybe it was a work-related injury, or maybe it was from a fight. Werner thought it must be from one of those bare-knuckle boxing matches he had heard so much about. They were legendary in underground circles amongst rival Gypsy families and Werner had heard that the fighters could become rich if they were to survive the 25-round matches.

"Evening, gentlemen, how can I be of service?" said Jacob.

"Well, we were just debating the election results and since the National Socialist German Workers Party got 44%, the Social Democratic Party of Germany got 18% and the communists got 13%, we wondered where you stood on the issues of Jews, homosexuals and Gypsies?" said Wolfgang.

"Well, I can't say I have that much to do with the Jewish community or any individual Jews. I see them when they come into the shop from time to time, but we never really engage in any kind of discussion. They all seem nice enough to me, always polite and curious. I don't get the hats and all the curly hair, but each to their own, I guess. As you all know, I have a little Gypsy in me, but as I am always telling my grandparents, new communities need to adapt and integrate into society if we are to be understood and if we are to prosper. I know what the average German thinks of the Gypsy, that we are all thieves and pickpockets, preying on the vulnerable, which, to a certain extent I have to agree with. I know people from the Gypsy population who have stolen and have no interest in becoming part of German society, and it saddens me. As for the homosexuals, well, you know that kind of behaviour wouldn't be tolerated in Gypsy society, we consider them as low as women; if I were to have a child who had decided to be homosexual, I tell you what I would do, I would drown him at birth!" said Jacob.

"So you agree that sometimes communities in society need to be removed for the greater good then, Jacob?" said Wolfgang.

"In terms of homosexuals, then yes, I have to say I do, Wolfgang," said Jacob.

"Oh, that reminds me, I did say I would drop by my grandmother's house on the way home, she's far on the other side of town so I best be on my way," said Jacob.

"No problem, Jacob, lovely to see you as always," said Helmet.

Jacob walked away from the group with a strong stride; he had a confidence in his walk, the kind only a successful man has.

"You see, as I said, insightful and very level-headed that one, look at what he said even about his own people, that they need to integrate. If only all Gypsies could be like Jacob there wouldn't be any need for the party to even have policies to deal with them," said Wolfgang.

"I am afraid I will also have to leave now, fellas; much as I have enjoyed our little discussion I have the last screening of Friedenstag to get to and you know how Penelope hates to be kept waiting," said Hans.

"Sure, you have a good time, Hans, and give Lady Penelope a kiss from me," said Helmet.

"I think I will also call it a night, gang, I have an early shift tomorrow and I can't be late again," said Werner.

# CHAPTER
## 2

The tram rolled into Ahrweiler. The place was a welcome oasis of peace for Werner as each part of the village held some kind of childhood memory. The green plush forest in which he would play with the other village children, the small shops which only ever seemed to have their products on certain days of the month. The dark, dimly lit cobble roads, streets that seemed like a time warp back to a by-gone era, and of course, the church and bar at the centre crossroads of the village, the two institutions that would always survive. The place had not changed and probably never would.

Walking past the post office Werner remembered his first kiss with a local village girl, called Heidi. It was nothing to write home about, he was only 13 and had no idea what he was doing at the time, but Heidi like any good German woman took charge of the situation and showed him the ropes. Heidi had moved when Werner was just 15 – her father was a farmer and was said to have relocated to the Bavaria region as he had always talked about producing his own beer. Werner wondered, where was she now?

Werner's father lived in a hilly area on the outskirts of the village, only a 15-minute walk from the tram station.

It had started raining and the night mist was settling in. Werner enjoyed the rain; it was the only time the streets were completely empty, the solitude always brought him comfort.

Werner cut through the Beckenbawer family's vineyard. The grapes had all gone by now, all that was left were the little brown bamboo sticks that the Beckenbawers used to keep the vines from hitting the ground. As Werner stopped for a cigarette, the rain did its best to extinguish his flame. He noticed some shadows moving in the window, their reflection dancing around on the back wall from the light from the fire. He couldn't see clearly but it looked like a father and his daughter embracing. What a feeling that must be, he thought, to have someone to hold, who had nothing but unconditional love for you, and you to them.

Walking up the garden path, Werner could see that the roses his father had once given such care and attention to were either dead or on their last legs, as was much of the flowerbed his mother had loved so much. The apple and pear trees were overgrown and had fruit rotting at their base. The wooden windows were peeling, and the stone walls were alive with green moss.

"That you, Werner?" said Werner's father.

Werner's father emerged from the creaking wooden side door. He still looked strong, but now used a wooden cane to help balance his movements. His hands were like old garden spades, large and strong but with cracks where his shrivelled-up flesh now remained. His face was still as stern as it had been when Werner was a child, his hair now a patchwork of black, grey, and silver. His eyes so piercing that Werner always thought he could burn a hole straight through a man's chest.

"Yeah, Dad, well who else were you expecting at this time?" said Werner.

"Don't get smart, and why are you dripping all over my living room floor?"

"In case you haven't noticed, Dad, it's chucking it down outside and as you had to go and buy the house furthest from the tram stop, I didn't have much choice."

"As I told you a million times it was your mother's idea. She liked to keep her eye on all the neighbours. She could be a real busybody, God rest her soul."

"She certainly did like to know what everyone was up to, that's for sure. It doesn't seem the same without her informing me what mischief Mr Hahn or the Hahn kids have been up to. The fire looks low on logs, should I go to the outhouse and get some more?" asked Werner.

"You might as well as you're all wet already, I guess, oh, and try to get the ones that are a little damp for the inner walls of the fire, it's better that way, you know. It means the dry ones will burn well in the middle and the damp ones will dry out over the next hours and then catch fire."

"Dad, I have stacked that fire a thousand times, I think I know which logs to get and which to leave."

"I was only trying to help, honestly you young people can be such hard work these days, you think you know it all with your flash uniforms and your goose-stepping around town like you were constantly on the march to London."

The outhouse was a hundred yards from Werner's father's house. The logs lay bare on the stone floor in the outhouse. The place had a musky smell, which made Werner think of the times he and his father would go on a fishing trip in the Grobe Dhunntalsperre region. His mother would pack them bratwurst and sauerkraut for lunch, which they would wash down with a bottle of Keufer and a ginger ale. They were some of the happiest times of Werner's childhood, the lake would be warm enough to take a swim and they would often come back with a good catch.

The moonlight was now fully laid upon the garden, shining on the slugs and snails that were slowly making their way also up the path towards Werner's father's door. Just then Werner realised that this was the perfect opportunity to have a couple of quick burns on a cigarette, especially if he was to endure his father's constant talking the whole night.

"Well, Dad, here you go: some dry, some damp. Should I put them on, or are you going to move out of that rocking-chair sometime this century?"

"I have moved, here I made you a cup of tea. You can have it if you give me one of those smokes you have been trying to hide all night."

"What makes you think I have any cigarettes on me?"

"Don't play dumb, I can smell the bloody things on you. I know the doctor says they are bad for my cough but if I can survive the war in France, I can manage a little tobacco. I don't want to hear any more about it, just hand me one over."

"OK, fine, Dad, you can have one, here. But don't be telling everyone in the village I made your cough worse,

I can do without their disapproving looks," said Werner.

"What are you talking about? The people in the village love you now you started working for the military-political wing of the party. They are certainly not going to criticise a son who brings his father a couple of guilty pleasures. Now drink your tea and tell me what's going on in the outside world. When is your dear leader going to beat those godforsaken Brits and take their empire?"

"There is a long way to go, Dad, we are fighting on all fronts right now and the leader knows what is best for Germany!"

"What about you and Catti? Any chance I am going to see some grandkids? You know you are going to have to make an honest woman of her someday, don't you, you can't have your cake and eat it, son. Remember she is the daughter of a senior official, it would be great for your career and she is a pretty girl to boot. My advice is to get her pregnant and married as soon as possible."

"You have told me this a thousand times, Dad, I know what you think, and I know you are right. Once this war is won, I can focus on me and Catti, but for now, I have to concentrate on my work. The party is very demanding and is frequently asking us to go above and beyond our day-to-day duties. We have just started on this new programme regarding the Jews. They are now to be relocated to southern Poland where they will be used for labour to help in the war effort; I think this should be a major turning point. We might as well use them, it's like the leader said ever since he took power: 'we need to take the useless, problematic, and unproductive and turn them into machines that can be used to make Germany a great European Empire'."

"I have been following this with some interest, Werner. I remember the Jewish family from the village, you remember you used to play with their son Isaac when you were a child? I wonder whatever happened to them. They were such a nice family, always inviting me to try the latest harvest – you know they made some of the greatest wines I have ever tasted? I remember Mr Goldschmidt telling me the key to a great wine was tender loving care from the moment you had the seed in your hand till the time you stepped on it with your foot. What a great man he was, I do hope he and his family are doing well."

"Dad, what have I told you? You shouldn't talk like this anymore. If someone was to hear, well we would both be in big trouble. The party does not look favourably on Jew-lovers and they definitely would not like to hear how a First World War hero was singing the praises of the local Jewish farmers!"

"Jewish this, Jewish that, what is the leader's obsession with the Jews? I thought we were at war to build a greater nation, not chasing down every minority we can get our hands on. And please do not call me a war hero, I am sick to death of you boys walking through my village saluting me like I was the leader himself. When I went to war, I was a young lad with stupid dreams of excitement, thinking I would return to a glorious nation, that would somehow provide me with all the happiness I ever wanted. Well, I will tell you what, Werner: it didn't happen. It was a complete lie and it was a bullshit war we shouldn't have even been fighting."

"Come on, Dad you don't think that, Uncle Hoffman told me of the day you picked up your medal for bravery, he said you were beaming from ear to ear."

"I didn't go to that ceremony for myself, I couldn't care less about that bloody medal. I went for the families of all those men I shared a trench with and for those who didn't come back from that stupid bloody war. I was no war hero. I never told you what I did to get that medal, did I?"

Werner could feel his hands starting to sweat and felt a little lightheaded, the kind of feeling you get when you have that early morning cigarette or a noon beer and the light catches your eyes too quickly.

"My regiment was involved in trench warfare, we fought at the Battle of Neuve Chapelle, it was a hellish place. There was hardly any food, we were constantly hungry, the rats were so big and so desperately hungry too that if you fell asleep with your boots off they would run towards you and take massive bites out of your toes or any other body parts they could spot. I saw so many young men die of treatable diseases, we used to joke with one another that the British should just leave us here and go home. We would be none the wiser and eventually end up eating each other. The worst thing though, Werner, the worst was the smell, and the mud – imagine rotting corpses and constantly trying to remove the black filth from your fingernails. Baths were non-existent and we used to collect rainwater from buckets we had set up on the roofs just to be able to wash our privates. It was like Hell on Earth.

"Anyway, the day I won that medal was much like any other. I had woken up earlier than usual as I was always catching my head on a rusty nail sticking out of the guy's bunk above me. That particular day I caught it right down my cheek – you see, you can still see a faint line down my cheek now."

"Oh yeah I always wondered what that was," said Werner.

"That's how I got it. Anyway, I was up and to keep busy I was doing some early exercises, then the sergeant came into our barracks and informed me that I and my regiment were going over the top that night. I woke the guys up and told them the news. They were just as scared as me, yet we didn't say anything. We knew the British guns were just over the horizon and that every regiment that had gone over the top had fallen without gaining any land.

"Honestly, Werner, that war was almost ludicrous; it would have been funny if it wasn't so tragic. We would take one step forward and two steps back, losing thousands of men, and the generals didn't even bat an eyelid. The evening arrived, and we fixed our bayonets in preparation to go over the top. I remember thinking what a farcical situation it was, I was attaching a knife to go against a machine gun and attempting to run over a field full of landmines. I heard the first whistle and the first round of soldiers ran towards the enemy. I couldn't see because I was at the bottom of the ladder, but I heard the machine gunfire and the screams of all those young boys. Then I heard the second whistle and it was my turn. In a flash I was running toward the British, firing as I ran, then I felt this rip and pain on my leg – I had hit some barbed wire, which caused me to trip and smash my face on one of the rocks. When I slowly came to my senses, I awoke to find the battle was over – everyone who had gone over the top with me was either gunned down dead or was seriously injured. I managed to crawl towards my barracks but as I did I came across Dieter, one of the youngest of my regiment – he had had half his face blown off. I managed to drag him over the top and to the safety of our barracks. I was sure the British could see me moving but I wasn't left with much choice – it was either stay there like a sitting duck or pull myself through the mud to safety.

"When our Oberst heard that we were the only surviving two he lavished us with praise. Dieter couldn't hear any of this as he was still shellshocked and had been transferred to the army hospital which was 20 miles behind the front line. The other soldiers credited me with saving Dieter's life and for managing to 'dodge the British guns', but in truth, all I had done was run forward, got knocked out, and crawled like a beaten dog back home. Now does that make me a war hero?"

"So, what are you telling me, that for all these years, you have been living a lie, just walking around pretending to be some great hero when all you really were was a lucky guy who happened to trip on some barbed wire? What a complete joke! So you are just a charlatan. All I can say is it's a good thing Mother isn't alive to hear," said Werner.

"I never asked for the honour, Werner. When I returned home all I wanted to do was raise a family with your mother; it was the army who pushed me into accepting it, and then I started receiving letters from all the families of the other guys who were killed that day. They wrote of how me being alive gave them hope and made them think of their sons. After reading them I felt that if it gave these people closure and helped them to move on, then it was worth a small lie."

"That's just it though, isn't it, it's all one big lie! How can you even live with yourself? Don't you hate yourself for not telling the truth? You could at least have told me and Mum what happened that day."

"Werner, often it's better to live with a lie than to hurt those around you, sometimes things are better left unsaid."

"I don't agree, I think you are one big faker who has relished the fact people looked up to him when deep-down you are nothing but a low life conman."

"Okay, well if we are doing this maybe I should tell you some home truths and then you can live a lie. You are so stupid you have been living one all your life and haven't even realised it, but I know the truth and I am telling you, you better learn to live with lies also."

"What the hell are you talking about? I have nothing to hide, I'm an open book!" said Werner.

"Do you remember Grandfather Steadman? Well, he was half Jewish, that's right, half Jewish! What are you going to do with that information? Something tells me you are going to keep it to yourself. I can't see the party being so happy that their most hated adversary is actually in their ranks!"

"This is pathetic. You know this is complete bullshit! If we had Jewish blood in our family's history I would have known about it!"

"If you don't believe me then check it out yourself, you can probably find it all in the local library! That's right, you are a JEW, JEW, JEW and there is nothing you can do about it!"

Hearing the words of his father, Werner's face constricted into a tight ball, red flashed over his cheeks and the vein was popping on his forehead.

Werner grabbed at the nearest object, which happened to be the steel fire poker, he struck it over his father's head with all the strength he could muster, each blow stronger than the last. His father fell, but Werner continued to strike him, blood and flesh flying, with every hit. Until his father was not speaking but just lying in a puddle of his own blood.

# CHAPTER 3

"Hey, Bridgette, I want to shut up the shop soon, are you done with all the stock-taking yet?" said Jacob.

The shop was a general store, located in a poor part of the city. It was not the largest business in the area for food and other essentials, but it had a friendly, welcoming feel. The large strip lights lit up the shelves, highlighting the bread, eggs, and flour available. Since the political situation had gotten progressively worse, Jacob had to dim the lights more and more just so that his customers didn't realise that the stock shortages were getting closer and closer.

"Be right with you, Jacob, I'm almost done," said Bridgette.

Bridgette was a shy, mouse of a woman who Jacob had employed for several years. She was very skilled in accounting and always had her nose buried in a book. Jacob remembered thinking that she must have gone through hundreds of books during the time from when he hired her. She had a slim frame and long brown hair. She was pretty in a classic way – her cheekbones were high and she had an infectious smile, which never failed to also make Jacob smile, despite how his day had been going.

"Good. I want to get off early today so that I can go visit my grandma, you know how she is, she's getting on a bit and I don't like to think of her all alone up there, especially ever since the neighbours started all their problems and accusations," said Jacob.

"For Heaven's sake what has happened now? She's lived there for years, hasn't she?"

"It's difficult to say. Ever since the party started their campaign for social change and inclusion, the villagers have become more and more hostile to her. They put signs outside her caravan saying 'go back to your own country', excrement smeared on her front door, and she even had a rock thrown through her bedroom window. I have to be honest, I am getting really worried about her safety, but she just won't listen to me – you know what old people are like, they just can't be reasoned with sometimes."

"Try not to worry so much, Jacob, the party has said that anyone cooperating with them will not be harmed and nomadic people will eventually be resettled in a proper house. People are just mad because they think all Gypsies are lazy thieves which we know they're not."

"I know, Bridgette, in many ways I agree with the party that the old ways and lifestyles are very much out-dated; the number of arguments I have had with my grandma about this, you wouldn't believe. She just will not move. I've asked and asked if she will move into my apartment in town, but will she? Will she heck!"

"Jacob, not all people are as adapted to German life as you are. I mean, you grew up here and don't have any of the old bad influences from Romania."

"Poland," Jacob corrected.

"Ah yes... Poland, exactly. So you see, your grandma is just doing what comes naturally, isn't she eighty-three as well? I bet she is simply happy to be getting up in the morning and at that age, who isn't set in their ways?"

"I guess you're right, maybe I am too harsh on the old girl, but she has to learn, the party has said that they aim to get all Gypsies out of the rural lifestyle and make them part of the new society they are trying to build."

"You just need to be careful, Jacob, things can change very easily these days and nothing is set in stone. Didn't you say that half the camp residents have already moved away from the site and even from Germany?"

"Oh come on, Bridgette, don't you have any faith in the law and the party? Can you not see what they are trying to build? It's a bigger and brighter future for our country, for our children, don't you want them to grow up in a great European empire?"

"I don't have any children and neither do you, so this is all academic, isn't it? And yes, of course, I have faith in the party. I just worry as to what the actual grand design is."

"WHEN we have claimed what is ours, we will use our new power to bring other nations toward the light of civilization. Look at what the British did in India and throughout Africa: they brought trade and commerce, roads and infrastructure, and most importantly, brought rule of law to those lawless places."

"I doubt the local people in those countries see it that way, and isn't that the point though, Jacob, look at us now: we used to have a democracy; in fact, the party was voted in through democracy and now we are a one-party country involved in a war!"

"This development is needed, Bridgette, if like I said before, we are to become a great nation. Honestly, Bridgette, sometimes your comments do worry me – if you were to say them to the wrong person you could get into serious trouble."

"We don't all have your faith in the party, Jacob. What can I say? Maybe I am a bohemian at heart."

"You certainly sound like one, that's for sure, and I wouldn't worry about the country moving ahead in a one-party system. I remember my granddad telling me that Plato once said 'the best form of Government is a benign dictator' – maybe calling the leader a dictator is too much as I am sure he listens to his chief counsel, but one couldn't argue that he does not care for us all, it's almost like we are his children."

"Well, you have convinced me, Jacob, I just wonder if you can convince your grandmother."

"I'm sure I will be able to, she is a stubborn old woman at times but occasionally, very occasionally, she does listen to reason."

"Rather you than me, that's all I can say. Anyway, I'm done here so we can get off whenever you're ready."

"Finally! I thought you would never be finished!" said Jacob.

\* \* \*

He saw candlelight through the window of the caravan and smelt the roast chestnuts cooking on the metal mesh stove. Walking up the small stairs, he noticed that Boxer was missing from the outside. In all his days of visiting his grandmother, even as a child, he could not remember a single time that Boxer wasn't there, he was almost a part of the furniture.

"Hi Grandma, guess who it is? Your secret admirer!"

"Oh Jacob, you silly boy, come in quick, this is not a time for jokes, just get in quickly," said Grandma Anhalt.

"What's happened to Boxer? He finally jumped the stable, not that the poor horse ever had one in the first place," said Jacob.

"That's just it, Jacob, I can't find him. He has been missing for a couple of days now. I have walked into the village to ask if anyone has seen him but people just ignore me these days, one of them even spat in my direction and told me to go back to my own country."

Jacob could see that his grandma was worried: the wrinkles on her face were tighter than normal and her lips were curled up. Her grey hair was falling from her bandana headscarf and looked like it hadn't been washed in days. She looked to be resting against the chair and her hands were almost buried into the wooden arms.

"You're joking, right? I wonder what has happened to him and who would have taken him. Come and sit next to me on the bed, Grandma; you know that old chair is covered in splinters. There's room for both of us and I hate the fact you always move away from the stove when I come over. I'm not five anymore, I'm a grown man, I can handle a little cold from time to time."

"You're a good boy, Jacob, you know I have always said that about you, don't you? Let me just get my stick from the cupboard, you know I can't function like I used to. I know I don't look it but I'm eighty-six you know."

"Funny, I always thought you were younger. I told you, Grandma, these villagers are not as sophisticated as city people. They are quick to blame anything on people who are different. I must have told you this a thousand times, but you never seem to listen; you should have moved in with me in the city last year when the war started."

"I'm not the untrustworthy one? They are the people stealing horses – what exactly do they want with Boxer? He's old and in no shape to work anymore."

"Maybe they have eaten him?"

"Don't even joke! This isn't funny. I have had that horse even since you were a boy. Your grandad bought him, you know, as a birthday present for me."

"I am sure he will come back when he gets hungry. He probably just chewed through his ropes and decided to take a little excursion to investigate some of the other fields. Christ knows he must have seen enough of this one."

"Boxer would never just leave me, and I told you not to be blasphemous in my home. Do what you like in your own, but in here we have some respect for him!"

"Look, I am sure he will come back, but if you want, I will go and have a look around the village at first light."

"So you are staying over tonight?"

"I thought I would if you didn't mind."

"Mind, of course I don't mind, you know you are welcome to stay anytime. Oh, this is good news, it's the best news I've heard all week. You get yourself settled and have a couple of chestnuts. I wasn't going to cook a proper dinner tonight but as you are staying over, I will prepare a soup, how does that sound?"

"That sounds great, Grandma."

As Jacob's Grandma changed the cooking pot on the stove, and Jacob watched her fumble about through the cutlery drawer looking for the right spoon to use, he realised she could no longer live like this. Her hands were constantly twitching these days, with skin all ruffled up like crumpled up paper and bones that were almost transparent.

"Here we are, son, get that down you," said Grandma Anhalt.

"Thanks, Grandma."

"It's no problem, dear, once we are finished I will set the spare bed up so you can get a good night's sleep, I bet you don't get one in that apartment of yours, sounds like a nightmare with all those cars driving past."

"It's alright, you can't normally even hear them when the windows are down. I am glad though that you brought up my apartment. I know I have asked you this before, but I think it's time for you to come and live with me."

"Jacob, I have told you countless times, I am very happy where I am."

"But you have to admit, it's getting more difficult to live here, what with the villagers giving you nothing but headaches, you having to walk just to get fresh water and now Boxer leaving. Grandma, what is there here for you?"

"It's my home, Jacob, you know that, and homes are not like houses, you cannot just up sticks and move your roots."

"I thought this was a working caravan, surely that's what they are for, to be moved?"

"Don't be sarcastic, it doesn't suit you! You know what I mean, a home is more than just bricks or in my case wood on some set ground, it's about where you feel at ease, where you can sit and relax and know you are safe from the world's troubles."

"That's just it though, isn't it, the world as it is, you can't just hide away where you feel comfortable. The war as it is will affect all of us and we need to stick together. You taught me that family is the most important thing in life and that's why I am asking. I wouldn't if I didn't think it was necessary."

"I suppose you are right, son, I can't say I have enjoyed living here over the last few months. The looks I got from the villagers yesterday, they looked at me as if I were something on the bottom of their shoe."

"There, see, if you come and live with me, we can look after each other and you would also be doing me a favour. I am always working late at the shop these days and having your beautifully cooked dinner to come home to would make things much easier for me."

"I suppose it would be nice to have some company for a change and if you do need my help then I can't say no, can I?"

"Oh, you would, Grandma, you really would. So it's agreed, you will move with me to the city? We can pack up your things tomorrow and come back for the non-essential stuff in the next few days, okay?"

"Ok, son, as long as you help me come back when the war is over, and we still look for Boxer in the morning. Anyway, let's get some sleep because I am not going anywhere until we have at least searched the fields for him."

"Great, don't worry, I will be up at first light, I promise. Night, Grandma."

Jacob kissed his grandma on the forehead and helped her to bed.

"Thank you, son, you know you are an angel to me. If it wasn't for your visits, I don't know what I would have to look forward to."

"Come on, Grandma don't talk like that, you know I love coming to see you and when we live together, well, we can see each other all the time, can't we. Just think, we can play cards, I can complain about the shop and you can keep me well fed. Surely that is something to look forward to, more housework!" joked Jacob.

"Yes, that does seem appealing, doesn't it, Jacob, gosh you really can be a sarcastic little bugger sometimes. You get that from your mother, you know! Now let's get some sleep."

\* \* \*

Jacob awoke to the sound of voices. At first, he thought he was still sleeping – he often found himself waking up from a deep sleep wondering if what he had just dreamt about had happened; but this was different. As the voices got closer, Jacob slipped out of the bed and grabbed his clothes. Spotting his grandma's wooden walking stick, he grabbed it, and held it high above his head, ready to swing. He then heard a gentle knock at the caravan door.

"Mrs Anhalt, Mrs Anhalt, are you in there?" said a deep authoritarian voice.

The noise awoke Jacob's grandma from her snoring that Jacob had endured for years.

"Jacob, who could that be at this hour? I'm coming, just give me a minute to put something decent on," yelled Grandma Anhalt.

When she eventually opened the door, she saw two well-dressed men in military uniform. One was a tall slim-looking guy and the other a burly well-built man with a fat pig-like face.

"Hello Mrs Anhalt, we are from the Department of Internal Affairs. I'm sorry about the hour but I was wondering if we could ask you a few questions, it is a matter of national security," said the slim man.

"National Security, well you better come in. Would you like some tea? Jacob, put the stove back on and boil some water," said Grandma Anhalt.

"Ah, you must be Mr Jacob Anhalt. I understand you are the grandchild of Mrs Anhalt and you live at number 18 Kalker Hauptstrabe, is this correct?" asked the slim man.

"Yes, I am, how can we help you, gentlemen?" said Jacob.

"Mr and Mrs Anhalt, my name is Wolfgang Sankt. I am the head of the Köln Regional Department of Internal Affairs. I have come here tonight because of the party's new laws regarding the rights of Gypsy people and their strategic advancement in the building of our glorious nation. Are you both aware of the new laws that were signed into force at midnight last night?" said Wolfgang.

"No, we haven't heard a thing about any new laws that relate to Gypsies. What is it now, are we expected to listen to the wireless all night just in case somebody decided to mention us? What you should be doing is going down to that village and finding out what has happened to my horse. If you people spent as much time chasing criminals as you do introducing new laws, you would have this country shipshape in no time!" said Grandma Anhalt.

"Please, Mr Sankt, forgive my grandmother's tone, she has just woken up and is very old. I have a much better understanding of the laws governing our land, I'm a party member you know. I have been since the very creation of the party and have been a solid supporter of the leader through his glorious rise to the position of chancellor," said Jacob.

"Fat lot of good it has done us too, we still seem to have men waking us at 1 am, can I just go back to sleep!" said Grandma Anhalt.

"Now, Mrs Anhalt, there is no need to get upset, we have come here tonight to explain the new laws and to provide you with some very good news. We are here because we have heard about the treatment you have been receiving from the local villagers, we heard there had been some nasty incidents where you had faced physical threats. We also heard that you have suffered verbal abuse. Am I correct that you had even had a rock thrown through your window?" said Wolfgang.

"Yes, all of that is correct, Mr Sankt, some of the more recent incidents only happened a few days ago – how is it that you know so much about all this? Have you been talking to the villagers about me?"

"Mrs Anhalt, it is the Party's business to keep a watchful eye on all our citizens, the party cares about you and your well-being," said Wolfgang.

"See, didn't I tell you, Grandma, the party only wants to help people like you. I was only explaining to my grandmother tonight that the party wants to help people from the Gypsy community, isn't that right, Mr Sankt?"

"That is correct, Mr Anhalt, the party wants to help all people from the Gypsy community. As I was saying, the new laws that govern the Gypsies came into effect at midnight tonight, and as we speak there is a massive effort to enforce them throughout the country. You see, we are merely having the same conversation that will be taking place all over the country right now. The new laws say that all Gypsy villages, and citizens who are operating on illegal land, are to be relocated to more suitable dwellings. The party wants to give all Gypsy citizens a new apartment in an area of the city where they can be with others from that community so that you can enjoy your cultural and ethnic practices together and not feel any persecution from the local populace. Do you not think this would be a wonderful thing? Just think, Mrs Anhalt, you can be with others such as yourself, sing your old ethnic songs and take part in your cultural rituals, safe in the knowledge that they won't be interrupted by people who don't understand or make fun of them," said Wolfgang.

"That sounds great, doesn't it, Grandma? You can be with people of your age and talk about the old country without fear of prejudice. I wouldn't mind living there myself you know," said Jacob.

"Mr Sankt, you know I think we have met before, it was about a year ago. You were sat with Helmet Sazburgar and another group of gentlemen discussing last year's elections. Do you remember?" Jacob added.

"Now that you mention it, Mr Anhalt, I did think I had seen your face before, I seem to remember you were a big supporter of the party and the direction they were taking in regards to the Gypsies. Your views, however, on the Jews were not so in line with the party," said Wolfgang.

"Ah, it was the homosexuals; I can remember that we both had similar opinions on that!" said Jacob.

"That is correct, Mr Anhalt, I remember now, how right you were with your comments that night, I couldn't agree with you more. What did you say, they should all be killed at birth, wasn't it?" said Wolfgang.

"Oh Jacob, I hope you didn't say such evil things, why would you hate anyone, what have they ever done to you?"

"Grandma, I told you, please let me handle this. Yes, that is correct, Mr Sankt. I also seem to remember we discussed these issues over a beer – perhaps we could finish this conversation in the same way," said Jacob.

"That would be nice but alas, we have many more houses to visit tonight and my work now rarely allows me to indulge in such vices. I am glad, however, that you are both being so cooperative. It's music to my ears that you said you wished you could join your grandmother at the area we have designated for the Gypsy relocation. We are obligated to also inform you that you are being requested to go with your grandmother to the relocation site."

"I don't think I understand, you want me to go also? I have a shop and an apartment in the centre of town and what exactly am I to do with my clothes and other possessions?"

"Do not worry about that, Mr Anhalt, your clothes, goods and other possessions will be brought to you once you are given a new home in the relocation site."

"Wolfgang, is there not some way in which exceptions can be made for people who are of use to society and can be best served to work amongst the general population? I have a business that pays tax to the government, my apartment that I have worked hard for, I employ German employees, I could be much more useful to the party in the city than stuck in some village on the outskirts," said Jacob.

"I am sorry, Mr Anhalt, orders are orders, and we have been ordered to bring all people with Gypsy blood to the relocation site; exceptions cannot be made otherwise the whole plan of the leader's goes out of the window and is a waste of time," said Wolfgang.

"So, what is the great plan then in the end?" said Grandma Anhalt.

"Irradiation and purification of the nation!" said the man with the pig face. The tone of his voice was deep and spoken with absolute authority. As he said the words, he looked both Jacob and his grandmother in the eye. His face was red with anger like it had been building up over the whole conversation and was finally allowed to escape through his hateful words.

"Enough of this talk, Wolfgang, we have other families to visit tonight and I am damned if I am going to have polite conversations with all of them. You two come with us, we are going to take you to the relocation site now," said the pig-faced man.

The pig-faced man made a gesture towards the door of the caravan, signalling for Jacob and his grandmother to walk outside.

As they walked from the caravan towards the road, Jacob took his grandmother's hand. Jacob could feel that she was trembling, her face stone-cold like she had been slapped across it.

"Now, Mrs Anhalt, you go in this van, and, Mr Anhalt, you please go to the other van."

"I thought you said we would be going together, my grandmother is old and frail – surely we should go together, so that I can help her to at least get on and off the truck?"

"The men are in one truck and the women are in another, you are holding up the proceedings, just get in your allotted van so that we can get on with the process. I don't want to be here all night dealing with you people, I have my own life, you know," said the pig-faced man.

"Wolfgang please, it's small favour and you know I have always been a loyal supporter of the party, please just do this one thing for me. I don't want to see my grandmother travel alone."

"I am sorry, Jacob, it is out of my hands, now please get in the van," said Wolfgang.

Jacob slowly started to crawl up the van's ladders towards the back where he could see a metal padlocked gate and other men inside. As he turned, he let go of his grandmother's hand, and as he did they both slowly turned to each other, looking deep into each other's eyes.

"Don't worry, Grandma, just do what the men ask, and I am sure everything will be ok."

Jacob's grandmother tried to say something comforting, but nothing came; her face was blank as the gravity of the situation slowly sank in.

# CHAPTER

## 4

"Darling Penelope, are you ready? The show starts in an hour and I don't want to be late. I swear sometimes I think I need an army to drag you from that mirror. You know how the generals love to be seen with the wealthy elite and that means we have to be there to do some back-slapping and hobnobbing," shouted Hans from the bottom of the main hall stairway.

Slowly climbing up the stairs, Hans could see her outline – even Penelope's shadow had a touch of class like it was dancing to a slow rhythm in the moonlight, flickering on her golden blonde hair which seemed to make it stand out like an African sunset. Her neck was swan-like, long with a slight curve to almost accentuate her body's outline. Her dress hanging from her body like it was still on the shop rack, her long legs pointing towards the floor like sharpened swords.

"Baby, I'm so happy you like the dress. I wasn't sure if red was your colour when I first saw it, but now I know it was one of my better ideas. You look amazing, dear, the way it shows the arch of your back, it is going to make the men's jaws hit the floor when they see you. The men won't be able to keep their hands off you; you know they are a bunch of sleazy old fuckers. I'm sure General Koln will end up having a few too many brandies and touching you up," said Hans.

"Nonsense, sweetheart, he only has a quick touch, and to be honest, we need the support of the Party so it's a price we just have to pay. I might add it's one us women have been paying since the dawn of time; you men, honestly, really, you're only a few years away from still being apes."

"Fair point, you know sometimes I think it has worked to our advantage, us not getting married. If we were, I do not think we would get half the dinner invites. I must be the luckiest man in Köln as I have you all to myself!"

"That's true, darling, they just get a dance and you get me all night, how right you are, you are the luckiest man in Köln! Now stop blabbing and help me with this necklace, I can never clip it without your help, I think it's the way pearls roll around in my hand!"

As his eye followed her long elegant neck down her back to the lower part of her back, he thought to himself how so many men would love to be in his place right now. His fingers slowly clicked her necklace in place. Their eyes met in the mirror – she was sat on her makeup stool whilst he stood behind. They were both blessed with blond hair and blue eyes, the kind of features any self-respecting Aryan would kill for.

"There, darling, you are all dressed up, shall we call the driver to get him to prepare the car?" said Hans.

"Hang on, honey; don't be in such a rush. Honestly, I sometimes think you were born with your shoes on. I still have my bracelets to put on and I need to put some rouge on my cheeks. What will people say if I turn up looking like something the cat dragged in? They certainly wouldn't be asking me to dance, that's for sure," said Penelope.

"I am not even sure if I will be in the mood for dancing, you know how those things tire me out."

"Oh come on, Hans, let me have my little pleasures, I let you have yours," said Penelope.

Hans looked at Penelope with a smirk.

"Alright, if I have to then I guess I have to, it can be such hard work with you. Sometimes I think I would be better off with another woman more suited to me."

"You wouldn't be able to find one, Hans, not one who is willing to put up with all your imperfections. I think the only people in the world who would put up with you would be me and Wilfred," said Penelope.

"Really, Pen, you don't half come out with some funny statements sometimes."

"Sir, sir, please don't forget this. I got the cognac for the Commandant, you know how much he likes it. I also got some caviar for his wife, that woman loves to eat. Honestly, though, sir, these little gifts are getting harder and harder to source, I had to speak to some different suppliers and even the most reliable traders are having troubles," said Wilfred.

"Wilfred, you are a star, you know when all this trouble is finally over, we will have to use your new skills and have you set up as Germany's premier supermarket. You do seem to have a knack for it, you know," said Hans.

"He's right, you know, I fear if it hadn't been for you, Wilfred, we would be out on the street; the favours these little presents carry can't be measured in money. You are the one looking down on this house, making sure we all survive this dreadful time," said Penelope.

"You are both too kind, but you know the saying, you can't teach an old dog new tricks and I dread to think what my age is in dog years. Now you both should get going and please don't forget to compliment the Commandant on his new command of Köln Aachen region. I have heard from many people that he now holds considerable power in the party," said Wilfred.

"Wilfred, you are as shrewd as you are resourceful, you really should be a politician. No, on second thoughts, you are way too honest for that bunch of snakes, they would eat you alive," said Hans.

"I think you might be right, sir, highbrow society is your area of expertise. I stick to what I know best, polishing the silverware," said Wilfred.

"Well, I know Hans wouldn't be able to get through the day without you, Wilfred, you are his life and soul," said Penelope.

"One last thing, sir, should I prepare the guest bedroom?" said Wilfred.

All three looked at one another.

"Yes, Wilfred, that would be a good idea, I'm sure we will need it, won't we, dear?" said Penelope.

\* \* \*

The back seat of the car was cold, the weather at night had dropped in recent days and the leather always seemed to absorb the cold. Hans had never liked the car – it was a reminder just how different he was.

"Did you see that, Hans, that boy looked filthy. I thought the new Germany was supposed to look after all its citizens, isn't that what all the posters say?" said Penelope, gazing out of the window.

"It is, dear, but you know what change is like, there are always people left behind."

"I know what you are doing, Hans, I am not stupid. You know I want children; they wouldn't be the burden you think they would. Wilfred could help with them and we could also hire some other people to help out with the wet-nursing and domestic chores."

"Pen, we have discussed this before, it's not that I hate children, I like them. I just think they will have a big effect on our way of life. Don't you like the way we have things right now? We get to go to all the best parties in town, enjoy the good life and all the niceties that come with it. I mean, how many couples do you know that live in a house such as ours, drink wine whenever they want, any time of the day, and go to the theatre twice a week? I would hedge a bet that we would probably go three or four times if it were not for power cuts.

"I do agree that marriage is a possibility, but I don't think we need to do that right away, do we? Nobody seems to have a problem with the situation the way it is, or are you saying you don't like it anymore?" said Hans.

"That's just it, Hans, you think nobody has a problem with it, but you can never be sure and it adds another layer, doesn't it? We can't keep up like this; eventually, someone is going to find out, and then we are going to be in really big trouble. It's better for everyone if we just conform to the social norms. The war will soon be over and if the party wins we will have to get used to living under their terms. I'm just worried about us and especially you; if anything were to happen to you, Hans, I would be heartbroken, so please just think about it and say you will give it some serious thought."

"I know, Pen, you are always right, and I agree, people would see us in a different light, it would leave no doubt in their minds. As for children, well I guess if we did get married then this would at least leave a few years for us to talk about it again down the line."

"That's true, but Hans, I want you to think about all this seriously, think about the world around us and where people like us are in it."

"I will, Pen, I promise, and I love you for even thinking about all this, you have always been the level-headed one in this relationship. I would be lost without you."

As they walked into the Köln State Theatre Hans could see the biggest and best of Köln high society – the Count and Countess were laughing with the Commandant and his wife and waiters hovered around the couples, celebrities, and anyone of any importance to fulfil their every need. Young, pretty single German girls would flirt with overweight, red-faced German soldiers.

Picking up a glass of white wine, Hans could see Penelope had broken from his arm and was already working the room. Just watching her filled Hans with joy, she had a grace that allowed her to almost float around the room, charming everyone she happened to meet. He saw that she had eventually landed by the main theatre door and was talking to the Commandant. He was a beast of a man, short and stubby, and always in a hunched-up position. This, Hans thought, was from his fat belly that stuck out of his shirt at every opportunity it got. His legs always looked a little bent, probably because they were constantly forced to carry such weight all day. He was constantly suffering from gout, which was said to be a rich man's disease but really, it was just another sign his body was on the way out.

"Hans, Hans, come over, I was just telling the Commandant you had a little gift for him," said Penelope.

"That is right, darling, I am glad you reminded me. Please, Commandant, accept these small gifts of our appreciation of the party and more particularly, your leadership," said Hans.

"Hans, you shouldn't have. I told you, didn't I, dear, Mr Lahmen is a real gentleman. He has impeccable taste, and this includes his taste in women," smirked the Commandant.

"You are too kind, Commandant," said Hans.

"Well, you know, Herr Commandant, I could say the same about you. It is a great pleasure to be able to share my little acquisitions with the likes of a great leader like you and your beautiful wife," said Hans.

"In comparison to you and Miss Penelope, Hans, we wilt into the background every time. You know you should stop this socialite lifestyle of yours and take a more active role in the party. A man of your wealth and stature could go far in the party – we need people with class and finesse. Just imagine when we have expanded our empire and have to deal with other countries, well you could easily be an ambassador or, dare I say it, even the foreign minister," said the Commandant.

"Commandant, you do paint quite a picture, I can't say I wouldn't be interested but right now I don't think I can give any more to the party than I already do. I have many commitments at home that occupy my time," said Hans.

"What could be more important than the party?" snapped the Commandant.

Hans could see that his refusal to be more active in the party had rattled the Commandant and knew that he needed to say something meaningful to throw him off-topic.

"Well, Penelope and I have decided that we are going to get married and we are going to start a family as soon as God has graced us with his blessing in the church."

"Oh well there you go, that is wonderful news, Hans, congratulations to both of you. This is also what the new Germany needs, bright young people like you bringing more Aryan race children into the world. Why with your blond hair and blue eyes I am sure your children will be the envy of mothers everywhere."

"You are too kind, Commandant. Come, shall we walk through to our boxes?" said Penelope.

As Penelope took the Commandant's arm, she whispered in Hans's ear, "Didn't take long to change your mind."

Hans whispered back, "You should know by now, Pen, the Party has a way of pressuring people into decisions whether they are the right ones or not."

Looking out over the theatre, Hans could see the performers on stage. A round lady was bellowing out a magnificent performance to the crowd's delight, the children were at the back of the stage singing in low voices so as to offset the high tones of the main performers. The lead male performer was in such sleek shape that Hans found it hard not to keep looking him over from head to toe, his bare chest beamed out to the crowd like a lighthouse shining its rays over the sea. Just then Hans noticed his watch, and he quickly leant over to give Penelope a quick kiss.

"I will be back in a few minutes, darling. I just have to visit the toilet," said Hans.

Hans walked past the toilets and towards the film closet door, a hidden section of what looked to be part of the purple wall. Once inside Hans could barely see, but he had been inside the room so many times he could just about make everything out. In the corner there were some outfits from various Shakespearian plays – the party had long since banned anything British and Hans had always thought it was a sad sight to see the costume of Richard the Third just dumped in some old theatre room. He saw the small lamp on the dresser but before he could get to it, the light switched on. There, sipping on his favourite Scotch whisky, was a slim boyish-looking man, his legs and arms crossed, his hands pressed against the chair arms in anticipation. Hans knew it was Michael, he could tell just from the smell in the air. Without saying a word, Michael and Hans embraced in a long loving kiss.

"God, I have missed you, it seems like ages since we last saw each other," said Hans.

"Hans, you are such a sensitive one, aren't you, it was only two weeks ago and you know I had to go out of town, I don't even like those business trips. It's all hotel, conference room, hotel, conference room, they are no fun whatsoever," said Michael.

"I know, but the minute I saw you enter the theatre I couldn't think about anything else. Will we be able to meet up later or do I only get you for a few minutes before the next act starts?"

"At the moment I am not sure, I am here with a group of German entrepreneurs and they can't seem to get enough of me."

"Don't tease me, Michael. I need to see you tonight. I have been so lonely since you left town."

"Hans, you can be so over the top, you have Penelope and it's not like you are sat all alone in that big house of yours; everyone here hasn't stopped talking about your exploits, seems like you have been out every other night. Should I be getting jealous?"

"Michael, you know nobody could take your place, I've been counting the days till you returned to Köln. I only go out so much because I miss you, it just takes my mind off us being apart; otherwise, I would just sit at home wondering what you were doing without me."

"I know, my love, I would be the same. I am not complaining, just poking fun."

"So, you will try and come tonight?" begged Hans.

"I will do my best, just leave the basement door open as usual."

They parted with another intense kiss. Michael left first. Hans watched him walk slowly down the corridor. Seeing the way Michael walked always made Hans smile, he was almost dancing the way he swung his hips into each movement. Just then Hans had a strange feeling, like when a door closes slowly, or a shadow appears in a corner of the room. He turned slowly to look behind him, ever so quickly catching a young soldier's eye. Hans said nothing, he just continued on his way; he needed to get back to Penelope as soon as possible if he were not to be noticed.

* * *

Michael had returned to his city flat. The moon was shining in from the skylight and lighting up the flowers he had recently bought. The place was a mess and it was all too obvious that a single guy lived in it. The dishes were overflowing from the sink and the bins hadn't been emptied since he was last in town. Michael grabbed at the window frame to get some fresh air in as the smell of rubbish was starting to waft around the apartment. He knew he should take the bins out on his way, but he was just too excited; he grabbed his razor from the bathroom sink and some clean clothes from his dresser.

Michael almost ran down to the street; filled with joy he jumped into a taxi and told the driver to be as quick as possible. As the taxi pulled away a second car's headlights beamed from down the street, its engine starting in unison with the taxi and set off keeping a distance of about a hundred metres.

Michael asked the taxi driver to drop him off about a hundred yards from Hans's driveway. As he paid the taxi driver, he noticed a car pull up in the distance and the driver seemed to be fiddling with something on his dashboard. Michael waited a few minutes and lit up a cigarette. The driver, still doing something in his car, suddenly started the engine again and then drove past Michael. Michael didn't get a good look at the driver, but he looked like a youngish man.

When he got to the basement door, he found the spare key in its usual hiding place, under the large rock beside the stone wall. Michael opened the door and walked up the basement stairs toward the main staircase that ran around the central hall. The stairs creaked with every step and the bannister was covered in dust – the wood used to make the staircase must have been hundreds of years old. Coming through the kitchen Michael could smell the quarried meats coming from the pantry and the faint smell of cabbage and potatoes that Wilfred must have cooked for dinner. There was a sharp cooking knife out on the chopping board on the table and some fresh crumbs.

Entering into the main hall was like having a lightbulb shined in his face; Michael always hated how Hans used to insist on having all the lights on even when nobody was ever using the hall – it wasn't like he was entertaining; it was just him, Wilfred and Penelope in the old place. The decorations also used to drive Michael up the wall – Hans's ancestors used to stare out at him like they were watching his every move, almost judging him in their wide-eyed stares. He wished that Hans would take them down and get a more modern look, but he refused to because of his parents. He must have so many issues, he thought to himself.

Michael found his way to the spare bedroom; it was a small place with just enough room to fit in a double bed and a nightstand. There was a small light and some dank old curtains that had seen better days. Hans was sat at the bottom of the bed and had been waiting for him. On seeing each other they walked quickly towards each other and embraced in the moonlight, whilst wildly pulling off each other's clothes.

Hans awoke in the spare bedroom to the sounds of Penelope's screams. He couldn't tell what time it was, but it was certainly early in the morning. He looked at the window and could see that although it was still dark outside the sun was starting to rise, as were the birds. Hans tried to grab his watch but dropped it on the floor; he was still half asleep and was finding it difficult to focus. He rubbed his eye and grabbed his watch from the floor – it was a quarter past three in the morning. What on earth, he thought, could be wrong with Penelope?

Michael was still lying next to him in bed and was just starting to also come round.

"Michael, wake up, something is going on," said Hans.

"What's going on, Hans, is that Penelope I can hear? What is it, what's happening?" asked Michael.

Just then the door swung open and a young German soldier holding a pistol aimed at Hans. The soldier had a look of disgust on his face, his lips squeezed tight and his face growing redder and redder. The markings on his uniform indicated that he was a low rank in the army and Hans could see that his head and his short brown hair had recently been shaved short.

"Don't take another step. My name is Private Vogel and I am here to inform you both that you are under arrest and are charged with indecent behaviour. You are both to come with me. Now get up and get dressed immediately!"

They followed Private Vogel to the large drawing-room. It was dimly lit and suggested that there had been a struggle: the table and chairs were knocked on their side. The walls were covered in a dark ocean-blue colour and almost like the crashing of the waves of the sea, Hans could hear some faint cries coming from the main chair by the fireplace. On closer inspection, Hans could see Penelope shaking in a chair. Her nose was bleeding and her face looked like it was developing fresh bruises.

"Pen, are you ok? What has he done to you?" said Hans.

"Never mind what I have done, it's you two that have committed an abnormal act and it's you who will be punished," said Private Vogel.

Private Vogel walked over to the telephone and picked it up. There was a pause. "Put me through to the Department of Internal Affairs." There was another pause. "This is Private Vogel. I've caught two male enemies of the state conducting acts of sexual depravity and one woman who had been complicit in their crimes." There was a moment of silence before Vogel replaced the phone.

"Please, you don't have to do this; you can take whatever you want. Please just let us go, we will leave the country tonight and you won't ever have to see us again," said Hans.

"You think this is about money? I don't care about your money, you scum; I care about my country and the future of my children. I want them to grow up in a clean safe society, a society that doesn't involve perverts like you!" said Private Vogel.

Suddenly there was a crash from outside the drawing-room.

"You all stay where you are. Is there anyone else in this house that I should know about?" said Private Vogel.

"My butler Wilfred is home, it must be him," said Hans.

"I am going to investigate, don't any of you move a fucking muscle or I swear I will put two bullets in your skull," said Private Vogel.

The door slammed behind him as Private Vogel walked out. All three couldn't help but look at one another, not knowing whether they should speak. Just then Michael looked at Hans.

"We need to make a run for it, Hans. If the Department of Internal Affairs finds us we will be taken to prison and will not get out alive. I am telling you I have heard stories about what they do to people like us in there and it is not good," said Michael.

"Couldn't we just deny it all? Surely, it's our word against his and he is just a private, it's not like he has any authority in the army," said Hans.

"But the rumour, Hans, one way or another it is going to come out and how long did you think we were going to get away with it? We need to be serious. I think we should grab him when he comes in, if we could just get the gun out of his hands then we could tie him up or, better still, we could get rid of him permanently and this would also keep our secret safe."

"What are you suggesting, Michael? That we kill him? I'm not sure I could do it even if I wanted to!" said Hans.

"Think about Penelope, Hans, she is also going to be labelled an enemy of the state; imagine the impact this is all going to have on her and her family, if our relationship were to be made public – we must stop him and escape," said Michael.

"It wouldn't help anyway, you heard him on the phone: he has already informed the Department for Internal Affairs. The only thing we can do now is damage control. Pen, I want you to say that you knew nothing about mine and Michael's relationship. I want you to say how much it disgusts you and how you had no idea what we were up to. Flirt with Private Vogel if you have to, do whatever it takes but make sure he believes you that you didn't know – at least that way you will be safe," said Hans.

"I don't want to, Hans, I want to be with you. You're the love of my life, how can I say such things against you? We have been friends for years – how can I just turn my back on you when you need me the most? Maybe I could call my father, he might be able to pull some strings and have this whole incident covered up," suggested Penelope.

"Do you think your father is going to want to be associated with homosexuals, Penelope? To the party it's almost as bad as being a Jew. We have to act, Hans; if you don't, I am going to, I won't spend my life in a prison cell," said Michael.

"Ok, I understand what you are saying, I do. I just need to make sure Pen is on board. Pen, please, for me, do as I say. I will speak to him when he comes back. I will explain how Penelope knew nothing of our affair, and once he understands we will make a break for it and leave Penelope here – that way her story looks even more authentic and believable. Is everyone agreed?" said Hans.

"Agreed."

"Agreed."

They heard a loud bang from outside, followed by a single shot. A second later Private Vogel walked in. Shaken and speaking in a fast, almost uncontrollable manner. "That stupid old cunt, what did he think he was playing at? I told him to stop where he was and put the shotgun down. Do you see what you have done? Now some old man is dead because of your sick actions! No doubt he knew of what you two were doing anyway, so I guess I just cheated the hangman, I probably did Germany favour!" said Private Vogel.

On hearing the word Hans jumped up from the sofa and launched himself at Private Vogel; he hit him with such a force that they both fell to the floor. Michael ran towards where Hans and Private Vogel were wrestling on the ground. All three struggled to try to capture the gun in Private Vogel's hand as they rolled around, shouting obscenities at each other. Finally, a second shot rang out. At first, Hans could only hear Penelope screaming and then weeping, but as he looked down he could see Michael lying still, blood was now gushing from his skull. He shouted at the top of his voice, urging Michael to wake up, but it was no use.

Hans turned to Private Vogel with rage in his eyes. He grabbed Private Vogel by the throat and started to strangle him. Tighter and tighter, he gripped his neck until he could see the fingermarks; his fingernails were now cutting through his skin and small bloody patches were appearing.

"Die, you piece of shit, you murdering fucking bastard! I will kill you; I will kill you, you fucking cunt!" said Hans.

As life was draining from Private Vogel's face, Hans felt a crash against the back of his skull, it knocked his hands from around Private Vogel's neck and allowed him to catch a breath. The adrenaline was not enough to keep Hans on his feet, they wobbled with insecurity; he could feel the blood rushing around his body and then the trickle of the thick liquid rolling down his neck, and suddenly he fell to the floor, slipping into a deep unconsciousness.

# CHAPTER
## 5

Werner's first stop had to be the local church. He was so tired but he knew he needed to get everything hidden. He had worked all night digging a shallow grave in his father's garden, in which he buried him. He had mopped up the blood that had been spilt, and cleaned as best he could the fire poker, which he had used to concave his father's skull. The clothes he had been wearing he had burnt, along with the mop in the stone fireplace. He remembered feeling so clinical – when you are running on adrenaline you just do what you have to, he thought.

When he got to the church, Werner found that the place was locked and that the priest hadn't arrived yet. He would have to wait, so he decided to walk around the grounds. The church was a small stone structure, with a wooden triangular shaped roof that was covered in green moss from years of neglect. The gravestones were the same; it was clear that nobody bothered to maintain the grounds now or to clean the headstones, even the crypts were decrepit. Werner couldn't help but wonder how much people must have paid to have these memorials to their lives built, only to be left looking in worse condition than a public toilet. What a pity, he thought, surely someone could come once a week with a rake and some garden clippers to sort the place out. Just as his mind started to drift, he heard footsteps from behind him.

"Young Ritter, is that you? I haven't seen you since you were a boy. What happens to bring you to our neck of the woods? Been to visit your father, have you?" said the Priest.

"That's right, Father, I stayed the night at his house, although he wasn't there, not sure where he must have gone; he doesn't get out much these days. You haven't seen him, have you? Oh, by the way, I am doing a little historical research and I was wondering if I could have a look at the church records. It's a project we have been doing within the party, kind of a game. We have a small wager on who is the most authentic German of us all – the winner not only gets to boast but also gets a free night out, dinner, and all the trimmings," said Werner.

"Well, I can't say I have seen your father in a while, you know he stopped coming to church. I put it down to old age, nothing personal, I hope. Hmm not sure I agree with gambling and alcohol, but it all sounds friendly enough. You know the safe money would probably go on you, Werner. Did your father ever tell you what your name means?"

"No? I just thought it was a name like every other name in Germany."

"Come now, Werner, all names have meaning, and all names give an insight into one's character. Your father didn't name you Werner for anything, you know. Your father named you Werner because it means 'army defender'; you see, he must have known that you were going to be a military man, just like he was. I bet your military friends would love to know that, wouldn't they?"

"You're right, Father, I am sure they will be very impressed when I tell them."

"They will be super impressed if you also tell them what your family name means, as that is the old name for a knight! So, you see, you are a knight defending the army. How can Germany lose the war when we have men like that fighting on our side?"

"You might have a point, Father. Now would it be possible for me to see those records?"

"Of course, Werner, let me just open. I'm not as fast as I once was you know," said the Priest.

When they got inside the church Werner could see the place hadn't changed since he was a boy. The wooden pews at the back of the church still smelt of damp and were rotting on the left-hand side due to rainwater that was coming through the broken lead slates, dripping onto the wooden roof. The kneeling cushions were almost threadbare and the altar had seen better days.

"You know, since the war began, the church has seen bigger and bigger attendance levels, I should be glad, you know, but between us, Werner, I would happily preach to an empty hall if it were to bring peace and end to this bloody conflict. I know the party doesn't want to hear these views from me, I have received the latest pamphlets the party sends to the clergy on how we should instruct our congregation, but I can't help asking myself what would Jesus do?" said the Priest.

"You should be careful, Father; if other party members heard you talk this way it could wind up ending with you going to prison for subversion," said Werner.

"I don't intend to, Werner, I try to do as I am instructed but when mothers of sons who have died come to me and ask me did their sons die for a just course, the spiritual guidance I give comes from my heart and I know I am lying to them. Jesus, you see, was a revolutionary, not like the kind you see in Russia – what's the guy who led the revolution over there, Lenin, I think his name was. No, not like him; he was a revolutionary because he turned his back on hatred and discrimination; he spent his life working towards improving the lives of others, helping the weak and the poor. I ask you, Werner, what would he say to all this death and destruction? What would he say to the party's policies on the Jews? Would the party have him put to death? He was a Palestinian Jew after all who renounced his religion; if he were still alive, he would no doubt be sent off to prison. Would that be right? Sending the son of God to prison?"

"Well, he was put to death back then, so maybe, Father, maybe."

"Yes, Werner, but what a depressing thought: mankind has struggled for nearly 2000 years and we are no better than back then. Come now, I think those records you asked for are here in the back cupboard, grab a seat and I will see if I can find them," said the Priest. "Here you go, Werner, I think these are the books you are looking for. They have the christenings and marriages of all families in the village. I think your family can be traced back over the last three hundred years."

"Thank you, Father, are these all the books you have?" said Werner.

"As far as I know that's them all. Why don't you have a look through them and make some notes for your project? I will go and put the stove on and make us some tea, that should get the grey matter working."

"Thank you, Father, that's very kind of you," said Werner.

The records were in various handwriting styles, obviously from the priests who had looked after the church down the ages. The books had also been badly neglected – Werner could see that they had suffered water damage and the spines were completely removed from the original books. There was no way he would be able to go through all the entries in the vain attempt to find his family lineage.

"Father, would it be possible if I borrow these for a week or so? I don't think I have time today to read through them all," said Werner.

"We are not supposed to, Werner, they have been in the church premises almost as long as the church itself. I would be in grave trouble if you were to lose them."

"You know me, Father, I promise to treat them with respect. I will have them back to you within a week and I promise to be extra careful when reading them."

"Well, I don't suppose anyone is going to miss them, not for a week anyway. Yes, ok, you can borrow them, but remember you promised you will look after them and that's a promise in front of the lord so it is to be taken seriously."

"I promise, Father, really you are a lifesaver and thanks for the tea," said Werner.

\* \* \*

Back in his city apartment, Werner felt a sense of ease flood over him. The place was just as he left it, books on the floor, the window ajar, clothes thrown around his bedroom, and the smell of garlic from the preparation from his last meal. Werner could hear a soft tapping at the wooden door – he knew it was the door automatically because the small glass window in the door always rattled when the door was hit. It had been that way ever since Werner once got so drunk that he needed to ram the door to finally get it open. Werner moved towards the door; not making a sound and walking on tiptoes, he saw from under the door a shadow of a man.

"Werner, are you home? It's Father Kuntz."

Werner breathed easy.

"Just a minute, Father, let me just put some clothes on, I was just taking a shower," said Werner.

Werner quickly stripped down to his underwear, hiding the clothes he was wearing under his bed. On his way back to the door he noticed the books sat on the side of his dining room table; he covered them with his jacket.

He slowly opened the door, still a little unsure if he had covered everything that could have linked him with last night and the books from this morning. Behind it was a smiling Father Kuntz; his face was flush, probably from the stairs, Werner thought. His appearance shocked Werner, mostly because he wasn't used to seeing Father Kuntz out of his formal robes. He was wearing a black military jacket, black leather gloves, dark brown suit pants, and some well-worn black biker boots.

"Hello Father, this is a surprise. What can I do for you today?" said Werner.

"Hello Werner, I was out for a walk in the area and I thought I would drop by to see how you are," said Father Kuntz. "How are things with you anyway? I heard your last presentation at the party meeting. It was very interesting, amazing hearing about some of the ground-breaking eugenics that the party is undertaking these days, isn't it?"

"Thank you, Father, it's a great honour to have a man like you give such praise. I agree the party scientists are doing some pioneering work and they are coming up with some interesting theories."

"You don't consider them facts? I thought all party propaganda was supposed to be accepted as scientific fact."

"It is, Father, it is. Just recently though, I... I don't know I have just had some things brought to my attention and it's got me wondering."

"I see you have just started the fire, maybe you could boil some water and make an old man some tea," said Father Kuntz.

"Of course, Father, where are my manners. Please also take a seat."

"My grandmother always says to me, Werner, 'manners cost nothing'. This is a thing that people seemed to have forgotten before the party came along. I remember kids running around the church like it were a soccer field, men never holding doors for women. If there is one thing the party has installed in this nation, it's the restoration of good manners."

"I guess you are right, Father, I have noticed that people seem to take much more pride in their own appearance these days; the party should be thanked for this," said Werner.

"You look troubled, Werner, come and sit with me and tell me what's bothering you," said Father Kuntz.

"Me, no I am fine, Father, honestly. I think I am tired from all the extra work I have been doing."

"Werner, the worry is written all over your face; come on, you know you can tell me. How long have we known each other? You can tell me anything. Don't worry, I won't judge and despite my age, you know I can still relate in my own way to young people like you."

"It's something deeply personal, Father, I am not sure I can discuss it with anyone, even a man of the cloth," said Werner.

"I am sure it cannot be that bad; you know what they say: a trouble shared is a troubled halved, and if you can't tell your priest, then who can you tell?" said Father Kuntz.

Father Kuntz laughed, he seemed relaxed. "Come on, son, you can tell me; whatever it is we can deal with it together. Two minds are better than one when solving problems. Is it something to do with you borrowing the family record books from your father's village church?"

A cold sense of dread fell over Werner; he felt shocked and unable to move. Cold sweat almost instantly began to roll down his back and his palms started to become clammy and moist.

"How do you know about them? I only borrowed the books this morning?"

"Werner, how many times have I told you, in the new Germany we are all expected to watch over one another, we are all sheep in the leader's flock, the church included. The leader has passed on strict instructions to all priests that anyone enquiring about family records is to be investigated by the party. As you borrowed these records from Father Lehrer, he was obligated to inform me, as the head of the Köln arch-diesis. You see, Father Lehrer was just doing his job in informing me, and I'm just doing mine in following up with you. I have to say, you taking the books did surprise me. Why did you want to borrow them?"

"It's difficult to say, Father. I want to tell you, I do, but I am afraid of what it might lead to, afraid really for what I am and what I have done," said Werner.

"Werner, what is it? It cannot be terrible, there is always a solution to any problem we face in life. The lord is there to forgive and with his strength, we can always make amends, no matter how bad the act may have been. Just get it off your chest, son, you will feel much better once you do."

"You see, Father, it all started when I went over to my dad's house yesterday. Honestly, now I think about it I wish I hadn't have gone to that bloody place. I had been in such a good mood, Father; I was all-upbeat. I felt like things were on the up and up yesterday, and now I am feeling lost. I don't know who I am anymore, or who I should be. When I think about what I have done I don't know if I can look myself in the mirror," said Werner.

"Werner, you need to tell me the full story before I can help you. Come on, let it all out, tell me exactly what happened with your father and I am sure I will be able to help."

"Well, I was telling my stubborn father of how the party was doing and of the advances it was making in its policies and programmes to help purify the nation. Then we started arguing about the Jews and the party's policies. You see, I wasn't expecting my father to be against the party, he always used to say the country needed a strict hand and what stricter one is there than the party. The way he talked, I couldn't believe what was coming out of his mouth – at first I thought it was old age but then I realised it was deeper than that, it was his opinion and what's worse it was an opinion that he had deliberated over for a long time."

"Carry on, Werner, keep going; it's good to let it out."

"He then started telling me how I was wrong, how the party was wrong and – this I couldn't believe – that there was Jewish blood within our family. That's why I was looking for the books this morning because I wanted to get rid of this. I wanted to forget about it, so that this evil part of my past was not there anymore, that I would no longer have to think about it."

"Well, I can completely understand that, Werner, of course, you are going to try and hide this; it's not exactly something you want people knowing. Please continue," said Father Kuntz.

"Well by this time we were really arguing, I was getting more worked up by the minute and he knew this, it's almost like he was trying to get a rise out of me. Like he enjoyed pushing my buttons! I just lost it, Father, I grabbed the nearest thing to me, which happened to be the iron poker and I hit him, I hit him as hard as I could over the head, over and over again and again. I didn't stop until my hand went weak; by this time I hadn't noticed that he had stopped breathing or that the poker was covered in blood. I lost it, Father, and before I knew it I had killed him then and there," said Werner.

"My god, Werner, you mean you killed your own father! What did you do after? Where is your father now? Still in the house?"

"It was late, I didn't know what to do, by this time I was running purely on instinct, so I grabbed a shovel from the barn and I dug a hole in the garden and that's where I put him. In the hole, with all that cold earth. Oh Father, what have I done? I am a complete monster and then to try to cover it up when I should have just come clean. Really, I am going to hell, aren't I?" said Werner.

"So what is next, Werner? What do you plan on doing now you know all this information and now you have committed such an act? At least I understand now why you took the record books – you were going to burn them and the clothes you were wearing, am I correct?" said Father Kuntz.

By now Werner was on his knees, sobbing on the floor uncontrollably.

"I really don't know, what should I do? Should I come clean? This would mean I would end up in prison, and most probably be hanged. Surely, I could be of much better use to the party if I were still a member and I just kept my secret to myself?"

"That is true, Werner, you have been growing in stature in the party and people would be devastated to learn the news that you were of Jewish heritage, especially given your passionate speeches on how they need to be eliminated from the new Germany the party is trying to create. It might be better for all concerned if we just kept your secret to ourselves."

"But, Father, I have killed a man! My father! How will I ever deal with the guilt, I buried him in the garden for fuck's sake," said Werner.

"Werner, this war will make men commit horrible acts on one another, we will all have to stand up before God in the end and confess what we have done. There are things I have done that I am not proud of, the thing to do is work toward doing better in the world, this will help you get over your past sins. Think about the difference you can make in helping shape the new Germany we all want to create. Now go and get your clothes from last night and the books."

As Werner went to his room to pick up his clothes and the books, as soon as he had them in his hand he felt as if a weight had been lifted from his chest. Thank god he had told Father Kuntz – his advice was correct: why ruin his own, Catti's, and everyone else's life just because his grandfather was a Jew? He didn't feel Jewish in any way, he didn't look Jewish; in fact, other than a few scribbles in some old books there was no evidence in the world he was Jewish.

He handed Father Kuntz first his clothes and then Father Kuntz placed the clothes on the fire and they both watched as his shirt and then trousers melted into black smoke. After about ten minutes all that could be seen from the clothes was some leftover fabrics and the metal buttons that were attached to the fly of his trousers.

"Werner, burning these books will eliminate the histories of thousands of families. We are sinning, it's a sign that I am sure God understands and would agree it is a necessary one, but I do feel we should offer a prayer to him as a way of acknowledging this sin and asking for forgiveness. Would you mind kneeling and joining hands with me in prayer?"

Werner nodded his head and knelt.

"Bless us, Father, for we have sinned. We come to you today in the knowledge that your son Werner has committed a terrible crime and ask for your forgiveness. We also ask that you forgive our acts in burning these records today as a way to cover up an even bigger crime, Werner's Jewish family roots; he is truly repentant. Come now, Werner, speak to God yourself, tell him what you need to, speak as if you were a son talking to a father," said Father Kuntz.

"Father, please forgive me for I have sinned, I have broken one of the Ten Commandments, 'thou shall not kill'. I know this is the worst sin a man can do, but I beg your forgiveness, I committed this sin in a rage of anger and passion. I will have to live with the guilt of what I have done and of what I am. From now on I promise to live a clean life, one that works towards the nation's aims, and I promise to be a productive member of society," said Werner.

"IN THE NAME OF THE FATHER THE SON AND THE HOLY GHOST AMEN," said both men.

Father Kuntz placed the books on the fire and they caught alight instantly. Father Kuntz placed his hands on Werner's head.

"You are now free, my son, you are at one with God again. You can now go enjoy your life safe in the knowledge that you can meet God with a clear conscience," said Father Kuntz.

"Thank you, Father, it's a blessing having you in my life, I don't know what I would have done if I hadn't had your guidance. I am glad we had this opportunity to speak to God together to let him know I am sorry for my actions and to make peace."

"You are welcome, Werner, these books burning in front of you symbolise the burning of your Jewish heritage, and you should take solace in this and remember this ritual when times are really tough. Now, I will leave you to your own thoughts, I have other business to attend in Köln Cathedral and I must be getting on. I am glad that we were able to do this together today."

Werner walked Father Kuntz to the door. Just as they kissed each other on the cheek, Father Kuntz said, "Remember, Werner, put your faith in the Lord, he is the only one who can be trusted and can save us from our own sins."

After Father Kuntz had gone, Werner opened the windows and filled the kettle to make another pot of tea. How lucky he thought he was to have people in his life like Father Kuntz. Today he decided would be a new beginning. He would go and see Catti, drop by the party headquarters and see what else he could do to make the nation great. He had a spring in his step, the kind one feels after a job interview or an unplanned night that ends up with you waking in a new woman's bed. Maybe it was his dance with death from the night before, but Werner was sure that he had never felt so alive in all his life. Maybe he thought this was a good thing, maybe it is only when you hit rock bottom that you can work yourself back up to the top.

Werner walked downstairs to the building's communal phone box on the first floor. As usual, someone had left it off the handle and there was rubbish on the floor and the foul stench of old cigarette butts overflowing from the ashtray. In seconds a sheepish voice came through and asked with whom he was trying to connect. Werner asked the operator to put him through to Catti's parents' home – he knew she would be there on the weekend. When she eventually picked up, she sounded warm, which reassured him that things were looking up; they agreed to meet at a café a few streets away from Werner's house. The thought of having coffee and cakes there filled Werner with joy – this was one of the first places they had gone when they had just started dating and the place would always remind him of Catti, and the yellow summer dress she had worn that day. He could hardly wait to get there and to tell her he loved her.

Just as Werner was about to grab his jacket and leave his apartment, he heard a knock at his front door. The knocks grew harder, then Werner heard a familiar voice.

"Werner are you still in there? It's me, I think I must have forgotten my scarf," said Father Kuntz.

Werner looked to see his scarf was resting on the back of the sofa.

"Just a second," shouted Werner.

When Werner opened the door, he could see Father Kuntz wearing a sinister smile. There was something about his face that had changed – he looked giddy, like he had won first prize at a church fete. The smile distracted Werner so much that for a few seconds he didn't see the two burly looking SS soldiers stood directly behind Father Kuntz. They were dressed in full regalia, long black leather overcoats, with shiny polished boots. They looked menacing enough through their facial expressions, but then Werner noticed that they were both carrying machine guns. The guns were cocked and were even shinier than the boots they wore. Werner felt a feeling of unease slip over him and then an aching feeling in his gut, like when the first shot of vodka hits an empty stomach; he almost threw up in his mouth.

"Werner, don't be alarmed. These men are my personal escorts and I have asked them to be assigned to you to make sure you have adequate protection for your speech to the party tonight," said Father Kuntz.

"Oh, I see, Father, that is very kind of you. For a minute there I thought I must have forgotten to have paid my party subscription fee," Werner joked. "Please, why don't you all come in, your scarf is just on the back of the chair where you left it. I was just getting ready to go and meet Catti, here, let me just grab my jacket," said Werner.

"Don't worry, Werner, we won't be staying long, no need for us all to go in?" said Father Kuntz.

Putting his scarf around his neck, Werner could see something was out of place when Father Kuntz raised his head: his giddy smile had turned into a scowl.

"Werner Ritter, you are under arrest," said Father Kuntz.

"What? I don't understand, Father."

"You're under arrest for the murder of war hero Gunter Ritter," said Father Kuntz.

"But, Father, I thought we had decided to keep this a secret, that with burning the records I could be free and that we wouldn't tell anyone," said Werner.

"Did you really think I would just accept you were a dirty stinking Jew? The party has put its faith in me to guide them to a righteous path, where good honest Christians can lead the world towards a life of order, peace, and prosperity. Do you think this can be achieved by having murdering half-breed Jews walking amongst us? You are just like any other Jew out there on the street; you need to be eliminated from our society so that you cannot pass on your dirty blood to anyone else. You are cancer in the world that needs to be cut out of existence," said Father Kuntz.

"But, Father, what about all we just did together, what about all we talked about? I thought you were my friend, I thought you understood that I didn't want any of this. You know I hate the fact I have Jewish blood in me, but what can I do about it? Please, Father, there is no need for this, I can still help the party, I can still help create a greater Germany."

"You! Do you think the party wants the likes of you? You are a half-breed piece of scum that must be treated as if you were like any other hook nose, money-loving Jew. Now you will go with these two men and answer their questions."

"Please, Father, I beg of you, please don't do this. I will lose everything," said Werner.

"You lost everything the day you were born, Werner, when your parents infected you with your diseased blood, you just didn't know it yet. Take him away," said Father Kuntz.

As the soldiers seized Werner's arms, he started to struggle. He swung a wild punch, which caught one of the soldiers on the side of the head. The soldier let out a shout in pain as it landed and Werner felt his right arm pull free. He used his now free arm to smack at the other soldier's hand, which was attached to his left arm; he broke free and tried to push through the men and Father Kuntz towards the door.

The soldier, still shaken from his blow to the head, grabbed his rifle and crashed it into Werner's stomach. The force of the impact caused Werner's body to inadvertently curl forward in a C shape. He felt another crash from the rifle, this time to the back of his head, and the power sent him hurtling toward his apartment floor. Hurt and in pain, he still had the sense to force himself to turn over, from where he scrambled to get back to his feet. He heard a click and saw the rifle pointing at him, the soldier's finger firmly on the trigger. Just as the soldier squeezed, he saw Father Kuntz's hand push the rifle. The shot set off a loud bang and then shattered some glass.

"No, I told you that he wasn't to be killed, not yet anyway. We need him for questioning and interrogation; there may be more like him. Now, Werner, we won't tell you again: turn on your front and lay flat or I will allow my colleague to put two rounds straight in that Jew's heart of yours," said Father Kuntz.

# CHAPTER

### 6

The van rolled through the streets of Köln, but Jacob couldn't see where he was going due to the heavy blackout screens that had been erected in the van. Sat on the steel benches he would feel the cold shoot up through his legs and bum, making it uncomfortable to sit still. The van was a standard military vehicle, the types that had become more and more common these days, they would swoosh through the streets where the children used to play. Inside the van, there were other men, some elderly, some middle-aged, and some as young as children. One man had on a brightly coloured vest, a type of traditional clothing; another was wearing a neck scarf that showed he was from the Sinti tribe.

The van had been stopping at different locations now for the last two hours and every time it was the same, a ten to twenty-minute stop followed by another group of men joining the van. Occasionally, a middle-aged soldier would stick his head through the leather curtains that held the back of the van closed and would warn Jacob and his companions to be quiet or face a beating. Jacob could hear two men muttering at the end of the van; at first he thought they might be coming up with a plan of escape or trying to put together their money so as to bribe their way out, but on closer inspection, he could just see it was a father trying to comfort his teenage son.

An old man sat opposite Jacob. He looked in his late sixties and was dressed in a two-piece suit. Jacob nodded to the man to get his attention. "Excuse me, but do you know where they are taking us?" said Jacob.

"I don't know but I imagine it will be the resettlement and interrogation centre they have built outside of Köln, near the Luxembourg border. I heard a few stories from others in the village and they said that they had seen other families being taken there," said the man.

"If you knew other Gypsies were sent to this centre you are talking about, then why didn't you run away? Surely it can't be that bad if you were willing to allow yourself to be arrested and go there?" said Jacob.

"Nobody wants to be arrested, and nor do they want to leave their home. I am doing what anyone else would have done, this is my country, and I am not about to run away from it like some criminal, just to become a refugee or a homeless bum in Austria. I am a proud member of the community I come from, but first and foremost I am a German. I'm not leaving my country; if you ask me, it should be the party to leave it, they are the ones obsessed with wanting change. I'm quite happy in my little apartment minding my own business," said the man.

"I like your suit; I have been after one like that for a while. What exactly do you do? I mean before you wound up in here with me?" said Jacob.

"I was a high school teacher for most of my life; since retirement I have spent most of my time indulging in my passions, gardening, and reading," said the man.

"What do you think will happen to us once we get to this relocation and interrogation centre?" said Jacob.

"Isn't it obvious?" said the man.

"Well no, not really!" said Jacob.

"The name is in the title, we are going to be interrogated and then once they have decided where to put us, relocated. I heard from friends that the centre has been operating for about a year now, at first it was only Jews that were sent there but now it seems the party has extended the centre to anyone who has been deemed an enemy of the state or a drain on the country's economy."

"What do you mean a drain on the economy? How can someone be a drain on the economy? Surely they can be used in the military somehow?"

"Think about it, have you not seen the posters that have been up around town? They have been up in my little village so you must have seen them in Köln. You know the ones with the doctors on them explaining the benefits of eliminating all useless subjects from society?"

Jacob racked his mind, there had been so many posters that had gone up around town that it was hard to keep track of what was what.

"Do you mean the ones with the doctor with the disabled child on his knee?"

"Exactly, that's the one; well, next to the picture was a statement saying these people cost the state 50,000 Marks a year, wouldn't your taxes be better spent building a better

Germany. That's what I mean by the party deciding whether you are a drain on resources and the economy or not."

"I guess I can see the party's point, they do cost the country money. I mean it might be harsh and nobody wants to do it, but just think about all the money the country could save by not having the disabled in society – we could use all that money for schools and education, mastering the sciences, and developing new industry," said Jacob.

"You know what you sound like, you sound exactly like them. Life isn't about money – if everything were to be based on just money, then mankind would be back in the Dark Ages fighting over which king controlled the most land. Do you think people like Leonardo da Vinci or Michelangelo painted and sculpted such beautiful things because they wanted money?"

"Ok, you have made your point; I understand what you are saying but I still don't see how this should affect the Gypsy. We can be hard-working members of society, all able-bodied Gypsies can be productive workers, and they just need the opportunities to do so. Look at me and you, you have been a high school teacher and I am a businessman. I own my own grocery shop, I employ a young German girl, we are perfect examples of what Gypsy people can do when they set their mind to it."

Jacob could feel the stares of the other men in the van; they had all stopped what they were doing and they were focused on his and the old man's conversation. He had found himself speaking more deeply and in a louder voice than he usually did.

"I admire your optimism, I really do, but I don't think it is as clear-cut as that when it comes to the party and particularly the leader's philosophy on where we are in the world racial pecking order," said the man.

"The leader is a wise man, and the party is trying to build a better society for you and me. I do not believe they would just waste time and more importantly resources just to try and get rid of a group of people who could be useful to them," said Jacob.

The van turned off its engine and pulled to a standstill. The old man used the van stopping as his cue to speak in a louder tone himself, looking past Jacob and towards the doors.

Just as everyone seemed to take a joint deep breath, a soldier's face abruptly stuck through the back of the van, and his piercing eyes stared at each of the men individually before fixing on the old man Jacob had been talking to.

"Men over 55 and children to the right, anybody else from the ages of 14 to 54 to the left, form an orderly queue, eyes down and no talking!" said the soldier.

Jacob and the old man did as the soldier instructed and parted into different lines.

The night was cold and dark. Jacob kept his eyes on his shoes as he was instructed. He could hear the sounds of muffled voices just in front of him, gazing forward but without lifting his head fully he could see that it was the man and the teenage boy.

"Dad, why can't I come with you? I don't want to go in that queue with all the old people," said the young boy.

"It will be ok, son, don't worry. Look down the line, there are other children in the line, just do as the soldiers say, we don't want any trouble, it's best to just do as they say. The last thing we want is to make them all angry now, do we?" said the father.

"Please, Dad, please don't leave. I want to stay with you," cried the young boy.

Jacob could see one of the soldiers had also heard their voices and was walking towards the couple. He tried to warn them by coughing and clearing his throat a few times, but they were both too enthralled in their own conversation to notice Jacob.

"Hey, you two, what's going on?" said the soldier.

The boy continued to squeeze his father's hand and now his cries had turned to a dull sob.

"Please, Dad, don't leave me, I don't want to go on alone," said the young boy.

"You need to be quiet now, son, you need to stop talking immediately. Can you see that soldier? He is not going to be happy with us if we continue to talk, so please just do as I say and shut up just for now," said the father.

The father then wrestled his hand free from his son's and gave him a slight push toward the other line, but it was no use: the boy was not letting go.

"Fine, you don't want to do as you are told, do you; well both of you, you are coming with me and I will make you wish you had done as you were instructed!" said the soldier.

The soldier grabbed the boy by the scruff of his shirt collar and dragged him toward the stone wall, simultaneously pushing the father with the barrel of his machine gun. Once up against the wall, the soldier took four steps back and unloaded about 10 to 15 bullets in their direction. Both lines jumped with the noise from the machine-gun fire, some turned their heads towards where the bodies of the boy and his father still lay twitching, others just looked at the floor.

The soldier looked down. "There now, you can be together forever," laughed the soldier.

Jacob felt sick at what he had witnessed; he was frightened to look up but felt a need, an urge even to look towards his right.

They walked past the bodies of the boy and his father, their bodies still leaking from every bullet wound. The boy had a scared wide-eyed look still on his face. The father's head was coming apart as one of the bullets had gone directly through his eye. No one in the queue said a thing, nor did they even look too long in their direction; they just kept slowly walking toward the stone arch that was the entrance to the resettlement and interrogation centre.

Jacob and the rest of the men in his line were walked towards a wooden building that looked like army barracks. When they arrived inside the first wooden huts, they were all instructed to strip naked and to leave their clothes on the table in front of them. He stripped and covered his privates with his hands in front of him. He was then instructed to pick up a pair of black pyjamas that were handed to him by an overweight German woman who looked disgusted at him when their hands happened to touch. When they were all dressed, another soldier walked up and down the line, giving out instructions.

"You men are now prisoners of the party and you are to do as you are instructed. You will see from your uniforms that you have a brown triangle on the front of your shirt pockets; this triangle is important as it identifies you to any German soldier of what you are. Brown means Gypsy, which is appropriate for you as your kind are used to living in shit. The first rule of the resettlement and interrogation centre is that you must never take this badge off, you are only given one set of clothes so you better take care of them or you will feel pain and suffering you never thought imaginable. The second rule is you do as and what the soldiers in this centre instruct of you, without question. Anybody questioning authority will be shot on the spot, do you understand me! The rest of the rules you will pick up as you go along. Now follow the two officers to your right and do as they instruct," said the soldier.

The men, dressed in their loosely fitting dirty pyjamas, were walked for a further five minutes to another wooden hut; inside there were men and boys already lying on individual wooden beams, some of the men had blankets, others did not. They were all huddled in the foetal position and nonchalantly glanced in Jacob's direction as he entered.

"Now, find a sleeping bench and go to sleep, you will be up at daybreak for your interview, you will answer every question you are given so I suggest you get rest right away," said the soldier.

Jacob found himself trying to get on the bench near the door, but they were already full and the men on them had no intention of sharing. Making his way towards the back of the hut, he could see a couple of benches free. Jacob ran to the back and jumped onto one quickly to mark his territory. Lying there for five seconds it became clear why these benches had been left empty – the smell of the open toilet not four feet away was overpowering, as was the buzz of flies around the rotting piles of shit. Jacob tried to muffle the smell with his sleeve, but it was no good, the toxic air was too much for a thin layer of material. He decided that despite the smell he would have to stay where he was for the night; the next morning though he would try to find a better place, but right now all he wanted to do was to lie peacefully and gather his thoughts.

* * *

"Wake up, you scumbags, you are not here to sleep, you are here to work. I want to see you all on your feet in one minute and I mean one minute," shouted the blond-haired boyish-looking soldier.

Jacob was still so tired; he had only had a few hours' sleep. His back felt as if it had been smashed with a sledgehammer – how he had even managed to get even a few hours' sleep was beyond him. He managed to pull himself from his bunk without putting his foot in the open toilet and wiped the sleep from his eyes.

He looked around to see how all the other prisoners were acting. They all seemed calm, they reminded Jacob of a book he'd read, 'The Magic Island', which described a zombie like state; they were putting on their caps and looked strangely at peace.

"Right, you lazy sacks of shit, you only have one real rule to follow and that is to do exactly what I tell you. When I say do something you do it, or by God help you there will be hell to pay. Now form a queue and follow me outside, where you will be given your work detail and before I hear any complaints, remember what happens to people who stick their nose into my business," shouted the boyish-looking soldier.

On hearing his instructions, the room shifted to absolute silence and there was a communal groan from the men that came out as a whisper. Jacob didn't dare ask the others what the soldier meant by his last statement, but he didn't need to – it was obvious someone had felt the wrath of the soldier for their disobedience.

"You, left, you're on steel mill detail, you go with him! Now you two go to the sorting rooms. Which one of you is Jacob Anhalt?" said the soldier.

"I am, sir," said Jacob.

"Good, you follow me and keep up!" said the soldier.

Following the soldier through the building courtyard he could see various parts of the resettlement and interrogation centre. One area was for the Jews – he could see a sign showing a large yellow Star of David, he couldn't quite make out the words underneath it, but it looked to be saying something like 'area strictly for the Jews, no prisoner mixing'. The Jewish people he could see in the area looked skinny and like they were suffering from malnutrition, in comparison to the ones in the Gypsy area he was in, whom although being skinny too did not have those dark round marks under their eyes and gaunt faces.

The soldier led Jacob through the main courtyard to a large brick building. On entering he could see that it was broken down into different wings, A wing was for interrogation, B wing was simply labelled the holding cells, C wing was marked as enhanced interrogation and D wing was labelled resettlement and freedom departure area.

The soldier walked Jacob into A wing and into a small room. The room was mostly empty, with just two chairs and a table.

"Sit and wait for your questioner," said the soldier.

After a ten-minute wait a man walked in; he was dressed in a pinstriped suit. Jacob stood from the chair and waited for further instructions.

"Please, please sit. Allow me to introduce myself, I am Professor Bonn. Bonn like the city."

They both sat down at their respected chairs and in doing so Professor Bonn leant forward and shook hands with Jacob.

"Now, Mr Anhalt, before we start could I offer you a cigarette?" said Professor Bonn.

"Thank you," said Jacob.

Jacob snatched a little when taking the cigarette; he didn't mean to but he half thought that Professor Bonn would take the box back before he got a chance to touch the packet. As he put it in his mouth the Professor produced a lighter. As the smoke-filled Jacob's lungs he felt a soothing sensation, the feeling only a smoker could relate to. His eyes focused on the burning end, which seemed to dance back and forth as he inhaled.

"Now, Mr Anhalt, I would like to discuss a few questions with you, and I would like you to answer them as correctly and as honestly as you can. Do you understand me?" said Professor Bonn.

"I do, Professor," said Jacob.

"You were born here in Köln, were you not?"

"Yes."

"And I have it here in my files that your family is from the Gypsy community, but that you have integrated into German society, is that correct?"

"There seems to be no secret of this, Professor Bonn. When I was arrested last night, I was visiting my grandmother; she still lives a nomadic lifestyle but as you say I have tried to integrate."

"That's correct. I see you have attended German public school from where you graduated, operate your grocery shop and my records also indicate that you have an apartment in the centre of Köln, is this all correct?"

"It is."

"Now, I want to ask you about your grandmother and your family heritage. Where exactly does your family originate from?"

"They are from Krakow, I believe."

"So, you are a Pole?"

"I am a German, Professor; I was born right here in this city."

The Professor smiled and stared at Jacob. He focused on Jacob's face; as he had smoked the cigarette he had given him right down to the butt, so much so that it was starting to burn the cotton in the filter.

"Would you like another one?" said Professor Bonn.

"I would, thank you," said Jacob.

"There you go, go ahead and feel free to use the lighter. Now, we were discussing your family heritage. You had said that you were German; well I have to tell you, Mr Anhalt, that due to the German Eugenics Centre for Research you are no longer classed in the German catchment and this is the reason why you now find yourself in front of me rather than in your shop with Ms Wolf. Are you aware of what the German Eugenics Centre for Research does, Mr Anhalt?"

"No, I have never heard of the place."

"Let me tell you, the centre was started by the party to address racial issues of national interest. You see, we all have different lineages and heritages that could, in theory, be traced back to other areas of the globe; the question the country now faces when deciding which individuals can be included in the great society is a difficult one. How long do you imagine it takes to get, say, the polluted Gypsy blood you have circulating in you right now? A generation, two generations, three maybe? These tough questions need to be answered and that is why the centre exists. The doctors and professors working there are some of the finest in Germany and they recently introduced guidelines on when the blood could be certified pure."

"Are you trying to tell me that I do not have pure blood and that these new guidelines make it impossible for me to be German?"

"That, Mr Anhalt, is exactly what I am telling you, you are no longer considered a German because of your blood. I do have to say, though, that I do feel for some of the gypsies I see, ones like yourself, who have contributed to society and have then had to adapt to the new guidelines. You have to realise, Mr Anhalt, that we do this research for the benefit of the entire nation. How can we build the society we all know we want without being strict on our policy? We have to listen to our scientists just like we did on the invention of the motorcar or the development of some of our new fighter planes. It's science that will take Germany into the 21st century and it is science that will help our leader finally realise his dream of creating the master race to its full potential."

"Professor, if you don't mind, I would like to ask you a question. If these guidelines are now in force, what are people like me to do?"

"You, Mr Anhalt, you have to accept that you are now a member of the world order that is lower than where you once were. You might have felt that you were German, but think about it, Mr Anhalt, it's not just about where an individual is born, that makes no sense. If I were to be born in deepest darkest Africa, would that mean I am African? Or let me put it another way, if a dog is born in a stable, does that make it a horse?"

"Professor, if you know all you need to know already, then why we are having this conversation?" said Jacob.

"Well, Mr Anhalt, one reason is that it is standard procedure to interrogate any prisoner that has been identified as having individualistic qualities. You see, most prisoners stick to their ethnic groups, religious groups, or social groups. That's why you are interesting because you have tried to leave yours and move toward that of a normal German. The second reason was to establish which country your family came from, which we have done by classifying that they were Polish.

"This is interesting because it can also affect how you are treated whilst you stay here in the resettlement and interrogation centre. You see, the Poles are almost as subhuman as the Jews. I hasten to say that if it were not for the Jews' existence, they would be the most persecuted people on earth for as you know the obvious reasons and similarities. So now that we have established this, I will mark your brown triangle on your chest with the letter P, so that everyone in the centre can identify you as being someone of Polish descent. This, as you can imagine, may not sit well with the German soldiers whose task it is to guard our little camp – they hate the Poles almost as much as the Jews, so I would expect things to get much worse," said Professor Bonn.

"Please, Professor, is there not something I can do to stop you from labelling me a Pole? I have money at my apartment, it's my life savings and I can tell you where it is if you please just help me."

"I tell you what I will do, Mr Anhalt, if you write me down the address and tell me where the money is hidden, I will go and get it. If the money is there then I will see you tomorrow and have the guards remove the P from your triangle badge, how does that sound?"

"Please, Professor, by then everyone will know I am of Polish descent."

"I am sorry, Mr Anhalt, the rules are the rules, and I would be bending quite a few just doing this small favour for you."

"Let me write down my address for you; the money is hidden under the bottom drawer in my bedroom, just pull the wooden drawer out and you will find it under there in a brown envelope."

"Good, well-done Mr Anhalt, I will visit your apartment tonight. If you are telling the truth, then you may find that your conditions in the centre will improve. You may go when the guard comes."

Professor Bonn stood to his feet as if he was about to get ready to leave.

"Professor, if I may just ask you one last question before we go our separate ways. If what you say is true and there are both superior and inferior humans, then how do you explain the FACT that all humans originated out of Africa? Surely this means we all have black blood deep down?" said Jacob.

Professor Bonn's face instantly went red and his face pulled together as a tight ball. "Are you trying to make me angry, Mr Anhalt? Because if you continue down this path you will, and I am telling you now, you do not want to make an enemy of me!"

The professor walked through the door and towards the soldier standing guard. Jacob could not hear what he was saying to the soldier.

"So, Professor, should I take him back to the Gypsy section?" said the boyish-looking soldier.

"No, this Gypsy is particularly in need of re-education. I want you to take him to B wing and, as he likes African monkeys so much, make sure the guards hang him from his ankles – this will give him plenty of time to

contemplate whether humans come from Africa or not!"
said Professor Bonn.

* * *

It had been five days since Jacob had been interrogated
by Professor Bonn; he was now suffering from three days
without food. Occasionally the guards would lower him
from the chains in which he had been hanging; his ankles
were now so sore that the rusty metal had cut through the
skin and was piercing the bones.

Jacob's first day in B wing was spent in solitary – the
guards had simply hung him upside down and then left
him for the next 24 hours. At first, it had just been the
pressure of the blood rushing to his head that had caused
him pain, but now he could feel every slight movement
from his chains around his ankles, each brush against the
bone made him cry out in anger and sharp pain. He just
wanted it to stop.

The problem was the guards were not interested in
a confession or a retraction – they had told him so on
numerous occasions, they were there to cause him pain,
that was their jobs and from what Jacob could see they
enjoyed it. A young private named Gurt was particularly
fond of administering beatings and revelled in the fact
Jacob was a Gypsy when he was punching him. He would
walk around Jacob, waiting for him to pass out from the
pain or simply be overpowered by the blood rushing from
one end of his body to another; when Jacob finally did
succumb to his body's urge to pass out, he would deliver

a solid strike to Jacob's kidneys. The pain was strong enough to wake Jacob up from his agony-induced coma, just enough to hear Gurt scream insults at him. It was on such an occasion on the fifth day of Jacob's torture that he was awoken by Professor Bonn standing in front of him.

"So, Mr Anhalt, have you had time to think about your theory on humans coming from Africa?" said Professor Bonn.

Jacob was startled to see the Professor – he had been expecting another blow to the back or ribs from Gurt; he was dazed and confused.

"Professor, please please, you were right all along, I know you were correct in what you said."

"Are you sure, Jacob? Are you sure you believe in the actual science or are you just saying this to change your current predicament?"

"No, Professor I know now that what I said was complete rubbish; please, I am a skilled man, a businessman, surely there must be something that I can say to you to make you know I can be trusted," said Jacob.

"Well, there might be something you can do but it would require a man of courage and conviction and I am just not sure you are the right person for the job!"

"I am, Professor, I can be, I am sure of that. Please just tell me what you need me to do and I will do it. You know I can be trusted; did you look in my apartment? Wasn't I telling the truth then?"

"You were and I did. I guess you have shown some willingness to cooperate. Very well. We need someone to go undercover in the Gypsy area of the centre and to pass all information regarding prisoners' movements, discussions, and report on any information that may be of use to the party. Would you be willing to do this, Jacob? I can assure you it is the only way you are ever coming down from that wall."

"I can do that, Professor, no problem. You just tell me what you need to know, where you need me to report to and I can do it. I promise you I can do it, please just let me down and I can do it."

"You heard the man, Gurt, let him down. Mr Anhalt is now working for the party in a consultant capacity. Do not dress his wounds or clean him up, though, we do not want the other prisoners thinking he has received any special treatment," said Professor Bonn.

Gurt lowered Jacob to the cell floor from where he slumped into a pile. The Professor walked over to him and gave him a packet of cigarettes and a lighter.

"Now you see, Mr Anhalt, you can be given some special privileges as payment for your newly found spirit of cooperation. From now on you will be brought to me once a week; you are to tell the other prisoners that you are trying to buy your way out of the resettlement centre and that is why you are given cigarettes. You can then use these cigarettes to barter and improve your life in the centre," said Professor Bonn.

Jacob was too exhausted to stand to his feet but managed to motion his eyes in agreement. Professor Bonn nodded in acknowledgement to the deal he had just made.

# CHAPTER 7

Hans was blindfolded, his legs were bound, and his arms were wrapped around his back with chicken wire. He tried to catch his breath.

"Oh, look who has decided to re-join us," said a sadistic voice.

Hans felt a punch that landed directly in his chest, causing him to lose control of his breathing again. He wanted to bring his hands to cover the pain, but there was no use since they were tightly bound and all he managed was a short jolt. The punch had come from Private Vogel; he couldn't see him, but he knew the voice as clearly as he could replay the events leading up to him being knocked unconscious. He felt a kick in his ribs from another soldier who was also in the van. He couldn't make out exactly what he said but it was something along the lines of him being gay. Another kick landed directly to his head, this time from Private Vogel.

"You heard that, you dirty little freak, you see everyone hates your disgusting, sick life," said Private Vogel.

The kick's impact was enough to knock Hans back unconscious.

\* \* \*

Hans awoke on a stone floor in a bare room. Some chains were hanging from the wall of what looked to be a holding cell. Old blood was becoming brown behind the chains and the flies were going back and forth to land on it. He tried to pick himself up but he couldn't manage, he was still in extraordinary pain.

Hans heard the sound of footsteps. He managed to struggle to his feet; he could feel the dried blood on his head from where he had received the kick. He tried to use some spit to wipe it away from his head and to slowly investigate the scar that lay below it. The blood was crusty, and tiny bits of flakes kept coming onto his hands as he touched it.

The door swung open and in walked three men. The first man was well-dressed, wearing a white jacket and spectacles; behind him was Private Vogel who was followed by a third soldier.

"That's him, Professor, that's the man I saw engaging in unnatural acts," said Private Vogel.

Hans struggled to his feet, trying to grab at Private Vogel. He had barely got one hand on his jacket before the other soldier delivered a striking blow to the back of the knees with his rifle; the force sent him hurtling to the ground in a heap.

"I warned you, Professor he has a hell of a temper too, I tell you if it wasn't for his fake girlfriend, I would be dead!" said Private Vogel.

"You stay where you are! Any sudden movements out of you and the next one will land on your skull, that I guarantee!" said Private Vogel.

Hans did as he was told. He addressed the Professor, but kept his eyes on Private Vogel. "What is it I am being kept for?" said Hans.

The Professor laughed. "Leave us." He waved at the two soldiers.

The soldiers did as they were told but before doing so, Private Vogel gave Hans a sly wink on his way out.

"Now, Mr Lehman, may I call you Hans? Well, I am going to. I am Professor Bonn and I worked at the facility where you now find yourself, and, if you are interested, it is my job to assess which part of this centre you should be kept in. Normally I would conduct the first part of your interrogation in our A wing area, but you, Hans, are a special case and I gave strict instructions that you were to go directly to the holding cells. I have to admit you and the other homosexuals baffle me as a scientist. I have often wondered what drives a man to engage in such depraved acts. You are to be my special project, you see, Hans, because you are by far the most interesting case I have had to investigate here."

"What makes me so special? And who is to say that Private Vogel is telling the truth about me? Surely it's my word against his and I might remind you that I am an influential figure in Köln and he is just cannon fodder for the party!"

"You make very good points, Hans, you do, and I am sure many officers would believe you or even be frightened of your position and power, but nobody knows who you are here now, and I haven't even filed your name with the centre, so I suggest you start to realise the gravity of the situation you are in. You see, your problem is you are talking to someone who knows people. I deal with them every day and trust me when I say this, I have an eye for a liar."

"Take Private Vogel, for instance, when he brought you to me last night, he told me that he had caught you in a sexual act with your partner, a gentleman I believe who was called Michael. He then informed me that when your secret was revealed that you took leave of your senses, grabbed his gun and proceeded to try to cover up your crime by attempting to kill everyone who was in your home last night. He also reported that you successfully managed to kill your butler, your lover, and him if it were not for your girlfriend's intervention," said Professor Bonn.

"And you believe such lies?"

"That's my point, Hans, I do not believe him. How could you manage to take a German soldier's pistol from his holster and kill two people, especially the ones I am sure were close to you. But you see, Hans, as I said, I know how to read people. Private Vogel comes from a very working-class family, the type of family you have looked down upon all your life. So, I can understand his hatred towards you, a man who has everything he could ever want. You're rich, good-looking, have a beautiful fiancée, or should I say had, live in a mansion, mix with the social elite of Köln. Who wouldn't want your life? But this, you see, Hans, this is why you intrigue me so much, it's because you have everything that makes me interested in why you would be willing to lose it all for a fetish. You see, in the same way, I can see that Private Vogel is lying and would do anything to see you fall from grace; I can also see that you are lying right now, I can also predict your next move – you are thinking that offering me a bribe might be the way to get yourself out of this mess. Indeed, if you were a common criminal or a normal prisoner that might be the way, but I can tell you my interest in you far exceeds any monetary value."

"I'm telling you, Professor, I am not a homosexual! I despise them; I think they are dirty foul beasts," said Hans.

"Another lie! Come now, Hans, you don't need to continue this charade for my benefit, I am here merely to interview you and to make my mind up with regards to where you should be sectioned in this facility. Guards! Mr Lehman is to be held here for a week, give him only bread and water, how often is up to you."

The guards entered the cell immediately. As the Professor left the room one of the guards grabbed Hans's leg and dragged him towards an iron shaped bar sticking out from the floor; it had a loop at the top which the guard fed a chain through and then attached the other part to Hans's ankle.

"Sit there and think about what the Professor has said to you! The Professor does not like to be messed around with, he likes to get his answers straight away and your continued lack of cooperation is only going to put him in a bad mood. The last time he was like this he conducted 45 experiments in a day, I was hosing down bloody bodies for a week after. So, you just make sure you do as he says, and it will be better for everyone involved!" said the Guard.

\* \* \*

Hans quickly became accustomed to the routine of sleeping on a hard cell floor; he had even got used to learning to lie with his left leg elevated so that the ankle bracelet didn't rub in the night against the floor. The guard who had accompanied the Professor with Private Vogel would still come into Hans's cell once a day to deliver a half-cup of water and a dried piece of bread.

It was seven days before the Professor came to see Hans in his holding cell.

"So, Hans, I am told that you have asked to speak to me," said Professor Bonn.

"That's correct, Professor."

"Well, what is it you want to say?"

"Professor, I have had time to reflect and I have decided that it is better to come clean. The fact is I have engaged in homosexual acts. I want to cooperate with you, but I do not want to stay in the centre any longer, I just want to go back to my house and restart my life."

"That could be a possibility, Hans, but only if you give yourself completely to me and the programme I have designed for men like you. You see, the leader and the party know that all you need is re-education – you are an example of how one of the master race can be led from the right path by choices in his lifestyle. What you have is almost like a virus; you are infected with a disease that needs to be purged from your body. I have developed a re-education programme that can address your disease and help you change so that you can re-enter society. So, Hans, are you willing to give yourself to this programme, will you submit to the entire test I have designed and not turn away when the going gets tough? Because I have to warn you now, the journey we are about to embark on is a long one, a virus such as yours cannot be cured overnight."

"I am willing, Professor. I will do whatever you want of me. You're right, I know you are right. I have a virus and must be cured of it. With yours and God's help, I will overcome this damn infliction."

"I am glad to hear this, Hans, I am glad you are finally ready to reintegrate into German society. All you need to do now is to put your faith in the party and we will be here for you. You are not the only homosexual man who has been helped by the party – my treatment has worked on hundreds of men who were once in your position. Many of these men now live successful happy lives and have families. They often write to me and say how much they appreciate the guidance they were given when they too finally realised they needed to do something about the disease they were suffering from."

"Thank you, Professor, I promise I will do everything in my power to get myself back as a member of society. I want to be normal again, I will do what you want, I promise."

"That is the spirit, now the first stage of your treatment will involve the need to address your past crimes and undertake a medical examination to make sure your body is in working order. You will follow the guards' directions and do as they tell you. Once the first stage is completed, you will then see me, and we will discuss the psychological terms of your illness. You will also receive spiritual guidance throughout from our priest. Guards!" said Professor Bonn.

Two guards appeared.

"Take Mr Lehman to the medical examination centre, tell the doctors he is to be joining the homosexual re-education programme and I want him prepared and ready for physiological evaluation," said Professor Bonn.

The guards nodded at the Professor and dragged Hans by the scruff of his neck towards the door. As they went down the corridors, Hans could see through small windows in other integration cells; the dull cries flowed after him as he was marched towards the medical examination area of the centre.

On arrival in the medical examination area, Hans was told to remove all his clothes and to lie down on his back on the doctor's medical table. Four doctors ordered Hans to provide a urine and blood sample, he was then made to sit up and say ahh. Just when he thought it couldn't get any worse, he was ordered to bend over the table and to pull his bum cheeks apart; the doctors spent what felt like a lifetime examining his anus for lacerations, every so often making comments and inserting a finger and feeling inside his body. The shame was almost unbearable for Hans – less than a month ago he was dining with generals and commanders; now he was being ordered to bend over naked whilst a random person decided to invade his body. How had it come to this, he thought. The humiliation then continued as the doctors examined Hans's penis, they rolled back the head, squeezing and poking and then stopping to make comments and scribble down notes on their clipboards.

During his medical examination, Hans had noticed that his clothes had been taken away by a nurse who had been observing the examination. When she returned she was carrying a pile of what looked like black pyjamas; they were the same as the ones he had seen other prisoners wearing around the resettlement and interrogation centre, apart from one small difference: his, he noticed, had a small pink triangle on the front jacket pocket.

"Excuse me, doctor, I don't mean to question the programme, but could you please tell me where are my clothes I came in with?" said Hans.

The doctors looked baffled. "Your clothes, Mr Lehman, were civilian clothes; you are no longer a civilian, you are a prisoner undergoing re-education for the illness of homosexuality. The fact that you voluntarily agreed to the treatment does not mean you are any better than any of the other prisoners here in the centre, it just means that you are willing to try and change. You see, you are no different, but you are lucky because, despite your depraved feelings and thoughts, you have the advantage of being born with Aryan blood. A Jew, you see, cannot change, he had no option to do so; he is born and therefore he is. So next time you feel like questioning why or what is going on, remember how lucky you are! Those poor Jews will not be so lucky, I can tell you, they will be moved when the time is right to southern Poland and will suffer a different fate to you that I can tell you," said the doctor.

"Thank you, doctor, I know I am a lucky man to be given this chance to undergo re-education, but why do I have a pink triangle?" said Hans.

"The pink triangle represents a person who has homosexual tendencies; you see the Jews have the yellow triangles over each other like the Star of David, the Gypsies have the brown triangles and so on. Now get dressed, you are to go back to your cell," said the doctor.

* * *

"Hey, come over here, sweety and sit on my knee?" said one prisoner.

"Yeah, let me have a squeeze of that arse!" said another prisoner.

"Fuck off, this is all a mistake! Once I'm out of here you'll see I will be making sure you fuckers suffer, along with these idiot guards and that doctor!" growled Hans.

"Do you think we're daft? We all know what a pink triangle means, it means you're a dirty cock sucking little bitch. Now why don't you get on your knees and do what you do best!" said one prisoner.

Hans had endured days of the same kind of treatment, since being labelled. The pink triangle only drew more attention to him even though he tried his best to keep it hidden at all times. By now he thought everyone must know.

"If you're looking for a fight then I will give you one! I'm not taking any more of your shit!" said Hans as his voice deepened.

Hans had been repeatedly beaten and taunted since being put back in with the general population. Sometimes it was by the guard, other times it was by the other prisoners, although they were often too weak to keep it going, whereas the guards would take their time over the beatings. They would often take it in turn, to punch Hans in the face and then kick him when he finally fell to the floor.

* * *

When Hans finally saw the Professor again, he was covered from head to foot in bruises. He was no doctor, but it had been almost a week since he could see out of his right eye and he wasn't sure if it would ever open again. He also was sure that at least two of his ribs were broken and he had developed a slight limp when he walked. Upon inspection of Hans the Professor ordered the Guards to bring in a doctor. The doctor administered an injection to dull the pain and dressed his cuts. It had been a while since Hans had used his mouth to speak since being labelled a homosexual and given a pink triangle – people in the centre had made an effort not to be seen talking to him; even the guards had stopped shouting abuse at him, they just now kicked him at will.

"So, Hans, how are you feeling? It looks like your re-education is going well," said the Professor.

"I've been better," snapped Hans.

"Clearly not lost your sense of humour though, have you. You may feel bad now, Hans. I understand how you are feeling, and I am sorry you have run into some trouble whilst you have been here at the centre. I am afraid some of the guards and inmates can be what you would call 'prejudiced'; this will change though as soon as you do. The first part of your treatment involves your medical examination; we have to make sure there are no big differences in your body to that of normal Germans. The second stage involves you coming to terms with your illness and the realisation of what society thinks about it. You are given that pink triangle so that everyone here knows you are different; when you finally pass your treatment you will be able to remove those clothes along with the triangle and never look back. But for now, the shame you feel for wearing them has to be endured. Trust me, Hans, it will make you a stronger man in the end and will force you to loathe yourself the same way that others do right now. Only through admitting you have behaved evilly before, can you make the change for the better," said the Professor.

"So, what's next?"

"I'm happy to report that you passed your medical examination, and the guards have reported to me that you have not caused any problems despite being provoked several times. This is good to know; it shows you are willing to accept your shortcomings and the authority of your superiors. Now I am satisfied that you have successfully completed these two stages, it is on to stage three; this can be the hardest stage for most prisoners and will require you to have strong willpower. Stage three involves you learning to love the female form and particularly female genitalia. You will be taken to Wing C of the centre; this wing is saved for prisoners who need intense assistance, some to combat their illnesses like you and others to help them remember information that might be vital to the party. But first I would like to ask you some questions and I want you to answer them truthfully.

"Before coming to this facility, you were a member of many of the elite clubs in Köln. The party is always interested in knowing where the gay community spend their time and, more importantly, which individuals are part of that community. What I want you to do is point to this photo sheet I have in front of me and mark with this pen any of the men you might have seen at these clubs, particularly any that came to your gay private members' clubs," said the Professor.

"Professor, if I help you will you please help me? I need the guards to go easy on me, I am afraid that if they continue to beat me the way they do, I will never recover. I could also do with some more food so that I can grow strong for when I am rehabilitated back into society," said Hans.

"You agreed when you decided to undergo this treatment that you would not question anything I asked of you. Having said this, very well, I will speak to the guards and ask them to be kinder to you despite their urges – you can't blame them, you know, it's only natural to want to beat and eliminate the filth from society. Here, take these cigarettes and I will speak to the centre cook to make sure you get a little more rations per day. Now show me who else in these photos you know to be a homosexual," said the Professor.

The Professor congratulated him on his accomplishments, he then told the guards to go and get coffee for them and some bread and jam.

The two men sat inside the holding cells, its bare walls a reflection of Hans's predicament. At first, they sat there silently sipping coffee and smoking cigarettes. Hans was desperate to eat but he didn't want to just grab at the bread; he hadn't eaten in so long, he was licking his lips, but he didn't want to give the Professor the satisfaction of needing what he had.

"Go ahead, Hans, you can eat," said the Professor.

"Hans, when evaluating my subjects, I like to try to understand how they came to be the way they are. You are an interesting subject because you had everything. Please, Hans, tell me about your first sexual experience with a man and how it came to be. I mean was there ever a time you decided to be homosexual?" asked the Professor.

"I had an experience with another boy when I was ten years old. We were playing soldiers with each other and rolling around in the dirt when I noticed that we were becoming incredibly close and I was getting aroused. Before I knew it, we were kissing and holding each other. Things never got any further than just kissing. I think the other boy just grew out of it, but I couldn't, Professor, I felt drawn to other men," said Hans.

"I know from previous studies that I have conducted that often homosexuality is heightened when an only-male environment exists, but you see what you probably didn't know at your age was that you were doing something wrong. When we get to a certain age our minds develop and we can judge what is right and what is wrong. You, you see, have something in your brain that makes you act differently to the rest of the males in society and this is why you must undergo the treatment so that we can get you back ready for the real world.

"I told you a little about stage three of the process earlier; well let me now fill you in completely. Stage three involves a highly sophisticated visual and sound programme that is aimed at making you ready to appreciate the female form in all its beauty. I will inform the guards that you will be undertaking stage three of your re-education programme in the next week and I will be sure to report how well your progress is going. I'm sure once those heartier rations come through that you will be feeling better soon. Keep with the programme, you are doing very well," said the Professor.

* * *

Over the next three months, Hans found himself in a routine that involved a daily visit to Wing C. The area was designated for enhanced interrogation, with specific sections designed for specific prisoners. The area Hans was brought to was painted white but with pink triangles near each corner to the beginning of each new wall; they were this way to add extra insult and humiliation to the prisoners who were undergoing the re-education programme. The walk from B wing to C wing was not a long one, but to keep his mind occupied Hans would often count the number of steps from his cell to the mini cinema where he would go for six hours a day. Once inside the cinema Hans would be tied to a chair, his hands and legs bound to the chair and his eyes held open by small metal bars. The metal bars were like having matchsticks inserted into his eyes – these were needed to facilitate the films that Hans was forced to watch for six hours straight. During the showing of the films, he would have heart and blood pressure monitors placed on his arms and chest; he would also receive an injection during the session. Hans was told that this was a mood stabiliser, but it could have been anything.

The films Hans was forced to watch were a collage of small, short pictures and films rolled into one long six-hour production. The pictures would sometimes be familiar, like German athletes from the Olympics or clips from propaganda films, blond-haired and blue-eyed boys and girls would run across the screen, then before Hans could focus naked women would appear, the film would flick back to the party flag and its soldiers marching across France. The films would play over and over again, whilst music from Wagner, Horst-Wessel-Lied or Die Wacht am Rhein played continuously. The sessions were draining but Hans found them manageable; it got to a point where he even knew when the music would change, and when the next film reel would start. The only thing that would add to his discomfort was the electronic wire attached to Hans's penis. The nurse had at first informed Hans that this was to monitor his sexual activity, analysing arousal and blood pressure. However, to Hans's amazement and often pain, the electrode had a secondary function: this was an electric shock that would be administered during sessions when Hans either started to drop to sleep through exhaustion or when he looked away from the screen for whatever reason. At first, he had found the pornography displayed on-screen upsetting and disturbing – it wasn't that he couldn't watch or that he found heterosexual sex awful, he just didn't see the point in it being shown in the tacky way it was being shown – surely, he thought, it was better to show a loving couple engaging in sex rather than the hammer and tongs action he was forced to endure; after all, wasn't the party trying to promote family values?

When the film sessions were over Hans would have to be taken back to his cell – the fatigue would often tire him out so much that he would not be able to use his legs coherently or be able to open his eyes enough to walk in a straight line. The way in which he was forced to watch the film led him to soil himself; the guards would often comment on his smell whilst dragging him back to his cell, and if he smelt particularly bad they would often stop at the showers and turn the hosepipe on him. The cold water would give him a sharp wakeup call but then he would pass out again, his eyes heavy like stone slabs. When back in his cell he would curl up into a ball and wait for the next session. The one thing that was positive to his re-education was the fact the Professor had kept his word and he had started to get bigger portions of food; he also got a packet of cigarettes delivered once a week. The guards, however, would steal these almost automatically, thus he would have to either hide as many as he could or smoke them all within the first hour. The film sessions would even infect Hans's dreams; often he would find himself dreaming about a certain part of one of the movies, himself playing the lead role or acting as an observer in the film watching the characters play out scenes.

* * *

"Hans, wake up!" said the Professor.

As Hans awoke from his film-induced unconsciousness he could see the Professor standing over him. He was examining him from head to foot, staring at Hans's face.

"Hans, I am here to tell you that you are progressing positively, and the nurses have reported to me that you are cooperating as best you can with the re-education programme. They also tell me that you are making physical progress too, that you are now a lot healthier, and that your mind is becoming better trained to accept and love the female form. I have to tell you I am very happy to hear this news. I was sure you would be an acceptable subject and you are not disappointing me," said the Professor.

Hans tried to open his eyes to focus on the Professor whilst he was talking, but the effort was just too much, like a man trying to stay awake in a long afternoon meeting he found himself nodding, slipping in and out of consciousness.

"Guards, bring us some chairs and a table, can't you see this man can hardly stand," said the Professor.

"I don't know why you treat them so well, Professor; if you ask me all this re-education is a waste of time, better to put a bullet in his brain and have done with it," said the guard.

"Yes, well I didn't ask you, did I? I gave you an order and as long as I'm in charge you will do what I say. If the authorities thought you were the brightest one in the room they would have put you in charge, wouldn't they? Now get a move on," said the Professor.

"Good, now pick him up and put him in the chair!" said the Professor.

"I don't want to touch him – he stinks, look at him; he must have shit and pissed himself five times over," said the guard.

"I'm sick of arguing with you, put him in the fucking chair and then go and get us some coffee and some cigarettes, there's a good boy!" said the Professor.

"Hans, wake up, come on, drink this water. Here, let me light you up a cigarette," said the Professor.

As Hans struggled to drink the water, he felt his throat burn – his bruises had yet to heal, and he could only manage short sharp sips. As he lit the cigarette the smoke slowly filtered its way down his throat and brought a slight relief from the pain. The nicotine rush hit him with intense shock; he felt woozy and slightly lightheaded.

"Hans, I need you to focus. You are feeling better now, correct?" said the Professor.

"Yes, forgive me if I am not myself, the re-education programme is intensive, and I am often drained beyond belief by the pressure it puts on my body."

"Indeed, it is, Hans, but as I have told you before, it is for your own good; only through intensive programming can you rid yourself of the illness that once consumed you. Have you been paying attention to Father Kuntz and his visits to the centre? I believe he has been to see you once or twice to provide you with spiritual guidance."

"Father Kuntz has visited me a couple of times and his visits have been very pleasant. He gave me a bible too and I have been trying to read it whenever I can."

"That is good to hear, Hans, I am so proud of the changes you are making and of your progress. You should treasure that bible, for when you finally leave this place to get back to everyday society you will remember how it helped guide you from evil to good. Now, let us discuss your next stage in your re-education. I am happy to report that you have completed the propaganda section successfully and you are in the final stages of re-education. A physical test will now follow and then you will be subjected to a final integration session with me. You see, Hans, you are nearly ready to re-join the new Germany we are all trying to create. You will be able to use your newly found vigour to build a place for yourself in the new Germany, and who knows, you may even be able to help the party with other homosexuals who want to change their ways and become good people rather than sinners."

"I am ready for this, Professor; I am ready for the next challenge. I am trying my best to do the programme successfully, forgive me if I am not going as fast as you think I should be."

"You are doing fine, Hans. If you think you are ready for the next test then I will inform the guards and we can schedule the event."

* * *

"You two go and arrange the final stage of this man's examination. He will need his strength, so I want you two to keep an extra attentive eye on him and make sure he gets enough food," said the Professor.

The idea of the new challenge excited Hans, he was that much closer to being a free man. All he needed to do now was to get through another physical, answer the questions correctly and he would be able to go back into society. Who knows, he might even be able to go back to his own home. Apart from Private Vogel, only Penelope knew that he was locked up in the resettlement and interrogation centre and he was sure she wouldn't have told anyone at how he ended up in here, the shame surely must have been too much for any normal person to bear.

"Well, I have to be going now, Hans," said the Professor.

He blew cigarette smoke all over Hans's face as he departed but did stretch out his hand in what looked like a gesture of friendship.

"Thank you, Professor, I won't let you down and I really appreciate you ensuring the guards treat me well; the extra food has definitely helped me build my strength up."

That evening Hans sat in his cold stone cell and dreamed of a better life. He had recently started to talk to himself in a desperate effort for company, and at night he would whisper:

"Soon I will be free, I have done everything they have asked, they must let me go now. I've nearly finished the course, oh how I can't wait to be out of here, to see the sky, to see life outside these walls."

"Keep your voice down, you don't want the guards to hear us – if they do we will be in super trouble," said Hans to himself.

"I know, I know I will. I'm just so excited, I can't wait, maybe when I pass the final physical, I might be able to move freely. I could even go to London or somewhere in the new world. New York would be great, yes New York, I could start a new life there. Nobody would ever know about this place or my past, I may even be able to live my life more freely, you know America is supposed to be much more open-minded than Europe," said Hans.

"Ok, come on, stop talking now, we are nearly at full strength, no need to go catch a beating and be back to square one, just go to sleep," said Hans.

That morning Hans was awoken by a steel door slamming.

"Come on, you, time to move, quick, on your feet before you piss me off. I can't believe I have to spend my time looking after wastes of space like you," said the guard.

Hans jumped to his feet quickly – the week of extra food and water had helped him recover and he had even managed to get a semi-decent sleep during his final week.

"Yes, sir, I will be right with you!" said Hans.

As they marched out of the cell and down the corridors, Hans couldn't help but ask: "Excuse me, sir, but where are we going?"

"You're going to C wing and after I have finished babysitting you, I am going for lunch, then a shit," said the guard.

Funny, Hans thought, that despite all their bullshit, despite all the propaganda, the beatings, the misinformed sermons from Father Kuntz, he still knew that he was homosexual and that nothing would change this; he had beaten the system.

* * *

"Hans, do you need to use the toilets down the hall or are you good?" said the guard.

"If it wouldn't be too much hassle then yes, I wouldn't mind," said Hans.

"Look, you finish your exercises and I will come back for you in five minutes to walk you there. You're doing good, you know. I can't speak for all of the guards but myself, I have to say, I am impressed; you really have changed my opinion, and so has the Professor with his experiments," said the guard.

Just then the Professor walked through the door, banging it into the guard ever so slightly.

"Hans, you are looking much stronger. I am glad to see this; your re-education is nearly complete. Are you ready for your final physical?" said the Professor.

"I am, sir," said Hans.

"Good, well take a seat. Firstly we have some questions that I must run through with you. I expect you to answer these truthfully, is that understood?"

"It is, Professor."

"Good, now my first question is would you say your opinion of the female sex has changed? That is to say, do you now find women attractive?"

"I would say it has, Professor, I can honestly say that I now look at a woman and I am attracted to her," said Hans.

"And how about your feelings towards other men?"

"I realise now that the life I was living before was wrong, sexual acts between men are wrong and it was due to my childhood and the all-male environment that I misjudged friendly child's play for something a lot different.

life I lived before coming to the centre."

"And what about the sight of another man naked? Do you still feel sexual urges toward them?"

"I don't, Professor. I have asked myself this question many times during the last six months and now I know that it was women all along that I should have been attracted to."

"Do you feel that if you were to be released that you would be able to engage in a sexual relationship with a woman? I mean, would you be able to re-join society, get married, and eventually bring good wholesome Ayran children into the world?"

"I believe I would, Professor, I think I am now ready to re-join society to spend my life working towards the creation of a new Germany, one that allows us to finally pass on the party's values to not only Europe but eventually the world."

"I am glad to hear that, Hans, of course, there is no doubt that we will win it, but it is always good to hear an inmate say such things. I think I have now heard enough, and I think yes you are ready for the final physical test. Guards, bring her in!" said the Professor.

The guards entered the room with a blonde-haired woman dressed in the same clothing as Hans. She looked skinny and gaunt, but it was obvious to Hans that she was still beautiful even though she was seriously in need of nourishment. The guards were holding her by both her arms, but she didn't look afraid; in fact, to Hans's astonishment she really didn't do anything, her face never even left the floor from where it was fixated.

"Now, Hans, firstly, let me introduce you to Anna. Anna is a Ukrainian Jew from Kiev, she was lucky enough to be working in Koln when she was captured by the party and sent to the centre. As you can see from her appearance, Anna is, I think you will agree with me, a very aesthetically pleasing female, despite her being of Jewish descent," said the Professor.

The Professor was right: Anna was a very beautiful woman, Hans thought, you could tell by her high cheekbones, she must have once looked like an American movie star. She reminded him of one of the Russian ballet dancers he had seen many years before the party had come to power. She could be an exact match if you were to take one of the ballet dancers and knock all the life and soul out of her.

"Your final physical, Hans, is to take Ms Anna here and have sexual intercourse with her. You can do it in any position you like, but I want to see full penetration and ejaculation to complete this part of your re-education."

"Professor, am I just expected to strip her naked and have sex with her?" said Hans.

"That is exactly what you are going to do, Hans. Now if she gives you any resistance you are more than within your rights to beat her as you see fit, but I am sure you will not get any opposition. You see, Anna is what we like to call one of the guards' 'comfort women'. She is used to taking care of the guards' needs if you know what I mean. Anna! Undress!" said the Professor.

Anna slowly started to undress. She removed her black pyjama shirt to reveal a bony body, covered in bruises that could have only been caused through punches to the midsection. She then removed her prison-issued pyjamas to expose her private parts and bony, sore-covered legs. Now standing completely naked she tried ever so slightly to move her hand to allow her to cover her private parts; the guards, however, did not allow her to do so and thus held her in place.

Hans walked towards the girl. He stopped dead in front of Anna and took her by the hand. He used his index finger to guide her face upwards towards his until they were looking one another in the eye. Anna had an empty look on her face, she was a shell of a woman. Even when they were eye to eye, she did not blink, did not smile.

It felt like an eternity, but Hans found himself staring at Anna, a million thoughts running through his mind. Should he turn her around and fuck her from behind? This might be the easiest way, he thought – at least then he wouldn't have to see her dead eyes. He knew he was on borrowed time, he had to get on with it; but it wasn't excitement he felt, it was shame and empathy – he couldn't get it out of his mind this was someone's child.

"I am sorry, Professor, but I cannot do it, I cannot do as you ask. I cannot rape this woman. I am happy to do anything else, I will watch the movies again, but I am sorry I cannot do this," said Hans.

The Professor's face went a dark shade of red, his voice elevated and now breathing heavily, he looked at Hans like a disappointed father.

"What? You cannot do it! You are so close to being re-educated and you risk it all for this piece of Jewish scum? You know what this means, Hans, you know there is no going back?" said the Professor.

"I cannot do what you ask of me, no; in fact, I won't do what you ask of me!"

"You either take this Jewish whore and fuck her now, Hans, or you will feel the full wrath of the party!"

Hans noticed a small flicker in Anna's eyes. She was still looking directly into Hans's eyes, but it was like someone had switched a light on in her head – she was alive again if only for a brief moment.

"I will not, Professor, I'm sorry but your programme has failed. I am gay and proud of it. I will not bring myself to your level; I will not commit this vile act on this young woman. Whatever else I am, I am not a common criminal and I am not some sick rapist. I ask you what kind of a person I would be anyway to go back into society having done what you ask!"

The Professor's face screwed up like a rolled-up piece of paper. "Guards! Get that whore out of my sight!"

As the guards dragged Anna naked from the room she finally spoke. It was in the lowest tone possible and could have quite easily been missed had it not been for Hans watching her every movement on her face. She simply mouthed the words 'thank you' as she was taken away. As the guards left the room Hans would hear a loud bang. After around 30 seconds they re-entered, with blood on their boots.

"Now take Mr Lehman to Wing C and we will see how long he survives without his extra meal rations and his special treatment. You both heard me, didn't you! I want him to suffer before he dies, treat him how you would a Jew; no, in fact, he is lower than a Jew and I want him to be treated as such!" said the Professor.

One of the guards pulled out his wooden baton and smashed it across Hans's face, knocking both teeth and blood from his mouth. When the other guard pulled his gun from his holster Hans thought his time on earth was up, but instead of putting a bullet between his eyes, the guard used the butt of the gun to deliver a crunching blow to the side of Hans's skull. The might of the impact knocked Hans to the floor, where he found the boots of the guards waiting for him.

One after another he received the full force of their kicks in all parts of his body, one landing in his chest, the other in his groin, and then to the back of his head. When the soldiers finally stopped, Hans was lying in a pool of blood, barely conscious.

"Take him to Wing C; once there I want you to implement programme D," said the Professor.

\* \* \*

The pain woke Hans up from where he had passed out. He was in total darkness; his hands were bound behind his back and rope was tied to his legs, allowing him no room to move. He tried to gasp for air but there was something inserted in his mouth and a black bag cloth pulled tightly around his head. As he wriggled to try to find his footing, he could feel pain shooting up him from various parts of his body. First, it was his groin, he was sure something was ruptured, and then he felt his ribs and back. His spine felt like it was going in different directions, and he wasn't even sure he could walk. Before he could feel for other injuries, he heard two men talking.

"There he is, now the chains are off. The Professor has given us free rein to do whatever we want to you before your miserable life comes to an end. What do you think we should do first to him, Gurt?" said the soldier.

"Well, Karl, I have always been in favour of a little water treatment," said Gurt.

"Good idea, put him on that chair and get me a bucket of water and a jug," said Karl.

Hans was trying to focus on breathing through his nose. Although he couldn't see he could hear the guards walking around the room, and a bucket being filled with water from a tap. After about a minute the water stopped, and he could hear it getting closer by the spillages made as the guard was carrying it. One of the guards grabbed Hans by the legs and dragged him, sitting him upright on a chair.

Once in the chair, he felt the guards wrap more rope around his chest and legs, then one of the guards tipped him back so that he was at a 60-degree angle, then he felt water being poured over his face. The dark black cloth that was tightly secured around his head started to become damp and hold the water, stopping his only airway. Hans gulped for air.

Just as he thought he was going to pass out he felt the water stop and one of the guards pulled the cloth just far enough from his face so that he could catch his breath; he gulped at the air almost trying to eat as much of it as he could. Just as he felt like he was able to breathe normally he felt a punch to the bridge of his nose, the pain shot to his head and the blood pouring from it started to block his only airway.

The guards again poured water over his face and the drowning sensation returned, Hans's eyes felt like they were going to pop out of his head, he couldn't breathe and with every breath, he could feel the blood run back and forth up his broken nose. The blood was now dripping into the back of his throat enough for him to taste.

This practice continued for the next 20 minutes, each one lasting slightly longer than the last. The punches too varied from face to torso to thigh.

When the guards did finally stop their sadistic water torture, Hans was fighting for his life. His lungs felt like they were flooded with blood and water, and he had to take quick gasping breaths just to survive. The guards lit a cigarette each and stopped.

"Jesus, this can be hard work, can't it. I am totally knackered, my arms ache and I think I might have broken a knuckle on that last punch," said Karl.

"You are out of shape, Karl. You have to make sure you knock the shit out of this scum at least twice a week if you are to get any kind of practice. What do you suggest we do next to him?" said Gurt.

"I know what we will do but not before we have finished these cigarettes and I am not doing anything until we take that rag from his mouth – it's no fun unless you can hear the bastard's scream," said Karl.

"Agreed, ok, I am almost done. Come on, then, let's get on with it," said Gurt.

The guards reached over to Hans and loosened the cloth around his head, then reached under to remove the rag from deep within his mouth. As soon as it was removed, Hans took in a massive breath that was almost too much for his lungs to handle. Before he could manage to try to look with his eyes, he saw the dark cloth go back over his head and go back into its original position.

"Hang on, before you put that out let's have some fun," said Karl.

One of the guards lifted Hans's trouser leg and pushed his still-lit cigarette into his leg. The pain was sharp and unyielding and forced Hans to let out a loud scream in agony. The guards laughed with pleasure and then shoved the other cigarette into his kneecap, forcing Hans to again scream with pain.

"Pass me that rusty lead pipe, Karl," said Gurt.

There was a silence in the cell. Then he heard the pipe being dragged around the cell on the floor, the walls, and then back to the floor. As he listened, he tried to figure out where the guard was, through the cylindrical sound the pipe was making against the stone floor. From nowhere he felt the pipe crash against his thigh; once he had let out a scream the noise continued, again being dragged around him in a circle back and forth, from behind him and in front of him. Once more he felt the full force of the pipe come across his body, this time impacting against his elbow. Hans screamed again in pain.

"Please stop! Stop, I beg you!" said Hans.

"Look, the little gay boy is still alive, Karl, and now he has found his voice. How dare you speak to us, you are scum, you are less than worthless!" said Gurt.

"Please I am begging you, please. I don't think I can take anymore."

"We will stop when we think you have had enough, boy!" said Gurt.

Hans felt the pipe strike him again around the face. The blow hit his front teeth, shattering them on impact. His mouth was now rushing with blood, causing him to spit the broken teeth and the blood from around his mouth. The gunk of saliva, blood, and smashed teeth had congregated in front of his mouth and was now running down the black cloth towards his shoulders.

"Please for the love of Christ, please stop this, I will do anything you want, please, I will cooperate in any way, please just stop beating me I beg of you," said Hans.

"That's just it though, isn't it, boy, you won't do what you are told, will you? If you had done so, you wouldn't have ended up in here with us. No, you would have given that Jewish whore a good fucking and would be well on your way out of here," said Gurt.

"I told the Professor that all those stupid experiments were a fucking waste of time. People don't change. How could he have expected this sick pervert to change – he doesn't want to fuck a woman, he wants some guy's cock! Well, I have just had a good idea if it's cock you want then maybe we can help you. Karl, untie him from that chair and fasten him to that table," said Gurt.

The guard grabbed Hans by the scruff of his neck and held him in place whilst they undid the rope around his legs. They then dragged him over to what felt like a table and bent him over it.

"Yes, that's it! Now tie his hands forward to the table so he cannot move and pull down his trousers!" said Gurt.

Bent over the table, his arms unable to move, Hans was acutely aware that the lower part of his body was exposed. He felt so vulnerable, he couldn't even use his hands to cover himself.

"Please, please," begged Hans.

Gurt walked over to Hans and shoved the rusty lead pipe deep into his anus. Hans screamed with pain, tears were flooding down his face and he was writhing from side-to-side in agony. As the pipe was pushed deeper and deeper into his body, he could hear the two guards laughing as it cut his insides.

Karl pulled Hans's hair so that his head was as upright as it could get and shouted into his ear: "I thought you would like this, I thought you liked things up your arse?"

"Yeah, you should be loving it, you fucking dirty piece of shit!" said Gurt.

The pain was unbearable; every push seemed to go deeper and further into his internal organs. The image in Hans's head of the dirty rusty lead pipe entering his body kept flashing into his mind like one of the cinema films he had been forced to watch. It was too much for him to take and for his body. As pain flared so did his mind eventually shut down, in a fuzz of white noise and tunnel vision.

# CHAPTER

### 8

"So how long have you been in this dark, flea-ridden hole?" said Thomas.

"I've been in the centre for about three months, I think, although it's a little hard to keep up to date when all you have to look at are these stone walls and the wooden bunk bed, isn't it?" said Werner.

"Although I have to admit, the time allows you to think, especially when you're wondering how the fuck you ever ended up here in the first place," added Werner.

"Well, why did you end up here anyway, Werner?" said Thomas.

"Well, you know, there were certain events that led me to be here, betrayal by me and by others springs to mind, but you know, in the end, the reason was hatred. Hatred for others and hatred for myself," said Werner.

"How so?" said Thomas.

"It was my hatred for the Jews that led me to this point in my life, and now I live amongst you all, how ironic is that?" said Werner.

"There is a certain poetic justice to it all I guess but you know that might not last long. There are many in here, Werner, who are out for your blood, hell I was when I first heard you used to be a party member. If I were you, I would learn to have eyes in the back of your head – the people in here hate you just as much as the party hates the Jews."

"I don't blame them, Thomas, why would they want to be in here with someone who persecuted their families and friends at every opportunity? We reap what we sow, and I am definitely living proof of that," said Werner. "I have to just accept my circumstances, Thomas, what else is there for me? If I get shanked in the back so be it, I can't keep living in fear in here, I am powerless to change anything."

"Things will get better, Werner; when you have sunk to rock bottom you can only go up."

"You're a good man, Thomas, I really appreciate you being so kind. I wonder if you could do me a favour whilst you're in such a good mood?"

"What is it that I can do?" said Thomas.

Thomas looked shocked by Werner's request for help, his pale gaunt face look perplexed, trying to figure out what he could do to help a man hated by everyone in the centre.

"Well, when I first got here one of the guards felt sorry for me, he gave me a packet of cigarettes as he noticed I still had my father's lighter. I used the cigarettes to barter for some food but now I am all out and I really need to find a good option so that I can trade the lighter. Do you know anyone who can help me?" said Werner.

"Oh, I see, well your best bet would be Isaac, but I'm sorry, Werner, it's not worth my life, they are just as likely to knife me for helping you. I will give you one piece of advice though: do not tell people you have a lighter – people in here kill each other for a slice of bread."

"I know Isaac. Thanks, Thomas, I will go and see him."

"No problem, just do not say you know me whatever you do. I have to be going; you take care."

Walking through the courtyard Werner could hear people talking about him as he passed their way, they would say things like: how can you turn on your own kinds, or party lover. Some would call him a traitor and others would spit in his direction or directly at him. Finally, he spotted Isaac talking to a group of men.

As soon as he approached the men, they all dispersed in various directions, making it abundantly clear that Werner was the reason for their quick departure.

"Werner, I have told you before, if you need to come and talk to me you must find me when we are not out in the open. I cannot afford to be seen with you out in public like this; you know half the people in here think you are an undercover spy, the other half just wants you dead, because of your past," said Isaac.

"I am sorry, Isaac, I did remember what you said but you see I haven't eaten for five days."

"And I am supposed to feel sorry for you, am I? The next time you are feeling lonely and hungry, try to think about all the Jewish families your actions have impacted upon, think about how many mothers are lonely without their children, because they have been killed by the very party you promoted. I am sorry, Werner, but if it wasn't for business then I would want you dead too!" Isaac

"I don't want your pity, Isaac, I am here about business but how the hell does anyone know my background anyway?"

"We all know you were sent here after the party discovered your Jewish heritage, it's no secret and we all know you must have killed a man too," said Isaac.

"How do you know that?"

"It's written right there on your chest! Your star has a big M written on it. The M stands for murder; I'm surprised the prison guards didn't tell you, you being all chummy with them! So come on, tell me who did you kill?" Isaac

"Look, I'm not here to discuss me, I am here about business. I have this solid silver lighter and I want to exchange it for some food. If you help me, I am willing to give you a small finding fee, how does that sound?"

Isaac took the lighter from Werner's hand and inspected it closely.

"I have to admit, Werner, this is a beautiful lighter, and it's all in good working condition. You know if you were to sell this anywhere else in the world other than in here, you would get a pretty price for it. Here though, here you might just get five potatoes if you are lucky." Isaac

"So you think you can shift it then for me?"

"Me? No, I don't think I can do the transaction, but I do know a man who I think can, he is very particular who he deals with, so he may want to meet you first. If you like I can take the lighter to him and then give you the potatoes in the next few days." Isaac

"Do you think I am stupid? Don't be daft, I am not just going to hand it over to you on your word that you will deliver the goods. I am holding on to this; like I said, if you set up the deal then you will get your cut."

"Ok, fine with me, but remember who is doing who the favour. I will come and find you in the next couple of days. Whatever you do, don't come and find me!" Isaac

\* \* \*

Two days went by till Werner saw Isaac again; by now he was beginning to lose all hope that he would be able to make the deal. Werner was starving and was unable to move quickly on demand; instead, he chose to stay all day on his wooden bunk bed. He had been lucky so far in that he hadn't been called for work detail for the last three days. Often, men were picked at random in the centre and led down the street by the guards to the surrounding factories.

"Werner, Werner, get up," said Isaac.

Werner awoke in his hard wooden bunk to Isaac's brown beady eyes staring at him. He was balding more and more these days through lack of nourishment and it was starting to circle on the top of his head. He looked even more stressed than usual, his hands were shaking, and his fingernails were thick with black dirt.

"He will see you now. Come on, get up and come with me, we haven't got much time. He doesn't just do business with anyone, you know, so don't fuck this up. I have stuck my neck out for you," said Isaac.

Werner forced himself off his bunk and upright. Isaac insisted that he walk ten paces behind him so that people would not get suspicious that they were together.

In a secluded corner of the courtyard near the iron barbed wire fence Werner could see Isaac stop to talk to some skinny young men. They all looked similar in their issued clothes, but different in their facial expressions; as he approached, he could hear them arguing with Isaac about Werner.

"Why have you brought that Jew-hater here, Isaac? You know Rabbi Shiltz is not to be disturbed," said Helge.

"Climb down from your high horse, Helge, he knows I am coming," said Isaac.

"But does he know you are bringing *him*?" said Helge.

"Not that it is any of your business, but yes he does know that I am bringing Werner. Now move out of my way," said Isaac.

Isaac and Werner walked through the group of young men and down a small alleyway. When they finally reached the end of the alley, they came to a small cul-de-sac that looked like an unloading bay, there were meat hooks everywhere and industrial type machinery used for god knows what. In the corner, he could see an old gentleman sat at a table with two other old men.

"Hello, Isaac, nice to see you again and this must be the mysterious Werner Ritter, I have heard a lot about you," said Rabbi Shiltz.

"That's right I am, but forgive me, I have no idea who you are," said Werner.

"Well let me introduce myself then, I am Rabbi Shiltz and I am the chief Rabbi in the centre. These two other gentlemen you see sitting with me are also Rabbis, together we act as a small council for the Jewish inmates in here. We offer spiritual guidance when we can, of course, we cannot do special prayers on the Shabbat or prepare Kosher food for our festivals anymore, but talking – well the party cannot ban that, can they, no matter how hard they try.

"I hope you don't mind me calling you by your first name. A man such as you, who has never helped anyone but yourself, cannot comprehend that some people work towards the greater good of their people and know the value of working with others towards a greater goal," said Rabbi Shiltz.

"Oh, and what might that be, Rabbi, to line your own pockets?" said Werner.

"Here, Werner I have your potatoes ready. We have determined that we will offer you four potatoes for your lighter. Now may I see it?" said Rabbi Shiltz.

"Four? Isaac told me I would get at least five!" said Werner.

"I didn't, Rabbi. I said I thought you would get five, but I never said you would get five. I swear to you, Rabbi," said Isaac.

"Werner, whether Isaac here informed you of five or four potatoes is insignificant, what is significant is that I am offering you four! Now can I see the lighter for myself?" said Rabbi Shiltz.

"Here, take it, you old crook!" said Werner.

Werner stuffed the potatoes in his jacket pockets whilst Rabbi Shiltz inspected the lighter. He knew he shouldn't be getting mad with the Rabbi as he was respected throughout the centre by the Jewish population and could have been a useful ally, but years of being told what thieves the Jews were was hard to suppress.

"If you don't mind me asking, Werner, where did you get such a beautiful lighter?" said Rabbi Shiltz.

"It was a gift from my father; he carried it throughout the First World War, his father gave it to him, and he gave it to me," said Werner.

"I am hesitant to take it from you, especially when it has such sentimental value, but you see, Werner, I will use this lighter to try to bargain with the guards to get more rations for all the prisoners. I collect things like this so that when I do go to the guards to ask for something, they are, let's say, in a better mood and their first reaction isn't to blow my head off. You see, your potatoes may be important to you, but this lighter has more use. One day you will see that," said Rabbi Shiltz. "You know your story does interest me, Werner. Me and my friends here, make it our business to collect as much information as possible on the inmates here so that we can identify potential threats and problems, but you baffle me. I would like to see you tomorrow one-on-one if you have time? Would you be willing to do this?"

"I guess I could, Rabbi, I can't say I have any major luncheons I have to attend," said Werner sarcastically.

"You see, men, that is one thing the party cannot take from us, our sense of humour. Very well then, young Werner, let us say tomorrow at noon."

"See, I told you I would be able to get you some food for the lighter, didn't I, now how much is my cut for making all this happen?" said Isaac.

"Well, I know we said half a potato for you, but I am willing to share them all with you if you like," said Werner.

"What? Why would you do that?" said Isaac.

"I am trying to say thank you, this is the most I have spoken to anyone and I know the Rabbi is trying his best to make things better for the people in here. I don't know, I just feel like I should try and do the same," said Werner.

"Well, I am not going to say no. Maybe you are not as bad as everyone says. I will accept your offer, Werner, but I have to tell you that it takes more than two potatoes to buy my friendship. Friendship needs to be earned over time, you know; it cannot be bought," said Isaac.

They both walked slowly back to the wooden sleeper huts, not saying anything but smiling as they did.

"I think we should ration these potatoes, Isaac. We cannot just eat them all at once; we need to keep our strength up as much as we can. They will only last a couple of days," said Werner.

"I know what you are saying, Werner but if we are seen with this food, someone won't hesitate in cutting our throats for them. I think our best option is to just get a fire going as quickly and secretly as possible and then eat them without anyone seeing. I say we eat them and continue our struggle for more food. You are going to see Rabbi Shiltz tomorrow; you can always ask him to help you," said Isaac.

"You do what you want then with yours, but I am going to keep one on my person at all times. As for someone trying to cut my throat, well, let them try! I may be weak, but I was trained by the party in hand-to-hand combat and I am sure I can fight off any of these starving bags of bones. Plus, fuck it, I am eating this one cold!" said Werner.

\* \* \*

That night they both went for a walk just outside the wooden hut areas of the centre. After building a small fire Isaac cooked the two potatoes on a tree branch they had found a few nights before, whilst Werner kept guard. Occasionally, someone would walk towards them; if it was a guard they would pretend to be huddling around the fire for warmth, the guards pointed and made vulgar remarks but never actually got close enough to smell the cooking food. When the potatoes were ready, they both ate them as quickly as possible, often burning their mouths in the process. After they had finished, they shared one of Isaac's cigarettes.

"I guess this now makes us friends?" said Werner.

"Colleagues for now, but I don't often share my cigarettes, I can tell you," said Isaac.

The next day Werner did as Rabbi Shiltz asked and headed to meet him at noon. As he walked to the alleyway he couldn't help tongue the lump on the roof of his mouth and wondered whether it would be better to rip the skin off or just leave it. As he arrived, he could see the men who were there the day before were now gone. The Rabbi was standing with a woman with jet black hair, thick black eyebrows, and hazel brown eyes. When he approached them, Werner couldn't help but stare at her – despite her skinny frame, she was the most beautiful thing he had seen, she was like an oasis in a desert of misery.

"Hello, Rabbi and Ms?" said Werner.

"Oh, hello Werner, yes we have a meeting, don't we. Werner, this is Jenny, she is my granddaughter. We were brought here together, and I was just explaining to her that we will soon be leaving together as well," said Rabbi Shiltz.

"Fat chance of that, Rabbi, we will die in here if you ask me," said Werner.

Jenny looked down at the floor and grasped her granddad's hand.

"I am sorry, miss, please accept my apologies, I didn't mean to make you feel uncomfortable. I am sure your grandfather is right, we will soon be leaving here; after all, it is a resettlement centre and the party won't want to keep us here forever," said Werner.

"I'm sure you would know if anyone does! Aren't you the one they say was a member of the party, were you not tasked with inciting hatred towards the Jews? Grandfather, I cannot believe you are even talking to this monster," said Jenny.

"Now, Jenny, we have talked about this. Mr Ritter and I have private business to discuss so please leave us now," said Rabbi Shiltz.

As Jenny turned and walked away from the men she scowled at Werner with a look of disgust.

"Rabbi, you wanted to see me, but I can't possibly see what we have to discuss? I don't have anything else to barter, all I have left is a box of matches."

"That's ok, Werner I didn't ask you here to take your last worldly possession, I still don't feel great about the fact I had to take your grandfather's lighter from you, but as I explained it was for the greater good of the inmates in this centre."

"It's ok, like my father it means nothing to me now anyway."

"I am sorry to hear that, Werner, one should always try to make peace with one's family; in the end, it is all we have, that and God of course. This is partly the reason I have asked you here today. Please come closer to the fire so we can keep warm as we talk. The first reason I have asked you here is to try to explain how important you can be for your cause and the cause of the Jewish people living in the general population. You see, Werner, you used to be an up-and-coming member of the party and it is for that reason you can help us. You must have noticed that the guards go easier on you then they do a normal Jewish inmate? Why do you think this is?"

"Go easy on me? I'm a half-dead skinny excuse for a human being, how the hell is anyone going easy on me?"

"You do not have to take on work detail, the guards have never beaten you, indeed I have even seen some of them smile at you whilst you are walking in the courtyard. You see, Werner, they feel pity for you, they know that it wasn't your fault and although the party has taught them to hate all Jews they cannot help but remember that you were once one of them. It is for this reason that you can help in our struggle."

"I am a slave and prisoner like you, what can I do?" said Werner.

"At first just make friends with the guards and see if you can win their trust. Once you have done this, opportunities will arise where you will have the chance to benefit from this friendship," said Rabbi Shiltz.

"What makes you think they will want to be friends with me? You know what the guards are like in here – if anyone even looks at them the wrong way they can end up getting shot."

"Start with the young guard who patrols your sleeping quarters at night. I have been watching him and I can see he is not cruel like the others; he has never beaten anyone and he has a look about him that says to me that all he wants to do is return home from this horrid centre to his mother. You said you still have your matches?"

"I do."

"Well then take these cigarettes and the next time he is doing the rounds you go outside, strike up a conversation with him and offer him one. This will create some trust. Talk about things other than the party, things you have in common. Women, football, how you miss having a beer, anything that will create a common bond between you."

"You seem to have this all planned out. What makes you so sure he will be willing to be my friend?"

"Werner, you do not spend half your life giving spiritual guidance to others without learning a little about human behaviour. The other reason I have asked you here is to talk about God."

"God? How can I talk about God with you? I was raised a Christian not a Jew. I was taught that your people killed the son of God!"

"Werner, you need to stop holding on to all this anger, please let me help you make peace with yourself; only then can you make peace with God. Now let me address your first issue. You see, it is not important which faith one believes in, what is important is that a person finds the peace and strength God can provide. What part the Jewish people played in the death of Jesus Christ is not an issue, if they played any at all – who is to know what happened two thousand years ago? What is important is his teachings of love and mercy."

"How can I just switch from one religion to another, like turning on a light? It just doesn't make sense to me."

"You are not changing religions, Werner, you have Jewish roots and you are a Jew. You just need to embrace this, and you will feel much freer than you have felt in years. If you will allow me, I would like to teach you about your Jewish heritage and the plight of the Jewish people over the centuries. Would you be willing to sit down and do this with me each day?"

"I am not sure, Rabbi, I want to trust you, but I have to be honest I hate myself for what I am, I hate being surrounded by Jews, the way you look, everything about you."

"This is understandable, Werner. If I sat you down, played your films, music and gave you propaganda to read about how Americans were the scum of the world then you would eventually believe they were. The party has brainwashed you with wayward science and propaganda to make you hate Jewish people, but over your time in here you will see that they are no different from the rest of humanity. In fact, through my teachings, you will be able to understand how they have helped shape humanity for the better, how they are an innovative and creative people who work hard and have survived much persecution."

"But how, Rabbi? How are the Jews even going to survive this war?"

"Werner, this current situation we find ourselves in is not the first time in history that we Jews have been persecuted for our beliefs. The Israelites, since Abraham,

Isaac and Jacob have always suffered persecution. Think about the history you were taught in school, the first crusade, the Spanish and Portuguese inquisitions, the expelling of Jews from Spain, England, France, and Germany. All these events involved the Jews being persecuted, the situation we are now in is no different to any other, the only difference is the scale we are in and just like those past events we will continue to fight on because we are God's chosen people."

\* \* \*

Two months had now passed since Werner first agreed to meet with Rabbi Shiltz. At first Werner only really went because there was often food and water, but after a while, he realised that even talking about anything had sharpened his mind, he loved to pick holes in what he was being told and the whole back and forth, he found he would often mentally play the conversations in his mind like a fencing match.

"Werner, you are here for your lesson?" said Rabbi Shiltz.

"I am, Rabbi, what are we going to be talking about today?" said Werner.

"Well, today I thought I would tell you more about the different types of Jews that exist in the world, today we are going to discuss the difference between Ashkenazim, Sephardim, and Mizrahi Jews and even about some of the smaller groups such as the Indian Jews, Bene Jews, Brei Menashe, and Cochin Jews. How does that sound?"

"That sounds great, Rabbi, you know how much I enjoy discussing Jewish heritage and how much I love the stories from the Torah."

"You mean your heritage, don't you, Werner?"

"Yes, Rabbi, I mean mine too."

Just then Werner caught something from the corner of his eye – it was Jenny watching the two men talk intently.

"You should spend more time with Jenny, she has warmed to you these months."

"Oh come on, Rabbi, just because she now says hello doesn't mean she's warmed."

"I might be old, Werner, but I can still tell when a woman is interested. Now tell me about how things are going with the guards."

"Well, I have good and bad news. The good news is you were right: the young lad is a nice enough guy and has stopped to have a cigarette many times with me. The bad news is that this has led the other inmates to suspect they were right about me all along and that I am a party spy."

"Don't trouble yourself too much about what the other inmates think, I have let it be known that you are acting on a secret mission for me and have told everyone that you are not to be touched under any circumstances. Does that put your mind at ease?"

"I guess, but boy do I get some dirty looks. I am sure the young guard likes me though, occasionally he gives me some extra food when he passes by."

"I know, I have seen you giving it to Jenny. I wondered why she was suddenly putting a bit of weight back on, she has a lot more colour in her cheeks."

"I'm happy to do it, Rabbi, she's a lovely woman, so caring. I guess she must get this from you and your teachings."

"I cannot take the credit, I am afraid; she has always been like that. I think she gets it from her mother."

Werner thought to himself how he longed to speak to Jenny, but he was afraid that when he finally did, she would find out about his past. How could a woman like her ever fall in love with a murderer like him?

* * *

"So, what is the latest with you and Jenny?" said Thomas.

"Well occasionally I get a chance to have a brief few moments with her, but I'm not sure I have made much progress, to be honest," said Werner.

"What? She must be a little impressed with you, what with this secret mission you're on, and bringing her all that extra food you have been getting. By the way, thanks for the apple the other day, I can't even remember the last time I had something so delicious."

"You know, Tom, I think I am really falling for her. I love her dark black hair, the curve of her long neck, but mostly it's her beautiful dark eyes. She lights up everywhere she goes, when I see her it's like she's shining."

"You better act fast, you know, you're not the only one who's interested in Jenny. I've seen other men trying to flirt with her. So, if you do like her then you are going to have to tell her at some point and you better do it quick. I heard the resettlement programme will be really ramping up soon and we are all to be relocated to southern Poland."

Werner had heard this before from the guards but only in passing; they had signalled that those that were willing to relocate to Poland were to be left in relative peace and would be part of new Jewish communities there.

"I know Isaac was sent there just last weekend, it's such a shame, we were just becoming good friends and then off he went. You know I didn't even get a chance to say goodbye to him, the guards just came for him in the middle of the night and he and about 60 others were not seen again," said Werner. "The Rabbi seems to think that once we are all relocated, we will be left alone by the party to live out our lives in a semi-autonomous State. I got to tell you, Tom, I think he is living in a dreamland. I know the party, and I'm telling you there is no way they are ever going to let the Jews live in peace. I'm just worried that any one of us could be picked up and taken away. Imagine if you, the Rabbi, or Jenny were taken without me knowing, I would be alone again in this hell hole."

"You worry too much about things that are out of your control. There is nothing me, you, or anyone else can do about it, so just try not to think about it, now give it a rest and let me get some sleep," said Thomas.

"Well, there is one thing I do know, I need to tell Jenny how I feel about her."

* * *

"Rabbi, now we have finished our history lesson I have something I want to discuss with you."

"More questions, Werner? I told you before you need to save all your questions up for our next sessions, that way we always have something to talk about. Have you ever heard the expression patience is a virtue?"

"Rabbi, please be serious, there is something I urgently need to discuss with you."

"Is this about you and Jenny?"

"You know about us? I mean to say you know that we are in love?"

"In love? Werner, I may be old, but I am not blind. I could tell from the first moment you two met that you were going to fall in love. Jenny always gets nervous when she likes someone and you, well you were like a childish schoolboy the moment you thought you had offended her. Kids today, you know in my day we would just go and speak to the girl if we liked her. You don't think I didn't watch the both of you awkwardly mumble a few words here and there, your eyes trying not to meet. Yes, Werner, I know about you and Jenny. I suspect you are here to ask for her hand in marriage?"

"Rabbi, it's like you have a sixth sense sometimes, yes that is what I want to discuss with you. As you know, Jenny and I have been spending a lot of time together over the past year and I have come to love her. I want to spend the rest of my life with her and I want to ask her to marry me, but I cannot do this without your blessing. Rabbi, I feel like you have saved my soul. Through your teachings and friendship, I have come to learn more and more and found a space in my heart for love when there was once only hate. I have you to thank for this and that is why I want, no need, your blessing if things are ever to develop to the next stage with Jenny. I wonder, Rabbi, could you do this for me, and could you ever think of me as a grandson after all I have done, could you?"

"Werner, I already do. Since you started studying with me, I am proud to see how you have changed and become the man I knew you could be. You have changed beyond recognition; it is for this reason and this reason alone that I will allow you to marry my granddaughter. However, there is one thing we need to discuss before you can go and ask her."

"What is it, Rabbi? You know I have been like an open book with you. You can ask me anything and for Jenny's sake I will give you an answer."

"Thanks, good to know, Werner, because what I have to ask will be personal to you, but you understand as a loving grandfather I need to know."

"You want to know why I have an M written on my yellow triangle, don't you?"

"You know I have never asked you before, Werner, because I never needed to know. It wasn't my business and although I know the M stands for murder, but I figure in here we have all served enough time to forgive any wrongdoings – but you are asking for the hand of the only person important to me. I hope you can understand that. Now when you are ready please, I would like to know what happened."

Werner looked down at his feet; they were thick black covered in mud. The hairs on them had grown to unimaginable lengths and the nails had either fallen off or were black and about to.

"I am ashamed, I'm not sure I can bring myself to tell you the whole story," said Werner. "Well, where do I start. Honestly, I don't know what happened that night, it was such a blur. I had been to the bar to see friends and then decided to travel to my father's house as I hadn't seen him in so long. When I got there, we started talking and as usual, he started baiting me about me being a party member and my new position within the ranks. You know he was a military man, Rabbi, a war hero to some and especially to me. I loved him, that's the honest truth."

"Go on, Werner, I am listening; don't be afraid."

"We started talking about the Jews, back then I was completely and totally obsessed. I believed all the party's lies, I even convinced others to believe them. It's not something I am proud of but at the time I have to admit I did enjoy it, I enjoyed that feeling that people cared about what I had to say."

"Power can be a corrupting thing, Werner, if it is not used for good. Please continue to tell me more about your father and what happened."

"My father started telling me about his views and how he didn't believe in the party's lies about the Jews. I told him that he was wrong and that there was scientific evidence that proved it, but he just paid it no mind, he kept disagreeing with me and at the time I felt he was provoking me on purpose just because he was bitter about my new position. I know now he was just speaking the truth and was trying to make me see sense, but I was too far indoctrinated to hear what he was saying. We argued until we were both blue in the face and that's when it happened."

By this time Werner was becoming physically upset, his eyes were tearing up and his lip was trembling. At which point, Rabbi Shiltz took Werner's hand and squeezed it tight.

"Come on, Werner, let it all out."

"He told me, he told me that I had Jewish blood! I couldn't believe it, I didn't want to believe it. It's like he ripped everything away from me that I held dear in one sentence, knowing that it would crush me. It was the last straw. I was so filled with rage and hatred that I just grabbed the nearest object and just started hitting him with it. By the time I had realised what I had done it was too late. I was standing over him, his head was concaved, covered in blood and I was holding a blood soaked iron rod. Honestly, Rabbi, it was like my soul left my body, it was a minute of madness, one incident that will haunt me forever. The shame I feel is sometimes unbearable, I think about what I have done every morning and every night."

Rabbi Shiltz closed his eyes and asked Werner to come closer to him. Werner wasn't sure if the Rabbi was going to slap him, but he shuffled forward slowly. In doing so he felt the Rabbi's arms around him in a tight embrace.

"Werner, you have a lot of guilt, guilt you must learn to forgive yourself for and guilt that you must lose before you can start your new life with Jenny. That isn't to say that you need to forget about your actions; after all, we humans are weak, we could never be as strong as God's will, but you can also not allow yourself to carry this huge burden on your back forever, you have to let it go. I am not going to change my mind, my decision is final and you have my blessing to marry Jenny. What I would like us to do first though is to do a cleansing ceremony, just you, me and God will take part. I believe only then will you feel able to ask for her love the way you have taken God's into your heart."

"Thank you, Rabbi, and thank you, God. I am so happy I will ask Jenny as soon as I have completed the ceremony."

"Ask me what? What ceremony?" said Jenny.

Neither Rabbi Shiltz nor Werner had seen Jenny approaching them as they were locked in the discussion. Seeing Jenny glide up the alleyway, her black hair blowing in the wind and her dark eye fixated on them both, left Werner and Rabbi Shiltz shocked.

"A secret ceremony, dear, one that I am afraid I cannot tell you about just yet. Werner, why don't you take Jenny for a walk and you can ask her about that thing you wanted to discuss," said Rabbi Shiltz.

"But, Rabbi, wouldn't that be better asked after we have completed that task?"

"Will you two stop talking in riddles, and tell me what the hell is going on?" said Jenny.

"Don't worry about that now, Werner we can do that tomorrow. First thing, whatever the outcome and I am sure it will be a positive one. Now you two go and leave an old man to his thoughts," said Rabbi Shiltz.

As Werner walked slowly through the dark wet back alleys of the centre, he knew it was time he got to the point. Self-doubt was eating away at his insides –why would she want him, why did he look so disgusting, and would she be able to see this, and why would she want a man who bore so much heavy responsibility for being in here in the first place?

"Werner, come on, what's with you today? You've hardly said a word for the last ten minutes."

"I'm sorry, Jenny I hadn't realised how rude I was ignoring you," said Werner.

"You just look so deep in thought Werner, is something on your mind?" said Jenny.

Taking Jenny's hand, Werner realised it was now or never. Standing in between two dank, old wooden huts wasn't ideal, but where was in the centre? It was now or never, he thought.

"Jenny, since meeting you and your grandfather my life has changed for the better. I now feel somehow at ease, I want to create a new life, I want to be able to love again, I want love in my life," said Werner.

Werner dropped to a semi-squat, as to try to drop on one knee without the guards seeing him.

"That is why it would make me the happiest man in the world if you were to accept my proposal in marriage. What I am trying to say is, Jenny, will you marry me?"

Jenny squeezed Werner's hand, motioning for him to rise to his feet.

"You know, Werner, when I was a young girl I used to dream of this moment, I used to think that one day I will be the talk of people in Köln. I imagined myself in a lovely wedding dress with all my family around me; now thanks to the party I have found myself in this miserable centre scratching out a life with only my granddad for company. That was until I found you. I no longer yearn for lavish extravagate wedding ceremonies and champagne receptions; I yearn for a man who will hold me as if I am the only thing he ever wants in his life. Can you be that man, Werner? If you can then yes I will!"

"I can, Jenny; I can with all my heart! I would say I am the happiest man in this godforsaken centre, but I know now that God is everywhere, he has touched me, and he has led me to you."

\* \* \*

"Good morning, Rabbi you didn't tell anyone, did you, that we would be meeting today?"

"I didn't, Werner, why? Are you embarrassed?"

"You know I am not, I don't know, I guess I am just still coming to terms with everything, I certainly didn't think I would end up here of all places."

"A journey of a thousand miles, Werner, starts with the first step, you have made this and you need to continue on this path if you are to re-join the rest of the world. Now, come sit beside me and let's begin the healing ceremony."

In a dark, smelly room on a concrete floor, stained with rainwater and with the hint of urine, both Werner and Rabbi Shiltz sat side by side, holding hands.

"Now, Werner, I want you to repeat the words I say and really try to feel in your heart their meaning and their value to you as a human being. Now, let's begin.

"May the one who blessed our ancestors, Abraham, Isaac and Jacob, Sarah, Rebecca, Rachel, and Leah, bless Werner, son of Adalbert since he has come up to the Torah in honour of God and Torah. May he merit from the Holy One of Blessing protection, rescue from any trouble or distress, and from any illness, minor or serious; may God send blessing and success in his every endeavour, together with all Israel, and let us say, Amen," said Rabbi Shiltz, with Werner following seconds after each word.

After the prayer, the two embraced in a warm, but still slightly uncomfortable hug.

"What now, Rabbi?"

"Now we will use this water and wash our hands and face, as a symbol of washing away the deed and the lies that accompanied it," said Rabbi Shiltz. "Now, Werner, our ceremony has come to an end, we have spoken to God and it's now up to you to move on with your life. This could be a life with Jenny, but this depends on you, my son. Werner, are you ready then?"

"I think so, Rabbi, I have to say though, I am a bit nervous."

"Marriage is something that one needs to be serious about, Werner, it's a special day. It binds a man with a woman so that they become one complete soul. You know many people consider marriage to be a person's personal Yom Kippur as it allows both a man and his wife the chance to forget and leave their former sins behind them. Come now, Jenny is waiting for you, we haven't been able to gather much but I found a white cloth Jenny can use as a Kittel and please tell me you have been fasting?"

"I have, Rabbi, I have also tried to avoid Jenny for the whole week, just like you told me. You know, to increase the anticipation."

"That's good, Werner, I am glad you have been listening to what I have been telling you; all this time I thought it was just falling on deaf ears but I can see now that you have been committed and this fills me with hope. I am just sorry that both your mothers are not here to see the ceremony and to take part in it, I always liked the Ashkenazi tradition for breaking plates. Still, we must do our best with who and what we have."

"Yes, Rabbi, we must, I appreciate what you have done to get as much as you have."

"Well, we couldn't get any materials to help make a chuppah but what I did manage to get my hands on, and you are not going to believe this, was a little bit of wine," said Rabbi Shiltz.

"Wine! You're joking right?"

"Do I look like I am the kind of man that jokes about such serious things? No, I pulled many strings to get this and by God, if we are going to do it, we are going to try and do as much as possible to make it right; Jenny deserves nothing less."

"Rabbi, are you sure that we are going to be safe whilst you conduct the ceremony? You know if the guards found out we were doing anything like this I'm sure they will kill us."

"Don't worry yourself now, Werner, it has all been taken care of. I have good men watching all the hallways and we have timed when and where the guards are going to be. Now come along and stand straight so that Jenny can join us."

Just then Jenny emerged from a back doorway that Werner had not noticed.

"Jenny, I am so happy to see you! This week feels like it's been a millennium. You look absolutely amazing in that dress, how did you manage to find makeup?" said Werner.

"You don't scrub up too bad yourself, Werner, and all a girl can do is try her best to look good on her wedding day," said Jenny.

Just then some of Jenny's friends joined the couple and stood slightly behind them whilst Rabbi Shiltz began to give seven blessings upon the cup of wine.

"Now both of you, I want you to take a sip of this wine and remember your sips symbolise the love and joy a man and a woman share for each other," said Rabbi Shiltz.

Werner held the glass with shaking hands, he was so nervous to be holding what seemed to be the most precious liquid in the world. As he looked into Jenny's eyes, all darkened from the slight coal dust she had rubbed above them to highlight her already beautiful eyes, he could see that she too looked nervous.

"Here, my love take a sip," said Werner.

As she took a small sip Werner saw her face change and a large smile start to spread across it. He then drank what was left of the wine and placed the glass on the floor.

"Werner, you know what is next, right?" said Rabbi Shiltz.

"Oh yes, Rabbi, I remember," said Werner.

With one fluid motion, Werner brought his decrepit boot down on the glass, shattering it into a million pieces.

"The broken glass symbolises the destruction of the temple of Jerusalem and now more than ever we Jews must be mindful of the past sorrow our people have endured. It is also said to be the last time the man gets to put his foot down – but that's another story!" laughed Rabbi Shiltz.

"Now, Werner, kiss the girl and may you both live a full and happy life for many years to come," added Rabbi Shiltz.

On hearing these words Werner took Jenny in his arms and kissed her soft ruby red lips, he felt their hearts beat in time and knew that he had once again found meaning to his life.

"Come now, you two, eat some of this food the people have brought for you. This is a happy occasion, but we must be vigilant, and you both must return to your sleeping huts right away," said Rabbi Shiltz.

\* \* \*

"Hello there, Werner, how are you today?" said Fritz.

"I am good thank you, Fritz, thanks for asking, and yourself?" said Werner.

"Would you like a cigarette? I have a fresh pack," said Fritz.

"That would be wonderful, thank you, Fritz, how are the wife and your boy?" said Werner.

Werner slid a cigarette out of Fritz's soft cigarette box and as fast as he could without trying to look nervous. Fritz was a young, blond-haired, doe-eyed soldier who for a reason unbeknown to Werner had decided to take pity on him and even speak to him on occasion.

"The wife, well nobody is content these days, Werner, so as you can expect she isn't exactly happy-go-lucky right now, especially with Michael needing more and more and there being less and less," said Fritz.

"I understand, it must be hard raising a young child in these circumstances," said Werner, as he exhaled a large cloud of smoke.

"You don't know the half of it, Werner; still though, it could be worse I suppose, I could be in here with you and all these other poor devils," said Fritz. "You know, I know why you are here. The other guards told me to look out for you when I arrived and what you had done."

"I always wondered, but if you knew that, why are you talking to me?"

"I don't blame you; I am not one of these lunatics who just think we should wipe out everyone, you know. Things change these days very quickly; you were not to know about your family's history and if you ask me, you did the right thing when you found out."

Pulling on the last bits of tobacco, Werner felt that same feeling again. Shame, mixed with a hint of happiness. He knew what he had done to his father was wrong, but it also made him happy to be treated with even the smallest bit of care and respect. It was clear Fritz liked Werner; the question Werner constantly asked himself was by how much.

"Thank you for the cigarette, Fritz, it was very kind of you to share one with me. I better go and let you get back to your rounds," said Werner.

* * *

Over the next week Werner looked out for Fritz doing his rounds – he knew 8 pm was always the time he would go past Werner's sleeping huts.

"Hey Fritz, how are things? How's Michael and Adalheida doing?" said Werner.

"Werner, come sit with me. I have a nice bit of cake here that might interest you, Adalheida cooked it just this week," said Fritz.

"Oh, thank you so much, Fritz, you know you are too kind to me, bringing me all these rations, I don't know how to thank you for your kindness."

"Think nothing of it, Werner; besides, you look like you could use all the extra food you can get. This place can eat a guy to his bones if he doesn't take care of himself. See, I bet that tasted good, didn't it?"

Whilst Fritz talked Werner shovelled the cake into his mouth as fast as he could; if anyone saw them it would be him who would be for the high jump. Fritz's kindness was now being a threat, a threat he couldn't control.

"It was haven, thank you, Fritz, and please thank Adalheida for me."

"Oh ha ha ha, she would go mental if she knew I was giving away food she had slaved all day to make to a Jew. No, I think it's best I don't thank Adalheida this time," laughed Fritz.

"Oh well, nevertheless I am very grateful, Fritz, your kindness over the past weeks has really lifted my spirits and I am feeling much stronger, mentally, and physically."

"Don't mention it, Werner, like I said I feel for you, ending up in the beastly place and you know you're one of the only civilised people in here. God knows those guards don't appreciate anything in life other than killing it. Here, have a cigarette, won't you."

* * *

"Hey Werner, I got a little something for you. Remember though, just make sure nobody knows that it's coming from me. It's a bit of cheese and sausage, I know you Jews aren't supposed to eat pigs but well, it's good food," said Fritz.

"That's not a problem, Fritz, thank you so much for all your help. The sandwiches, the cured meats, the bread, you know you have been so good to me these past weeks, I can't thank you enough for all that you have done," said Werner.

"Well, you do look better that's for sure, my god when I first met you, you were this skinny dirty runt of a man, now you're just dirty," laughed Fritz.

"You're right, I am feeling a lot healthier and stronger, but still the same with the dirt. I try and try to keep clean but it's not easy in this place."

"Look, I will try to bring you a little soap next time as well and a rag so that you can at least give yourself a clean. You use the showers, right?"

"I do but now the centre is getting busier and busier we are allowed to shower less and less."

"Yes, the centre is now running at full capacity, that's the way it's going to be from now on, but I have heard there will be a solution to all this, and an order that will come from the very top soon. That should create more room here."

During his walk back to the other end of the centre, Werner wondered to himself what this solution could be – to his mind the place could only get fuller and now relocation would stop the masses from coming in their droves. Just then he realised the cheese was very smelly and he started to sweat, wondering if anyone would notice it hidden up his jacket sleeve.

"Jenny, get Rabbi Shiltz, I have something special and we need to all share it," said Werner.

"Ok, I will go and get him now," said Jenny.

"Oh, and bring that bit of bread you have saved – we are going to make our own sandwiches," Werner said with a beaming smile.

"Werner, why have you called me over?" said Rabbi Shiltz.

"Rabbi, quick, get your knife out and cut these for me," said Werner.

"Well you know, guys, we shouldn't be eating this sausage as it's made of swine but at the moment we must put survival above all other customs. Jenny, rip the bread into three pieces, would you, dear," said Rabbi Shiltz.

As they all ate their cheese and sausage sandwiches, Werner looked at Jenny's and the Rabbi's face, they looked content for just a second. Werner thought to himself that if it were not for their awful situation they could have been in a park, with children running around playing football and sharing a picnic.

"Hang on, did you hear that?" said Rabbi Shiltz.

"Wait here, I will go look," said Werner.

The mood had changed in an instant from slightly content to being terrified. If the guards were to catch them they would almost certainly be questioned and shot, and if the other prisoners found out they were getting extra rations, well that would be even far worse.

"It's nothing, must have been a rat. Quickly though, get this down you sharpish and we can go on acting like nothing is untoward here," said Werner.

"Here, there is a little leftover, you and Jenny eat it," said Rabbi Shiltz.

"Oh no, you always do this, you need it more than me, Rabbi, please take it," said Werner.

"If our people are to survive this, you both need to eat up, how else are you going to repopulate our people on this earth!" said Rabbi Shiltz.

"Ok, ok, why is it we need to go through this every time I get something for us?" said Werner, as he took the last bit of cheese and passed Jenny the last bit of sausage.

Werner watched the groups of men get off the old steam locomotives. They all looked at the rails and steps as they disembarked the train, never making a sound. It was strange to think that these trains could have been carrying them to their summer holidays in the mountains or a lakeside retreat but instead, they were carrying them to their death. The trains were strong heavy machines with four large red wheels and what seemed to be hundreds of smaller wheels, all chugging along in unison, the round faces of smiling brutes awaiting their orders. As soon as the fresh loads were unloaded, others would be poked, prodded, and pushed into the carriages. Werner watched Jenny's face when this happened – at first she used to look horrified, her month used to drop open and her cheeks would be red with anger; but over time her face became numb to what they were witnessing. Life, Werner thought, has a way of doing this to you: seeing something truly disgusting once can have an impact on you forever, but seeing it over and over just becomes mundane. It was the monotony of it all, yes, that was the real killer, seeing something over and over again just makes it normal and boring.

"Jenny, there is something I have been meaning to discuss with you. I think we need to start planning to get out of this place and get out of Germany," said Werner.

"How do you propose to do this? Walk out the front gate?" said Jenny and she laughed sarcastically.

"It won't be easy, I know, but you must have seen the people leaving by the hundreds daily – if we wait too long, we will be one of those people and may never see each other again. I heard from Fritz that there are three different camps in Poland where Jewish families are being sent and it can be a lottery when being allocated a camp; often people from the same families can be sent to all three camps being split up."

"I have heard these stories too, Werner, I would like to say they are not true but honestly I wouldn't put anything past the party. God only knows what they have waiting for us in Poland."

"Exactly, Jenny, we need to act quickly. I think I should ask Fritz for help; I know we don't know him that well, but I believe he's a good man and will help us escape."

"Werner, are you crazy! Fritz may like you and he may even throw us some extra food, but there is a massive difference between giving someone a few scraps and helping an enemy to escape a guarded facility. Think of it from his point of view – he has everything to lose if you are caught trying to escape on his watch; even if you did he would have to account for you being missing; you know what Germans are like, with their lists and counting. They are meticulous, whether it's people, rations or pots and pans."

"WE, Jenny, we! I would not leave here without you, I thought you would know that. I also plan to take Rabbi Shiltz with us."

"I know you did, Werner, but think about what you are saying now. It's gone from sneaking one person to a group of people out of here. Even if we did get out of the centre, where would we go? We are dressed in prison clothes, with no one to help us on the outside."

"Jenny, I know you are scared, but if we are to survive, we have to make difficult decisions. You married me and I need you to let me think for the family now. My father always kept the family gold hidden at his house under the loose floorboard in the basement; if we could just get to his house, we could get it and pay to be smuggled over the border."

"Over the border to where?"

"Switzerland!"

"Switzerland, and what makes you think three starved Jews are going to be welcome there? Have you not heard the stories of how they are getting rich from this war at the Jews' expense? They pretend to be neutral farmers but what do you think, mark my words they are not! I don't know about your experiences with farmers, but mine is that they are often some of the most hateful, intolerant people on the planet. Do you think their little farming towns where they all look alike want some Jews turning up playing happy families?"

"Jen, you are making excuses, you know we cannot stay here. Switzerland would only be a stop-gap, I intend for us to get to London and then America."

"London and America? Have you really lost your mind? People in London already have a massive refugee crisis and their own problems, and as for America, what makes you think we can get there or that they will care at all about us and our freedom?" said Jenny. "They are just as bad as the Swiss, they are looking after their own interests, watching as Europe destroys itself."

"Jenny, we need to do something and I have decided that this is our best option if we are to survive this war. If we don't die on those trains to Poland, I am certain we will die in their camps. Do you really believe the party wants to house us all in our own little Jewish utopia, leaving us to do what we want?" said Werner.

"No."

"Then it's decided. I will speak to your granddad and then Fritz. If he agrees to help us, we will make plans to move quickly. I am sure he will be accommodating; if he won't do it out of goodwill, then I am sure the gold at my father's house will change his mind. Please trust me, Jenny, I know what I am doing."

"I do, my love, you know I do."

\* \* \*

"So, what do you think? I know it's a long shot, but I think if we plan it right it could just work," said Werner.

"I don't know, Werner, you and Jenny would be taking an awful lot of risks and you know anyone who has ever tried to escape has been shot on sight," said Rabbi Shiltz.

"The trains are leaving more frequently than ever now, who knows who's next to be put on one. I must take this chance, I must try, surely you understand that. What is the point in staying here and dying? That's what they want, all of us dead; well I'm not going to have it and I am not going to do what they want!" said Werner.

"I understand, Werner, I do, but none of us knows if that's what they want. They have said over and over that we are to be relocated, nothing more."

"If you believe that, Rabbi, then you are a fool; we are doomed, all of us. The only thing that is keeping us here is time."

"Well one thing I do know is that you can't stay in Europe, it's not safe for our people here, you must go to America, it's the only place you two can make a clean start."

"I know there are underground organisations that help people escape. I heard the Party talking about them many times when we were discussing strategies on how to destroy the enemies within."

"I have heard of these too, but how would you even go about finding where they are based. It's risky, Werner, and I fear you might be risking too much dragging Jenny with you."

"I have heard stories from people who have escaped the country before, there was this one guy who managed to get to Switzerland and is now at the forefront of helping

Jews escape. If I could get a message out, maybe we could be the next success story."

"Or the next cautionary tale," said Rabbi Shiltz.

"The difficult part would be getting over the border – if we could manage to change clothes and get a ride to the border then we could have a chance, even if it's a slim one," said Werner.

"You are going to need money, a change of clothes, help, and a whole lot of luck if you are both to pull it off."

\* \* \*

Werner had become used to standing next to the wooden huts. Its damp rotten outer walls had become as familiar a smell like his mother's baked biscuits. He used to stand for hours and watch the different types of insects crawl back and forth and wonder whether they knew what they were doing or whether it was just all intuitive. His favourite part of smoking there was not the sharp drags but blowing smoke on the bugs so that he could watch them react. In many ways he thought they were just like humans – some ran to get away, others stopped dead, curled up and tried to protect themselves, and finally, some just dropped off the walls. When the time comes, he wondered, which of these would end up as him.

Suddenly he saw a big beaming smiling face turn the corner. It was Fritz, his face red from the cold, his yellow-blond hair wet from the pissing down rain. Werner always felt a little uneasy at the sight of Fritz – he never knew if this was going to be the day, or whether one day he would be turning him. Just then he noticed Fritz was carrying something in his right hand; he couldn't make it out, but it was a package of some sort.

"Werner, we must stop meeting like this," said Fritz.

"Good evening, Fritz, how are you today?" said Werner.

"Just the same, you know this war, when will it end! You know the British are pounding places now almost nightly, it's funny you being in here – it's probably one of the safest places to be, well unless they make a mistake and think this place is a weapons factory. Oh, before I forget, here are a couple of left-overs I packed for you. It's not much but you understand even us Germans are finding it hard to keep food in the pantry right now," said Fritz.

He offered Fritz one of his last cigarettes.

"Do you need a light, Fritz?" said Werner.

"Nope I am good thanks, so Werner, tell me what exciting things have you been doing in the camp today?" said Fritz jokingly.

"You know as well as I do, Fritz, there is fuck all to do in here. Avoiding the guards keeps me busy."

"Yeah, I think you're right. I am not sure I could cope in your place, these dirty conditions, and constant eking out a living. How your life must have changed from being a party member."

"It's a shit hole but then when you get used to a place it just becomes home. Fritz, I have something to ask you but I don't want to offend you in doing so."

"Offend me? Well how much worse could it be, you know I would be in a whole heap of trouble if anyone knew about our chats."

"I know, Fritz, and I am grateful, I cannot express to you how much your help has inspired me in here. It's not just the food or the conversations we have; you have given me hope in the Germans, that not everyone wants us all dead, that not everyone wants to enjoy suffering. It's because of this hope you have given me that I must take liberties and ask you to give me even more hope. Fritz, I need your help, me and two other inmates want to escape from the centre."

Fritz choked on his cigarette smoke.

"Werner, are you crazy? Do you know what will happen to me if I were caught helping you escape? You know even asking me could have you shot. And who are these other two inmates you want to escape with? Why don't you just ask me to break out everyone?" said Fritz angrily.

"I know it's a lot to ask, but you are my only friend here. You know what is happening now, you know that even tomorrow I could be selected and put on a train. I don't know if everything I have heard is true, but I am certain you know that where those trains go is not a good place."

"Look, Werner, I feel for you, I do, and yes although it seems impossible that a German and a Jew could become friends, that is what we are. But what you are asking, I do not think you have calculated the risk involved for both of us. If anyone even heard us having this conversation, we would both be shot, and what of these other two companions, who are they?"

"I am sorry, Fritz, but I cannot tell you. I trust you and that is the only reason I am asking you now, but please understand it's safer for both of them that you do not know their names right now."

"Three seems like an odd number to me; isn't it two's company, three's a crowd? Why would you want to leave with this odd number?"

"As I said, I cannot tell you right now, but I do need your help. Do you think you can find it in your heart to help me? I have gold saved at my father's house. If you help me you can have it all."

"Oh yeah and how do you have all this gold? Been saving up whilst you are in here?"

"It was my father's, you can have it if you help me get out of here."

"It wouldn't be worth my life to try and help you for just some small amount of gold."

"Please, Fritz, I don't know how much is there but it's yours. All you need to do is get me and the two others out of the centre and into Köln. Surely there must be some way I can convince you?"

"Werner, you do realise I could have you shot for even asking me to help you. Out of respect for our friendship, I will not tell anyone about this conversation. Now, I think it's time you went back to your sleeping quarters."

"Please think about what I have asked you, there must be something we can do or I will die in this place."

Fritz stubbed out his cigarette on the wooden hut outer wall and walked away without acknowledging Werner; it was just then as he walked off into the moonlight that Werner realised the severity of what he had just asked.

\* \* \*

"So, look I spoke to Fritz yesterday and well frankly it didn't go well. He was shocked, but I think I can still get him on side, if only I had more time with him," said Werner.

"Time is one thing we don't have," said Jenny.

"Do you think there is no turning him, Werner? He must want something, or he must have some kindness – he could be reprimanded even for talking to you," said Rabbi Shiltz.

"Go back and speak to him again, darling, if anyone can convince him it's you," said Jenny.

"Jenny's right, if he is willing to speak to you and help you out, then he is willing to go that extra mile; you just need to convince him it's the right thing to do," said Rabbi Shiltz.

"Maybe we should think about other options – we might not want to lay all our eggs in one basket," said Jenny.

"What else is there though? We have no way of influencing the selection process, which means any of us could get called at any point and shipped off," said Werner.

"Even if we were to somehow influence the selection process, we would never be allowed to live together or even be relocated together. No, it's this way or nothing at all as far as I can see," said Werner.

"You're right, it's the only solution for us but I still don't like it! We are betting everything on a child," said Rabbi Shiltz.

\* \* \*

Standing in the gloomy shadows of the bathhouses, Werner had observed that Fritz had been missing for the last couple of weeks. The raw shit had been coming out from the bowels of the bathhouses due to the heavy rain and the smell was unbearable. Nevertheless, Werner knew that by volunteering to help dig out the sewage he would at least have the opportunity of a chance meeting with Fritz.

"Excuse me, officer, would you happen to have a lighter?" said Werner.

"I do but how the hell do you have cigarettes? You Jews are not supposed to have possessions in the centre. You will give them to me and I might not have you up in front of the firing squad!" said the guard.

"Please, I didn't mean any offence, officer, I'm just asking because I wanted to offer you one. I was given them by the general, I think he must have been in charge of the facility and he said he knew of my family," said Werner.

"He knew of your family? So, you must be Werner Ritter, the German turned Jew? So, I am meeting a celebrity. Well, then, what the Hell! You stay here with me for a second and have a cigarette. I have been wondering about your case. Tell me how is it you ended up in here? They say you are a Jew and now a Jew lover, but you don't look Jewish to me," said the guard.

"Well, how long have you got?"

"I have as long as it takes, I've been dying to know how this all came to pass."

"Well, it was my father who first told me about my Jewish heritage; until that day I had no idea. Once the cat was out of the bag, well then it all got very serious very quickly and that's how I ended up in here."

The guard listened contentedly to Werner as he spoke, pulling various faces as his tale progressed.

"So you had no idea, wow, that must have been extremely confusing. So, you were doing a great job for the party and then you ended up here with the scum of the earth. I can't imagine how awful that must feel to know you have worked hard for your country to eliminate these vermin and then being told you are one of them."

"You're telling me, so you see now I find myself in here and I don't want to mix with these rats."

"I guess that's life, it can throw us in some strange directions."

"Wise words, officer, well I better be going. We are not supposed to be out here, I only came out to have a smoke. Hey, isn't there normally a different guard doing this round?" said Werner.

"Yeah, there is, but I don't know where the lazy fucker is, he hasn't shown up for work in the last three days, if he is not here tomorrow I am going to write an official complaint to the director, do they think I want to be here any longer than I have to!" said the guard.

* * *

The next night Werner wasn't sure whether he should bother going outside again – if the new guard saw him lurking around he might get suspicious of him. Once, ok fine, but twice this might look fishy, so he stayed in his bunk, the whole time wondering if he should have been outside or not. When he finally did drop to sleep, he had an uncomfortable feeling that perhaps this was it, that things couldn't get any worse and that it was inevitable that he and Jenny would end up in Poland. An hour into his RIM cycle he felt a slight touch against his leg, then his name softly whispered in his ear. First, he thought he was dreaming but then he saw a familiar face standing over him. It was Fritz, he said nothing but pointed to the door leading outside to where they usually talked. Werner followed Fritz.

"Fritz, where have you been? I have been waiting to speak to you for the last four days, I thought you might have transferred shifts after what we discussed," said Werner.

"No, Werner, as I told the administration I have been at home in bed with a cold," said Fritz.

"You have, I'm sorry I shouldn't jump to conclusions."

"No, you are right to have assumptions, you see I have thought about your request and after talking it over with my wife we have decided to help you. Over the last three days I have worked out a plan to get you and your friends out of here."

"That's fantastic, what made you change your mind?"

"Many reasons, but let's not start kissing my arse just yet, Werner, we haven't got you anywhere yet. Now shut up and listen to what I think we can do for you."

"Ok sure, I am all ears but right from the start let me thank you," said Werner.

"Tomorrow night I am going to leave three guard uniforms under the water tank near the toilets, you know where that is right?"

"Yeah, it's the big green drum, I've seen it but won't the uniforms get ruined under there? I've seen water spilling from it many times."

"Don't worry about that, that's not the point, the point is I have a plan and if you will shut up asking stupid questions, I will tell you it."

"Ok, you're right, please go on."

"Tomorrow, I will do my normal shift at work, and as I said I will leave you the guard uniforms. What I want you to do is to put them on and meet me by the entrance. Now, you will have to change outside, so this will need to be quick and I have only managed to get one size for the men's outfits but that should be ok as you are skinny. I will then pick you all up and we will walk through the front gate together."

"Are you mad? We just walk through the front gate? That has to be the worst plan I have ever heard!"

"Don't lose your fucking temper and keep your voice down! We are walking through the front gate because I say we are walking through the front gate."

"OK I understand, but what will we do once we get outside, we can't just start walking, can we?"

"I am trying to explain, please just shut up for a second and I will tell you! When we get outside my wife will be waiting for us in her car, a few hundred yards down the road. She usually picks me up so there won't be any suspicion of the car or its plates. What you need to do is make sure your friends can handle the pressure – if one was to crack then we would all be caught. Do you think they will be able to make it?"

"I do, but even if we make it to the car, won't we stand out? I mean, look at me, it's clear I am not in good shape."

"I have thought about that! When we get to the car you will all change into civilian clothes. My wife will bring them with her. They won't be anything fancy but they will be enough to get us into town. With the new clothes and the cover of the night, we might just make it. Then you will take me to collect the gold."

"I see, but then how will we make it to the border?"

"Look, I understand your concerns, Werner, but please don't worry; I have thought about it all. I would not have suggested or even contemplated doing this if I did not think we could get away with it. The reason it has to be tomorrow night is that there is going to be a big party at the officers' mess hall, there will be guards and soldiers coming from different territorial areas and this will allow us to move more freely as the guards on the gate will be overwhelmed having to check so many identification papers and there will be a lot of new faces, including yours."

"But what if they do check our papers? We won't have anything to show them."

"The guards outside never check the papers of other guards on the way out – why would they? No guard in his right mind would try and help anyone escape from here."

* * *

"Hey guys, come here quick; I have something to tell you," said Werner.

"Whatever is the matter, Werner?" said Rabbi Shiltz.

"What's all the commotion?" said Jenny.

"Listen, I talked with Fritz last night and he has a plan, a plan that might just get us out of here!" said Werner.

"Can you trust him to help us?" said Jenny.

"He will and he is going to! I don't have time to run through all the specifics, all you need to know is you have to be ready as we leave tonight," said Werner. "The biggest problem we face is you, Jenny, we need to get you into the all-male dorm so that we can move quickly to the toilets and to pick up the uniforms."

"Uniforms?" said Rabbi Shiltz.

"Yes, uniforms. We will put them on and follow Fritz to the main gate," said Werner.

"Werner, are you sure about this? Are you sure he can be trusted?" said Rabbi Shiltz.

"You are always telling me to put my trust in people, well now we all have to. If we don't take the opportunity, then we might as well give up completely. I haven't, have you?" said Werner.

"No, honey, I haven't. I say let's go for it. What do we have to lose?" said Jenny.

"Only our lives," said Rabbi Shiltz nervously.

"Hey Christophe, can I borrow a razor and some spare pyjamas?" Rabbi Shiltz shouted to a prisoner keeping guard.

"I have only the one pair of pyjamas, but I think I can get another set for you, Rabbi. I'm not sure where I can find a razor though," said Christophe.

"Just find them for me, Christophe, there's a good lad. I know you can do it," said Rabbi Shiltz.

"I will, Rabbi, leave it to me," said Christophe.

* * *

"Great job on getting the razor, I knew I could rely on you," said Werner.

"Well, it was Christophe we should be thanking, he's a resourceful boy that one. He could find a needle in a haystack," said Rabbi Shiltz.

"Jenny, come here and, Rabbi, pass me the razor," said Werner.

"Werner, are you sure this is necessary? I mean couldn't I just wrap my hair up into a ball and wrap some cloth around it?" said Jenny.

"You know we need to do it; we need to make you look like a man. If anyone notices you in the dorms, then the whole plan could fall through. So please, I know you don't like it but just trust me and do it for me," said Werner.

"Listen to him, Jenny, he's talking sense. I know it's awful, my dear, but it's a small price to pay. Here, pass me the razor, Werner, I will do it," said Rabbi Shiltz.

As small curly black hair fell to the floor of the courtyard, Werner could see that Jenny was physically upset. Her eyes were tearing up and the wrinkles on her forehead were showing. At that moment he took her frail hand.

"Jenny, we need to do this. Once we are free you can grow your hair to your heart's content. You know it's the first thing I noticed about you when I first saw you walking across the courtyard," said Werner.

"Werner, you tell me it's something you noticed about me every time you want me to do something for you," said Jenny.

"You have me there, but what can I say? I fell in love with the whole package and therefore I noticed it all," said Werner with a wry smile on his face.

"There is something else we need to do, you are not going to like it, but it also has to be done. Jenny, I want you to take off your top! Come on, now, this isn't the time for being shy," said Werner.

"Why, what more do I have to do?" said Jenny.

"I got the extra pyjamas because we needed the legs. We are going to wrap them tight around your chest. People must think that you are a man and therefore we need to make sure nobody notices your breasts," said Werner.

"It's ok, Jenny, I will turn my back and give you a little privacy," said Rabbi Shiltz.

"Werner, you are making me feel so stupid! This better work!" said Jenny.

After all the preparations were complete, they moved to Werner's dorms and waited for Fritz's signal. He was supposed to give a gentle tap on the wall close to Werner's bunk. Waiting in the dark, all three held hands. Werner could feel Jenny shaking with fear, she looked as how he felt. He was just about to quietly lean forward to kiss her when he heard a short sharp tap. Then, again and again, the tap continued, then abruptly stopped. They all looked at each other, not wanting to speak or even to breathe.

"Right, come with me and remember, not a word from anyone," said Werner. "Ok, here are the uniforms, put them on and not a word; just stand in the shadows with me quietly."

"Sure," whispered Jenny.

They all stood silently, even breathing felt like making too much noise.

"There you all are. I see the uniforms fit, come on, we haven't got all night, follow me," said Fritz.

As they walked through the dimly lit courtyard Werner could see that they were entering a new section of the camp, one that didn't look as beat down as the Jewish quarter.

"Are we still in the same centre?" Werner whispered to Fritz.

"We are moving into the gypsy section; you can see the difference in the day because of the different colour triangles on the prisoners' pyjamas. You can also tell by the different coloured striped paint on the walls, that's so the guards know where they are entering too," said Fritz.

A group of soldiers walked towards Werner and the group; they had all been drinking. Their cheeks were red from the alcohol and they smelt of sweat and what Jenny would later describe as old cabbage.

"Hey, you, where are you all going, the party is this way?" said one of the soldiers.

"Oh, we are just finishing a few things up before we join you all. Looks like you have all started without us already," said Fritz.

"That's for sure, the only way to get through being in here is being drunk. I don't think I've been sober yet," said another soldier.

"Werner, can you see the main gate? It usually has two guards on the surrounding towers but tonight there is only that guy over there and he looks shitfaced, look at him staggering about," said Fritz.

"I can see him, come on, let's just keep going," said Werner.

"Werner? Werner Ritter? Is that you?" said a distant voice from behind Werner.

It was a lank skinny man dressed in prison pyjamas talking to a soldier calling his name.

"Werner, it's me, Jacob, do you remember? We used to drink in the same bar, the Bear and Shield," said Jacob.

"Jacob, yes, I remember you. It has been a long time, hasn't it, well, I am sorry I cannot chat, I must be on my way, I don't want to keep the general waiting," said Werner.

"We were just waiting for the general so you can wait with us," said Jacob.

"Jacob, please one second, I will just inform my colleagues," said Werner.

Werner walked two paces forward to address Fritz but move him away from Rabbi Shiltz and Jenny.

"Listen, Fritz, this guy knows me from before, and he thinks I am still working for the Party. I told him I was going to see the general and now he wants me to stay with him so we can see him together. What should I do?" said Werner.

"If you stay here, Werner, he will know you are lying and you will be charged with trying to escape. We cannot stand around here anymore, any longer and they will make out who we all are, we must keep moving," said Fritz.

"But if I leave without saying hello to a general it will almost certainly lead to us getting caught. There is only one solution: take the other two and go on ahead without me. Their names are Shiltz and Ritter. Please take them to the border and tell them I will join them later," said Werner.

"Ritter? But that's your name?" said Fritz.

"I know, Fritz, tell my wife that I love her. Now go, please, and whatever you do don't look back," said Werner.

Fritz didn't reply, he just nodded his head in agreement.

As the three of them walked towards the guard at the front gate, Werner could see Jenny trying to pull away from Rabbi Shiltz, who had a firm grasp of her arm. Her head was almost at a 180-degree angle as she tried to make eye contact with Werner. As they walked through the front gate and out of sight, Werner's face started to fill with tears.

"Hey Werner, what is the problem? You look like you have seen a ghost? Are you ok, can I help with anything?" said Jacob.

"No, Jacob! You have done enough!" said Werner.

# CHAPTER

*9*

Waiting in the corridor, Werner could feel himself shaking; he couldn't bring himself to look at Jacob even though he knew he had to. Instead, he stared longingly at a rock on the corridor floor. Suddenly a large bold man appeared from a side door Werner hadn't even noticed.

"General, can I introduce you to Werner Ritter, he is an old friend of mine from years ago, we used to drink in the same bar, isn't that so, Werner?" said Jacob.

"Do you take me for a fool, Jacob! Werner Ritter is a Jewish prisoner of the party, everyone in this centre knows that. What the hell are you both doing out here anyway, and why are you dressed in a guard's uniform? Guards! Arrest these two men immediately!" said the General.

"He is what? How can this be, General, he is wearing a guard's uniform?" said Jacob.

"Jacob, I don't know what you were doing with this man or why he is wearing one of our uniforms, but something tells me you were involved with it! I should have known giving you a position here would lead to you abusing it. Tell me how much he paid you to help him escape?" said the General.

"He didn't, I swear, I didn't even know he was in here! Please, Werner, tell him I knew nothing!" said Jacob.

"Is this true, Werner? You might as well confess because I am telling you now you will not be leaving this centre until I have all the information!" said the General.

"General, would it be possible to go someplace else and talk?" said Werner.

"Oh, don't worry, Werner, we will be going somewhere else, you mark my words. You will tell me everything either the easy way or the hard way, but I am telling you now you will tell me and my associates everything!" said the general.

"Please, Werner, please tell them the truth," said Jacob.

"General, I would like to inform you that Jacob was helping me to escape and that he is the reason I even have the uniform in the first place. He said he had stolen it off an officer he had swindled in an elaborate hoax," said Werner.

"What, what are you saying, Werner? You are lying, tell the general you are lying, do you know what this will mean for me!" said Jacob.

"I knew it! Guards take both these pieces of shit to Wing C, I want them interrogated immediately. I want to know who was involved in this plot, who helped Werner Ritter and how many others Jacob has helped escape. Most of all, I want you to make sure they both suffer for trying to make me look a fool," said the general to a group of soldiers that had gathered upon hearing the commotion.

As the guards marched Werner and Jacob down the dark, damp bricked tunnelled walls toward C Wing, Werner knew that this could be his end. He felt like he couldn't breathe, his legs were almost frozen to the ground from the shock of what had happened. In that time he should have been looking for an escape route, but instead, all he could think about was Jenny and what had become of her.

"You come with us, you in there and no talking!" said one of the guards.

The guards shoved Werner and Jacob through the door of the holding cell.

"Werner, why, why did you lie?" shouted Jacob.

Before he got a chance to carry on shouting at Werner, Jacob received a heavy fist straight to the bottom of his nose. The impact sent him falling back against the wall. When he raised his hands to his face, he could see the blood seeping through his fingertips.

"I told you to shut the fuck up! He is the least of your worries," shouted the guard at Jacob.

Jacob could see there was no point shouting anymore, Werner was being dragged away by the guards, who were now beating on him in a frenzy of attacks. For a slight second, looking through the blood running down his hands and face, he could see a pair of eyes fixated upon him. It was Werner; he seemed to be impervious to the punches and kicks, all he seemed focused on was Jacob. It was only fleeting but Jacob could see it wasn't anger on Werner's face, it was a smile, a smile directed in his path.

"Get him out of those clothes. I want to see him stripped to his bare ass! Do you know why I want to see you naked, Jew? Because you don't have any right to be wearing those clothes, you are not a soldier, you are not a part of the party anymore, you are nothing and before long I will put a bullet through your stinking miserable brain; but first I want to know exactly who helped you and how Jacob Anhalt was involved," said the general.

"It was Jacob, he was the mastermind behind it all. I simply followed his orders and did as I was told," said Werner.

"That's all you're telling me? I want all the information, not just stories! Gurt, make sure Werner here knows I am serious," said the general.

One of the guards walked forward and punched Werner full-on in the face, the impact knocked Werner to the floor. When he landed on the floor, the guard pulled his legs apart, and in one fluid motion kicked him in the genitals. The pain shot through his body like an electric pulse, the force knocking the wind out of his sails.

"Now, Werner, you will tell us how this plan was put into place and where exactly you got that uniform," said the General.

Werner lay on the cold cell floor, writhing in pain and agony, clutching his privates; his balls felt like they had been kicked into his stomach.

"I will not speak to you, General; you can torture me all you want," said Werner.

"Oh don't worry, Werner, I intend to! Guards, get out the crib," said the general.

Werner tried to get back to his feet, but the pain was just too overpowering. He touched the areas that were in pain and noticed his testicles and penis had shrivelled up almost to the point of disappearance. Then he saw the metal bed frame being erected in the cell, the guards were attaching electric jump cables to each corner of the bed and were then connecting the jump lead cables to an electrical generator.

"Put him on the bed! Now, Werner, we will see exactly what you know and what you don't know!" said the general.

"There, put him on the frame and make sure he's on his back. I want to see his face, then we will see who's smiling," said the general.

"Please, General, I take it back, I will tell you everything you want to know, please!"

"You think we have set all this up just to frighten you, Werner, no, no, you are about to feel just how 'shocked' I was to see you tonight," said the general.

Werner was strapped to the bedframe, the rust and dried bits of blood from the people before pushed into his naked skin.

"That's it, now, Gurt, show Mr Ritter here how we treat prisoners who try to escape," said the general.

Gurt attached the cable to the electric generator; within a flash Werner could feel a pain zap through his body. Like a thousand blades all going up and down his body, Werner could feel the electricity pulsing through his body. The power of the electric volts caused Werner's body to contract and arch without his control.

"There we go, Werner, how did that feel?" said the general.

Before Werner could answer or even realise the electricity had been turned off, Gurt flicked the switch again.

"Ahhh, you fucking bastards, you fucking cunts!" Werner shouted out in pain.

"Still a little fight left in you, that is good to see. It's a shame your body isn't as strong as your mind, Werner, you are not a man, you are a child, just look at the mess you have made!" laughed the general

"Oh my god, that is disgusting, it's all this pig deserves, to lay there in his own shit," said Gurt.

"Give him another zap, Gurt, I'm not sure his bowels agree," laughed the general.

"No problem, General," said Gurt.

"Please, please no, I will give you whatever you want, just please, no more, I beg of you," said Werner.

"I hear a lot of talking but nothing useful, just ramblings of a soon-to-be dead man, Gurt increase the power!" said the general.

The pain was now so unbearable that Werner could smell his flesh burning onto the iron frame of the bed. It smelt like week-old fried chicken.

"What, you think you are going to sleep, no, no, no, and miss all the fun, I think not. Gurt, the water!" said the General.

Just as Werner's eyes began to close, he got a cold slap to the face from an ice-cold bucket of water! It hit him with a rush of adrenalin, enough to jolt him back to a semi-conscious state.

"Please, I will tell you anything, anything you need to know! Just make him stop."

By now the water had mixed with the rust on the metal bed frame and was helping to conduct the electricity so well that parts of Werner's hair was starting to burn and the smell clung to the air.

"Werner, you idiot! Nobody tortures for information. We all know you will tell us anything now, this is not why we do it, haven't you figured it out yet? It's our excuse to make you suffer! You see, you are now ours to play with until you bore me, and we are done with you," said the general.

\* \* \*

"Werner, wake up! Wake up, you lying cunt!" said Jacob.

Slowly opening his eyes, Werner could see Jacob lying on the floor at the opposite end of the holding cell. He was badly beaten, naked and covered in burn marks, and was black and blue from head to foot.

"I would come over there and kill you myself, but I can't. Look at what they have done to my leg! It must be broken in several places. What have I ever done to you? Why am I here with you? I need to know, I need to understand why you hate me so much to have sent me to this place!" said Jacob.

"Shut up, you fucking prick, I don't hate you, you idiot! It's you who should be apologising to me! You have ruined my life and you are so stupid you don't even know it," said Werner.

"What, what did I do? I only said hello after not seeing you in years! I was minding my own business and you wandered past, all I said was hello. Please tell me how the hell did I ruin your life?"

"I was on my way out and you stopped me. What did you think would happen when he saw me? I could have been escaping tonight if it wasn't for you," said Werner. "Why are you in here anyway and why work for these fuckers!" said Werner.

"I could ask the same about you! The last time I saw you, you were a factory worker and in love with the party. Now I see you wear a yellow triangle with an M on it – since when were you a Jew or a murderer?"

"A lot has changed since we met, and what the fuck is that brown triangle you're wearing?"

"You should recognise it, you and people like you, are the reason I am in here in the first place, with your hateful speeches and your bullshit pseudoscience."

"Well, it looks like we have both found out the hard way that nobody is perfect!" said Werner cynically.

The door opened and another man was dragged in. He was still dressed in his prison-issue pyjamas, but it was obvious to both men he had been savagely beaten. There was a large red patch of blood at the back of his trousers, which appeared to still be bleeding.

"Dump that piece of shit with these two soon-to-be-dead pigs. Funny, isn't it, I think this is the first time we have had a gay, a Jew, and a gypsy all in together, it sounds like the start of a bad joke. We should open a freak show and charge people. Well, you can all keep each other company now, can't you! Give them a week of no food to think about it. That will help you find your voices," said the older solider to the younger guy manning the prison door.

All three men lay on the floor together, too injured to move.

"Werner, we need to help this man, he is bleeding from his backside. Christ, I wonder what they have done to him," said Jacob.

Jacob turned the man on his side so that he could look at him more closely; the man was delirious, speaking but not making any logical sense.

Jacob was examining Hans's body, looking at the fresh scars and bruises. He stopped when he got to Hans's lower half of his body. At first, Werner wondered why but then he saw Jacob's eyes fixated on Hans's pink triangle.

"I don't think I can do it, Werner. I don't think I can help this man, he's a gay. He must be, look he has a pink triangle on his chest," said Jacob.

"Who cares what he is. You can let him bleed to death for all I care, mind your own business! As usual, you are sticking your nose in where it doesn't belong," said Werner.

"Come on, Werner, look at him, we need to do something even if it's just to stop the bleeding – who knows what diseases these people carry," said Jacob.

"I'm too weak to move; if you're so concerned, you look after him!" said Werner.

"It's me who should be ripping your fucking head off, Werner! The least you can do is help me move him away from me!" said Jacob.

Werner crawled slowly to where Hans and Jacob were lying on the floor.

"Oh my god! I know this man, and I think you have even met him. His name is Hans Lehman, he also drank in the Bear and Shield. Don't you remember him?" said Werner, startled from the shock.

"No, I don't, but I think I would have remembered a gay guy drinking in the Bear," said Jacob.

"Wait, we are not even sure he is gay and even if he is, I am telling you he is a good man, or at least he was when I knew him," said Werner.

"Well, I used to think you were a good man and you helped me get locked up in this fucking cell, so forgive me if I am lacking in a bit of trust," said Jacob.

"Jacob, if you want me to help you stop the bleeding then you are going to have to help me too," said Werner.

"I want him moved but I don't see why the hell I should help you with your gay friend, you sold me out and probably would do again given half the chance," said Jacob.

"Please, Jacob, please help me save this man's life. I need to use the sleeve of your pyjama top to stop the bleeding, can I have it? I need to wrap it around his anus and bottom so that the pressure will stop the bleeding," said Werner.

"You can have it, but I am not helping you touch that gay's arse! At least if you stop him from dying, we won't have to share a cell with a rotting corpse; here have it!" said Jacob.

Werner grabbed the rag from Jacob and slowly lowered Hans's trousers. His lightest touch caused Hans to shake in a nervous discomfort. Werner rolled the rag into a tight ball and gently applied pressure to Han's bleeding anus, whilst holding his other hand on Hans's head.

"Hans, it's Werner, your friend. Do you remember me? I don't know how you managed to end up here, but don't worry; we are going to help you. I won't let you die in

here, we are going to get better and make it out of here,"
said Werner.

"You won't!" snapped Jacob.

"Jacob, I have something to say," said Werner.

"What is it now, more lies to get me in more trouble? I
think you've said enough!"

"I thought you said you wanted to know why I hate you?"

"I do!"

"Well, the reason you are in here with me and this poor
guy is that when you stopped me to talk to me, I was on my
way out of the camp. I had planned the whole escape and
the two soldiers you had seen me with were not escorting
me anywhere, that was my wife and her grandfather. So,
you see you completely messed everything up for me. I
could have been away with them now but, instead, I'm in
here with you and will probably never see them again! And
it's all thanks to you, you and your fucking stupid need
to stop me."

"You're joking, how the hell could I have known! You
mean to say you cast me to the dogs for something that was
completely accidental! You are a massive cunt, you know
that, Werner!!" said Jacob.

"I was angry and what was I supposed to do? If I
hadn't created the commotion with you, they would have
also been stopped and that is something that I wasn't
willing to do!"

"That still doesn't excuse what you've done to me!
How could you, how could you throw me under the bus
just to save them! You're a fucking twat and you deserve
everything they will do to you!"

"Jacob, if you do want to understand then let me tell you how I came to end up in here in the first place," said Werner.

* * *

"That might explain your actions, but it doesn't excuse them!" said Jacob after hearing Werner's story.

"Well, now you know and now you know why I ended up here and why I needed to get out! But ask yourself, what would you have done in my position, just given up and had everyone you love end up here too?"

"If that was what was needed, then yes!" said Jacob.

"You're full of shit and you know it! You would have done the same as me. For fuck's sake you are a camp informer, like you haven't sold out hundreds to save your own skin. I could tell the moment I saw your face that you had been doing something shifty, you must be the only prisoner in here who doesn't look starved to death."

"I did what I did to survive, you know what people are like, they would never trust a gypsy anyway, so why not look after myself!" said Jacob.

"Well then you have just proved my point, yeah why not look after yourself, that's what I did and you are the end result, so stop going on about it!"

"You don't know what you're talking about, Werner, all I did was tell little bits of information here and there, I never made-up blatant lies about someone just so someone else could get away. You might as well have handed me a death sentence when you did that and you know it!" said Jacob.

"We all rationalise what we do, we all find ways of justifying. In the end, you know I am right and you know you probably sent hundreds of people to Poland because of your 'little bites of information'. So go fuck off if you can't handle the truth," said Werner.

That moment, Hans started murmuring louder than normal; he had for days let out little moans of pain now and again but on the whole, had remained relatively silent, slipping in and out of consciousness. On hearing Hans, Jacob rolled back over so as to turn his back on them both.

"You know, Werner, before getting in this cell I wanted to kill you. But now I know we are cut from the same cloth; we are both in here because we are seen as different, and we both have flaws that do us nothing but harm in the long run. I guess we should just thank our lucky stars that we are not in the same place as this poor bastard right now," said Jacob.

\* \* \*

Werner awoke to the sound of the cell door unlocking. He could see from where he was lying that Jacob was still lying on his side from where he had fallen asleep the night before and that Hans was still face down. He was still making little weeping sounds but had stopped his incessant mumbling.

A guard's head poked around the cell door; it was a guard he had not seen before, and Werner pretended to be asleep. The guard stared at all of them one by one, scanning them and then muttered something.

Werner's eyes met Jacob's as he awoke, with which he greeted Werner with a frown.

"So it is real then. For a moment there I thought I was having a nightmare and was locked in a cell with two men who wouldn't give me the time of day before. I should have stayed asleep!" said Jacob.

"Jacob, the guards said we are going to be in here for at least a week, it has been seven days I have counted, and we are still here. I think we need to work together and find a way to get out of here," said Werner.

"You think I am going to work with you to try and escape this place? Do I have to keep reminding you that you were the one who put me here?"

"Jacob, I know I have wronged you, I know that, but please let us work together so that we can get out of here," said Werner.

"What about him? He is going to slow us down," said Jacob.

"We can take Hans with us; all we need to do is get out of here. I am telling you I was almost out of here when I ran into you, if it can be done once then it can be done again," said Werner.

"Yeah, but how? You are kidding yourself if you think he is going to be able to walk anytime soon. We would be better off strangling him now and saving him from further pain," said Jacob.

"Don't even joke about such things, we cannot do that to Hans; he is a friend of mine, or at least he was. I know he is a good man and didn't deserve what the party has done to him."

"He's obviously been fucked up his arse, you can see it from his injuries. He is going to be in for more of the same. I wonder how many guards fucked him before he was thrown in here with us," said Jacob.

"We don't know that, all we know is he has a pink triangle on his shirt pocket and that he's been tortured badly. The shirt could have been given to him by anyone."

"Werner, I am serious, he is in pain, let's put him out of his misery. Isn't it kinder that way, surely when a dog is on his last legs you take him out to the barn and shoot the thing? We should be doing the same here – you know Hans is just going to get tortured again, they may even rape him again, do you really want that for your friend?"

"You know I don't want that for him, but I cannot consider euthanasia; if the party's actions have taught me anything it's that once you step over that line it's difficult to stop. I mean, look at Hans, he could recover and who knows what the party will have in store for us, we could be sent somewhere, we could escape, we just don't know what will happen in life. A year ago, I never dreamed that I would end up in here and especially not with you or Hans. Look at the way the party made these arguments; first it was the disabled, the dwarfs, the spastics, and the people with Downs. Then it was the Jews because they were our money-grabbing slave masters. Then what, the communists and the trade unions, many of whom were only just arguing for fair wages. Then we had people like you, the gypsies, then it was the Jehovah's Witnesses and then we had pretty much anyone the party considered a danger to the development of the war effort and the creation of the new country.

"I am telling you I once did take part in this but now, Jacob, I have changed my life and I cannot agree with that kind of thinking. You need to think hard about what you have suggested and think about whether taking that path is the right answer, because I am telling you I won't go back to turning a blind eye to it anymore, if I have to die for my beliefs then so be it," said Werner.

"OK, OK, no need to give me a speech, Jesus! You may not be a party activist anymore, but you certainly do still like to get on your soapbox, don't you? I just thought we would be saving him from a short life of pain. Do you really think we are going to survive this place?" said Jacob.

"I know one thing, we are better off working together than against one another. I told you how I came to be in here, why don't you do the same? It's not like we are going anywhere, and I can assure you neither I nor Hans is going to be able to tell anyone."

"Well, it all started with me being stupid, I guess; I should have listened to my grandma," said Jacob.

"Well, go on, you are going to have to give us more than that."

"I was a fool, a fool to believe these fuckers, you know, Werner I did everything, everything they asked, to assimilate, I even dressed like them and turned my back on my culture and my history, and for what?"

"That's how they get you, Jacob, they make you think that everything is normal and that there is no point resisting, it's just easier to go along with what they want."

"I know and then worst of it all is that, had I have listened to those with wisdom and knowledge I wouldn't be in this mess and neither would my grandmother, wherever she is. She warned me, she warned me not to believe in their bullshit, to be my own person, to have independent thought, not just follow their dogma and what did I do. I joked, I laughed at her warnings, I said she was the misguided one that needed to modernise! God is playing a cruel joke on me, Werner, and I deserve it all."

"We have all been fooled, Jacob, you are not the only one. We all saw the posters go up and the way they were treating the Jews – hell, I used to hand those posters out! They take what you have to offer, and they chew you up and spit you out."

"But my grandmother, Werner, she has paid the price for my pathetic need to fit in, to be respected. What about her, I have ended her life."

"You don't know that, Jacob, you don't know she's dead. Don't cry, what good is that going to do you?"

Seeing Jacob was becoming physically emotional, Werner felt the urge to go to put his arm around him, but Jacob was a gypsy, and even though he truly did feel for Jacob, he just couldn't bring himself to embrace him.

"Just pull yourself together, Jacob, we will get through this. Don't let those bastards see you like this, you're a mess. Wipe your nose, for God's sake and dry your face before they come back," said Werner.

He wanted to show compassion, he wanted to show empathy, but years of hatred cannot simply be washed away like a dirty pair of hands. Washing one's soul is a different matter, he thought. The one thing he could do, he thought, was to pray for him.

"But you see, Werner, it's my fault she is now lost to me. I don't even know if she is in this centre, I have asked many people, and nobody has seen someone of her description. She could be anywhere for all I know, I don't even know if she is dead or alive. Look at what has happened to us, then think of how an old woman would cope in these conditions."

"We are both guilty of sending people to their deaths, Jacob, either inadvertently or directly. The thing we need to remember is we need to forgive ourselves to move on in life. Please, why don't we get on our knees now with Hans and say a prayer?"

"Say a prayer, are you crazy? If the guards catch us, we could be shot on the spot, and how can we get on our knees with Hans, he is a stiff cold slab on the floor. I mean, look at him, if he survives the night it will be a miracle."

"Come on, Jacob, please just trust me; we need to rid ourselves of the sins we have committed. We need to drop this hate; I know I still feel it in me, and I know I need to flush it out if I can truly move forward. Try not to be cynical about it, just go with it and see if it helps. Now let us pray."

Werner closed his eyes and started to recite the beginning of the healing ceremony Rabbi Shiltz had performed with him. Before he could continue, however, Jacob broke the short lived silence.

"What the hell is this? What language is this even, it sounds like something the Arabs would say."

"Jacob, it is Yiddish. It is a healing ceremony I once did with my grandfather," said Werner.

"And you expect me to just be fine with this? After years of you telling me we need to rid the world of these people and their language, now you of all people want me to join you in a Yiddish prayer?"

"I've come a long way, Jacob, and I know you have too. Trust me, please, it isn't which language you use, what religion or what denomination we are from, what does matter is the need to be able to put our sins out of our minds, to get them off our back. Please, Jacob, trust me, it helped me a lot and I am sure it will do the same for you."

They both settled down, kneeling opposite one another with Hans laid out next to them on the hard concrete floor. Werner repeated the words he had been taught by Rabbi Shiltz, the whole time watching Jacob's expressions cross over his face. First, there was a look of scepticism, then there was confusion, and finally a strange mix of disbelief, anxiety, and bewilderment. Werner held his hand against Hans's head to involve but also comfort him.

"I never thought I would say this but that was ok. You see there is more to my story, I was a party informant in here; I have lied, misled, and condemned men to their deaths through my actions. I am no better than you and what happened with your father, the only difference is I didn't swing the poker," said Jacob.

"Jacob, when this war is over many on both sides will need to look within themselves to ask for forgiveness for what they have done. We need to take solace in the fact we are taking steps, steps that are putting the past behind us. Now we need to decide how we are going to take action,

action that will get you, Hans, and me out of here. Come on, let's look around this cell and see if there is anything we can find to help us plan," said Werner.

Jacob managed to limp to his feet, putting most of his body's weight on his undamaged leg, whilst leaning against the cell wall.

"There is nothing here, Werner, we are fucked! It's four concrete walls and a floor," said Jacob.

"Look, what about the outflow over there? Do you think we could dig our way through there? I mean these wooden floors can't be that strong, the wood is mostly rotten," said Werner.

They both looked at the floor so intensely Jacob felt for sure his eye was going to burn a hole in it. If only that were possible, he thought.

"Digging? Are you crazy? There must be like ten feet of ground to cover and that's even before we breach the concrete walls. Not to mention the building foundations and the courtyard. Face it, Werner, we are totally fucked and there is nothing we can do!" said Jacob.

"We could dig with our hands, Jacob, come on, surely it's worth a try," said Werner.

"Werner, get a hold of yourself, you are grasping at straws right now, where would we even dump the dirt? It would take weeks, and don't you think the guards might just notice a hole in the cell when they come in? No, we need to think of something else, something that we could actually do!" said Jacob.

"Well at least I am trying to be positive," said Werner.

"If we are ever going to get out of C Wing we need a real plan, Werner, something real. What about if we called a guard and steal his gun?" said Jacob.

"It's not a bad idea, but what if two guards come, they have guns as well and if there is a hint of something dodgy taking place, they will shoot us dead, no question about it," said Werner.

"That's all true, but if we stay here and do nothing, we are dead already, and honestly what have we got to lose. Plus, like you said they have guns – if we can overpower a guard, get his gun, we could shoot our way out," said Jacob.

"Since when did you become Mr Strongman?" said Werner.

"Well, it's better than digging our way out, honestly how fucking stupid. That kind of thinking would definitely land us dead or worse in D Wing!" said Jacob.

"Jacob, you don't honestly believe the stories about D Wing, do you? And that Professor Bonn, that can't all be true," said Werner.

"Werner, I have heard rumours, of Professor Bonn and his team doctors conducted eugenics experiments on the disabled, gays, the crippled, twins, and anyone else the party had deemed of not worthy to the new Germany. It can't all be hearsay," said Jacob.

"I've heard the stories too, truly shocking stories. Things like pregnant mothers having spikes shoved into their stomachs to induce an abortion, twins tested to see if the pain received by one, could be felt by another, and people being injected with petrol right to the heart to study the effects. Do you think that kind of cruelty can take place here?"

"Werner, you are so naïve, of course it is being carried out here. God, you can be so stupid sometimes."

"Alright, let's just not, shall we. This bickering is pointless. Seriously though, even if we get the guard's gun, that will only leave us six shots against hundreds out there."

The room fell silent, a realisation that they were both doomed ran over them like a river slowly breaking its banks. They both slumped back onto the concrete floor; Jacob tried to use his arm as a pillow for his head, but it was no good.

"You know, Werner, I distinctly remember Hans saying he hated gays and always talking about women. Do you think he was living a lie all this time?" said Jacob.

"He must have been, well you could say the same about me, couldn't you, Jacob? I was an activist who eventually realised the joke was on him. Look at me, I am everything the country detests. The only person who wasn't hiding anything, Jacob, was you, you knew who you were the whole time."

"Werner, you might think that, but the truth is, I hated myself for being a gypsy, my grandmother always told me to embrace it, to know where I was from, but honestly I didn't want to know. My own kind disgusted me and still do deep down! Since being here I have informed on my fellow gypsies, I have given the party names of people who were looking to overthrow the party and break out of this centre. I know it's wrong, I feel guilty for almost certainly sending people to their deaths, but I can't help looking at them and thinking how pathetic they are. They are like sheep, walking around asking for help, being shepherded from one pen to another and I don't just mean in here either. The culture teaches about how we are a proud community of strong-minded travellers, but I saw no great adventurers, I saw no strong men in those gypsy camps, what I saw was a load of men asking for handouts, stealing what they could, and beating their families when things didn't go their way."

"You still think that now? Even after all the suffering, you have seen? Even after all the party has done to you?"

"I don't want to think about it, Werner, I wish I could be like you. I wish I could forgive my own people and hate the party, but you have to admit in this new world, surely, it's like Darwin said, 'survival of the fittest', isn't it?"

"Disenfranchised people do not have the same opportunities as others; when you live on the margins of society you are at a disadvantage already. How can someone from the gypsy community compete for a job with a white Aryan blooded male who has had the best schooling in Germany? The German is going to have better qualifications, better education, and better chances in life; this all adds up to the gypsy not feeling he has many opportunities in life, therefore he opts out and becomes part of the underclass of society."

"So how do you explain me then, Werner? I was born into that life, and I managed to make a success of myself. I know I was no business mogul, but I had my own shop, my own apartment, and even employed a staff member."

"You were the anomaly, Jacob! That Darwin quote you mentioned wasn't that actually by Herbert Spencer? And wasn't it: 'survival of the fittest, best suited to his environment'. Think about it, that means, all things being equal then the strongest will survive. If you were dumped in an all-Jewish community and asked to live as the locals do, you wouldn't survive, and you would be the weakest. A lion might be the king of Africa but in the freezing winters of the Arctic Circle, he would stick out like a sore thumb and thus not be the strongest or fittest to that environment. Look at the New World, if the stories were true and opportunities and riches were easy to get in America, then why are so many living in slums, poverty, and left to die on the slag-heap?"

"If what you are saying is true then, how can we ever really know who is the strongest, fit for survival?"

"The only way I think we can do it is by creating an equal playing field where all humans have a fair opportunity to compete with each other. I doubt we could ever get there though, even if there were to be some big world governing body, like the League of Nations, Europe has made things so lopsided that people from Africa and Asia could never compete. The banks, universities, and empires all sit in Europe and the new world – how is someone from China going to get to Heidelberg University? We in Europe are breeding elitism which has and will last thousands of years," said Werner.

"So if what you say is true, then how could this so-called level playing field ever come to fruition?"

"I don't know, Jacob, these are all questions that are above my mind's capacity. I wish I had my grandfather here to advise us, he was so knowledgeable on these kinds of matters. All I know is that if you look at history, one thing is for sure, all Empires collapse. This war may create new empires, if the British win then they will probably increase theirs. If the party wins then the New Germany may take all the French and British territories and own half of the world. Even if this does happen though, it won't last. How many maps have been redrawn over our small lifetimes? Most of these countries we are fighting for were not even countries 150 years ago – look at Italy."

"I'm not sure that is true, Werner; you think the British will collapse, that is laughable, they have been an empire for hundreds of years, if they win this war they will take more and never look back," said Jacob.

"Well for us it doesn't matter who wins the war, all that does matter is today and how we are going to survive tomorrow. I need some food; I am so hungry that I could eat my own arm off," said Werner.

"My grandmother would say 'she could eat the leg of a low flying duck'. What do you suggest we do? We can't just shout for the guards, can we and just ask – what if we end up back on that electric bed!" said Jacob.

"I tell you what, let's play snick, snack, snuck for it and the loser has to ask the guards," said Werner.

"Ok after three...snick, snack, snuck!" they both said in unison.

As Werner drew his hand into a round ball, he closed his eyes, within the blink of a second he looked down to see that Jacob was holding his fingers in the scissor configuration.

"Well it looks like I am it; I will go and shout the guards. Can you give me a hand getting up towards the door?" said Jacob.

Werner helped Jacob to his feet and towards the door.

"Don't ask for anything too big, just tell them that we need something, something to get us through the next couple of days," said Werner.

"Guards!" Jacob yelled.

It took Jacob shouting for a few minutes before the guard finally appeared; he seemed surprised to see Jacob standing near the door and instructed him to back up before he came into the cell.

"What is it you scumbags want?" said the guard.

"Please, would it be possible for me to get some food? We haven't eaten in days and we just need something to keep us going, anything will do," said Jacob.

"Food, food is it. Do I look like a waiter? Why yes, sir, I will go and get the oysters and champagne. You cheeky little shits, what makes you think you are different from any of the other lowlifes we have in here. Why should you get any special privileges?" said the guard.

"Please, anything will do, just anything," said Jacob.

"Well sure, no problem. Let me show you my pantry then you can help yourselves. Come along, let's go," said the guard.

The guard walked towards the hallway and waited for Jacob to follow him. Jacob turned to Werner and hugged him, whispering in his ear, "Don't worry, Werner, I know none of this was your fault. I promise I will be back as soon as I can. I know now that I am just as guilty as the rest of them."

"Don't worry, Jacob, I am sure he is just trying to scare us. I will see you soon," said Werner.

"Look at you two, I am touched, and I thought he was the gay one. Now put down your boyfriend and come along, I haven't got all day!" said the guard.

# CHAPTER
## 10

"N ow you sit in here and wait for someone to come for you. I don't want to hear another word from you either, especially not about food," said the guard.

Jacob found himself in a larger holding cell. He hadn't been marched far by the guard but he knew he was no longer in Wing C of the resettlement and interrogation centre; he hadn't seen this area before but he was sure it was Wing D, which meant only two things: resettlement to Poland or freedom through the path of a bullet. Still, a bullet would be the better option given the choices in Wing D.

Walking through the corridors he could glimpse a peek at the dimly lit room, most having a surgeon's table in the centre. As the guard pushed him with the butt of his rifle Jacob was pushed towards a wooden door, with the number 13 on it. As the door swung open, Jacob was abruptly forced through the door into a room which reminded him of a doctor's waiting room. There was a bench on one side, the room was painted white with a red stripe just below where the centre of the room should have been. Jacob looked for a guard but at first glance couldn't see anyone, then his eyes focused on the floor. A dwarf walked slowly towards him; his face was red with fresh burns.

"Are you ok? You look in pain!?" said Jacob.

"I will be alright, I have been through worse," said the dwarf.

"What happened to you?" said Jacob.

"I don't know how much you know about this place, but this is where people are sent to either be resettled or killed; you are one of the lucky ones if you get taken to the firing squad. The unlucky ones end up like me, spending their days enduring whatever sick punishment the doctors here can come up with. Imagine, I used to be an entertainer, performing to crowds across Europe, now I am poked, stabbed and experimented on like some lab rat," said the dwarf.

"Oh, sorry, I forgot to introduce myself, my name is Oscar, Oscar Voss," said the dwarf.

"Good to meet you, Oscar, my name is Jacob Anhalt. I had hoped that I wouldn't be brought here – you see, I asked the guard for some food for me and my cellmates and this is where I ended up."

"Bad mistake, Jacob, you should have known better than to ask these monsters for anything. Can you pass me some of that water, I need to cool down my face."

"What is it they did to you, Oscar?"

"Bonn is obsessed with testing on dwarfs to see whether they suffer pain the same as any other person. Imagine, isn't it obvious, that if you pour boiling water over someone's face they are going to cry out in pain?"

"Is that what he did to you? Is that why your face is burnt red?"

"That's only the half of it, he had poured boiling water down one side then freezing cold water down the other. There is no science involved at all; I had a friend who came to the centre with me. We used to work together in a travelling circus, we toured everywhere together. Of course, we were sent here together when we arrived. Professor Bonn is infatuated with dwarfs and little people. What he did to Elizabeth! First, he pulled all her fingernails out one by one, then they poured salt in her open wounds, just to see how she would react. They are absolute cunts!" said Oscar.

"That is awful," agreed Jacob.

"Well, you better get used to pain in here. The difference between here and Wing C is, the integration process in Wing C usually means they will at least stop after a while; even torturers get tired of doing the same things over and over again. In here, the doctors enjoy finding new ways to make someone suffer, but they call it work. Poor Elizabeth had her eyelashes pulled out one by one. Eventually, they got sick of testing on her and shot her through the head. That's it, you see, to them you are like an animal, they work you, they test on you and once you are no longer useful you are then sent off to the back yard to be killed like a rabid mongrel or a lame horse."

"Is it all dwarfs here?" said Jacob.

"I can see from your triangle that you are a gypsy, but trust me, you get people from everywhere in here. As you can see, I don't need a triangle on my jacket as it's rather obvious why I have been sent here, but the guards saw fit to give me one, that's the Germans for you. You see how you have a brown triangle; whilst I have a black one with the word inside saying 'bold'. This means I am part of the group labelled asocials, the bold means that I have also been labelled mentally retarded, which isn't the case. When I was at school I was top of my class! It just happens that my genius comes in a little package, not that these philistines would know anything about genius; what kind of people burn books anyway! Only the weak minded," said Oscar.

"So that's what your triangle means? I have seen many different ones around the centre but I don't know what they all mean. My previous cellmates in Wing C had a pink one and a yellow one, these were rather obvious but the others I have no idea about," said Jacob.

"It's simple, the group I belong to could include anything from tramps, cripples, dwarfs, lesbians, prostitutes, and people who have had sexual intercourse between Aryans and other races," said Oscar.

"Lesbians? I thought they would be given a pink triangle?"

"The party does not consider them in the same category as male homosexuals, probably because there is no penetration, I imagine, but who knows what goes through their minds when they make this shit up; it all defies logic," said Oscar.

"So, what are all the others then?"

"Green is for criminals, red is for political prisoners, like the commies the party has arrested. Let's see... then there is the blue triangle for immigrants, and lastly, we have the purple triangle for people involved in the wrong kind of church or what the party calls bible researchers. That is to say that they belong to a religion outside of the mainstream Catholic or Lutheran church. People often think this only applies to the Jehovah's Witnesses, but I have met many people from other areas of the Christian faith who have ended up in this centre."

"Wow, I never knew the party hated so many and had marked them for arrest. To think that they have even come up with a system. Do you think this applies everywhere?"

"Who knows, it's not like they can get rid of all of us, there are just too many in the world to do that."

"I do hope you are right. How's your face feeling now?"

Jacob helped Oscar apply a cold-water cloth to the side of his face. His skin was starting to blister.

"Come, let's sit and I can tell you some more of the stories of this place, that will cheer you up," said Oscar.

"To be honest I am not sure I want to hear any more," said Jacob.

"Trust me, it's better it comes from me than taking you by surprise. You know, I have seen so many come and go. Some have injections of all sorts stuck into them. Others, well they receive special experiments that happen once and that's it, you're done."

"Like what?"

"Well, I heard about one guy being put into a pressure container, you know like a pressure cooker. They just kept increasing and increasing the pressure in the tank until, well it had to happen. He popped, blew up like an egg that been left on the boil."

"My God, that's awful, how can they do such things?"

"People do all kinds of things in the name of science."

"Well, that's true, I guess, but just treating people like toys is crazy," said Jacob.

The stories filled Jacob with mixed emotions, they made him feel physically sick but he also couldn't stop asking for more. Like an alcoholic and his first drink of the day, he thought, you know you shouldn't but once you have broken you just need more.

"So, what makes you so strong, Oscar? How can you stay in here and not have it get to you, are you not afraid?"

"Of course, I am scared, of course I know I could go at any time, but you see, Jacob, it's because I am a dwarf that I have lasted this long."

"I don't follow you, how so?" said Jacob.

"Well, Professor Bonn is obsessed with dwarfs, that is why I have lasted so long and it's why I can keep going. One day, you see, Jacob, we will have our revenge."

"You know the day after I arrived here, I saw a Jewish family who lived on my street being processed. They were all sent to one of those cargo trains bound for Poland. That, Jacob, is one place you don't want to be."

"I've heard different things about Poland, I heard the Jews were fine there."

"Don't be so foolish, they are going there to their deaths, Jacob, everyone in here knows that."

"How do you know? I simply can't believe the party even has the manpower to kill them all, and where would they put them in the first place?" said Jacob.

Oscar and Jacob talked into the night. The guards looked in on them from time-to-time but hadn't paid much attention to either of them.

"You know, Jacob, there were times when travelling around Europe with Elizabeth, we performed for kings and queens, politicians and dignitaries, we were a hit, everyone wanted to see us. The crowds used to go mad for us, particularly Elizabeth's solo performance numbers. You know, one time me and Elizabeth danced to a performance on the stage at the Staatsoper Unter den Linden theatre. It was such an amazing time, Jacob," said Oscar. "You know, Jacob, if I am to die tomorrow that is the one thing I regret. I never told Elizabeth how I felt about her; we were friends, colleagues, but I had wished we were much more. I always wanted to tell her, I thought she must feel the same about me, but my pride and fear of rejection was too much, and I never told her how I felt."

"You were not to know, Oscar, don't beat yourself up about something that you had no control over. Nobody knows how this war will end, let's just pray we can make it through till the end, then we can start to have regrets, then we can start to think about what could have been; now we just have to survive. You have so much strength to endure what you have already and still manage to fight on. Please don't torture yourself thinking about Elizabeth and what could have been; the party is torturing you enough for a lifetime," said Jacob.

\* \* \*

"Right, which one of you is Mr Anhalt?" said the guard.

The guard's call woke Jacob up abruptly.

"Me," said Jacob, rubbing his eyes.

Jacob awoke to find a big brutish man standing over him. Jacob was immediately drawn to his beady little eyes that looked too close to his nose and his long over-shaped forehead that seemed to slope from one end of his face to the other. His little sharp teeth snarling at him through his nasty words.

"Good, one less gypsy to hang around here. Don't worry, imp, Professor Bonn won't be parting with his favourite toy just yet. You come with me!" said the guard.

Jacob didn't have time to say anything to Oscar before the guard grabbed him by his arm and dragged him out of the cell into the hallway. As the door slammed shut, Oscar tried to get to the window to see the outside area but due to his size, he couldn't reach the bars over the window. As he stood there deadly silent, he heard some walking outside, then he heard a single shot.

* * *

It had been days since Jacob had been taken out of Werner's cell and Werner was starting to wonder if he was ever going to see him again.

"Still not much life out of this one, I see, let's just give him a nudge to see if he's still alive. You up, gayboy?" the guard shouted as he kicked Hans in the chest.

"Please leave him, can't you see he's dead?" begged Werner.

"You want to think about yourself, not this freak. You're lucky I hate gays just as much as Jews!" said the guard as he landed another kick into Hans's chest.

Werner wanted to say more, he felt he owed it to Hans, but he just couldn't find the words. What difference did it make anyway, they were not going to listen to him, they hated him just as much as they hated Hans.

"You know, you I can understand, your race can't help it but these people, they choose to be sexual deviants, it's not normal. It an abomination!" said the guard.

"I used to know this man, he used to have a girlfriend. Honestly, I think you must have made a mistake," said Werner.

As he said the words he knew he should not have opened his mouth – as the last one left his tongue he knew it would only mean more problems for him.

"A girlfriend! That's even more disgusting! This one deserves to die in here, infesting everyone with germs; no wonder there are so many diseases in the world. You hear me talking, I'm talking to you! You're the disease!" said the guard as he walked out of the cell.

The guard's words shocked Werner but also made him think. This is once what he believed, it's what he used to promote, and it was also something he knew he needed to think about more.

"Hans, wake up," said Werner.

Werner often spoke to himself when he was trying to move Hans or even show him compassion. The fact was that he hadn't moved in days and that even when the guards kicked him, he had stopped crying out in pain and now was just staying deadly silent.

"Come, Hans, let me help you to the toilet, you must need to go now," said Werner.

When Werner tried to approach Hans he would move away fast, crawling into a ball like a frightened child.

"Come on, let me change those bandages and help you to the toilet, it won't take but a moment," said Werner.

"Please, Werner, please help me," Hans whispered to Werner as he helped him.

As Hans tried to use the toilet, he let out an almighty scream.

"Werner, please can you help me," said Hans.

"Sure, it's no problem. You know all men get caught once or twice with their pants around their ankles, Hans, it's not just you."

"You always were a funny guy, Werner. Where is Jacob?" said Hans.

Werner helped Hans away from the hole in the ground that was their cell toilet and back to the other end of the cell. The smell was starting to make them both retch, he would often find himself dry heaving

"The guard came in and took him out about three days ago, although I don't know really how long ago it was, I've lost all sense of what day it is or when it is. All I know is they took him," said Werner.

Over the next two days the guards started to change their ways ever so slightly, they had started bringing food into the cells now once every few days; it wasn't much, just a few stale crusts of bread, but it was something and any type of nutrient was welcome to Werner and Hans.

"Hans, why do you think they gave us these new prison uniforms?" said Werner.

"I have no idea, Werner; all I know is it's a damn sight better than sleeping half-naked on a cold floor," said Hans.

"Look over there, I saw another."

"Werner, do you need to do that. It's disgusting, I still can't believe you made me eat them."

"Look, do you think we can manage on old bits of bread? We need protein and cockroaches are packed with this, so if I catch it you're eating it."

"They come from the toilet hole, Werner, you know that, right?" said Hans.

"Of course, I know that, where else are they going to come from? It's just a shame I can't catch one of those nice fat rats I keep seeing at night."

"That's it, I draw the line at eating uncooked dead rat!" said Hans.

"Hans, you are in much better shape than you were a week ago and that's because we have been building up your strength. How else do you think that possible? Just close your eyes and imagine it's a juicy steak or something."

Werner then proceeded to grind up the broken cockroach parts over their stale bread.

"See, it doesn't taste that bad when you put it on the bread; if anything it makes it taste better," said Werner.

"Oh yeah, it's like eating caviar on crackers!" said Hans. "You know, Werner, I can still remember how Helmet used to tell us about his old war days and crack his lousy jokes. You remember the barmaid too? How we all used to bet on who could sleep with her, those were great days we were living."

"They were good times, weren't they? If only we could go back to them. It is crazy that we all ended up in here together, who would have thought it, what a coincidence, and who would have guessed what we would have been in here for," said Werner.

"What was Jacob in here for? Was it just for being a gypsy? Or had he been involved in some kind of illegal activity?" said Hans.

"What makes you say that? Is it because he is a gypsy?"

"I don't know, most are criminals, aren't they? Sorry, I shouldn't say that, it just came out. Isn't it funny how even when we have been punished for being different, we still cannot change how we think?"

"There are ways to do it, Hans, I know I have changed mine through embracing my religion, not ignoring or hating myself for it. I am happy now and if I die in here so be it; at least I have made my peace."

"I am not religious, Werner, I don't believe in God. I have always considered myself an atheist of sorts, I hate all that church mumbo-jumbo. Whenever I went to church it was all thou shall not do this and thou shall not do that, this is a sin, that is a sin. I'm surprised anyone could go about their day without not committing a sin."

"You are looking at religion all wrong; what I have found is the spiritual side of my faith. You don't need to go to church, temple, or the mosque to have faith in a higher power, I haven't once been to temple with my Jewish brothers and I am not sure I would even like to as I am not a fan of formal religions or those kinds of institutions; at least, I know I wasn't when I was a Christian. Still, I think you need something in your life to make you think that there is a good way to live it, I have heard of some people who live off the Earth and that Mother Nature is the one they find faith in, if that works for you then so be it. All I am saying is you need to think about what you are and be comfortable with it before you can try to find inner peace."

"Inner peace? What the fuck are you talking about?"

"I know that not everyone wants to hear about inner peace and spiritualism. Let's talk about something else. Hans, there is something I have wanted to discuss with you since I saw you here with me. You mentioned earlier that we used to joke and chase girls in the Bear and Shield and that you enjoyed this. Is that true? What I mean to say is, do you find women attractive? Or were you always lying to us when you said you wanted to fuck them? And what was your story with Penelope?"

"Werner, there are two things I am not ready to talk about. One of them is how I ended up in this establishment and the other is what took place in the other cell down the hall. If you are ok with not asking me questions about these two things then I am happy for us to chat, but if you want to know about that woman then I am sorry I cannot do what you ask. Do we have an agreement, or should I just shut up now?"

"Hans, it's ok, honestly I know we do not owe each other anything. You can tell me what you like, I only asked before because I was curious. But one question and then I will leave it. I have to ask, have you always been gay or did you choose to be it?"

"There is no choice involved, Werner; do you question your mind when you find something beautiful? I have always had feelings for other men. It was only in boarding school that I acted upon them. I think all men in some way have homosexual feelings or have at least thought about what it would be like to be with another man. The difference with gay people is we know what we want, and what's wrong with that? As you know, Werner, I used to be very interested in Greek and French philosophy, do you remember?"

"Yeah, I do remember you always talking about the Greeks now you mention it. God, I haven't thought about those kinds of things for a very long time."

"Exactly, well I used to read a lot on the subject of philosophy. I was always fascinated with the rights of an individual; you know, natural law and that kind of thing. Well, when I used to read it to myself I used to think, if we as humans have rights then how could being a homosexual be any different to being straight; surely I have the same rights to love another person as much as a straight person? And what if I wanted to get married to another man? It seems to me that religions and other institutions are the barriers to homosexuals having equal rights."

"Married? Hans, really you must be joking. People are taught from birth that being gay is wrong, do you ever think that the major religions will ever allow this to happen?"

"Why not? Yes, now it is the wrong time, but eventually, with time I think human beings will develop, and one day people like me will not be seen as anything different. The religion that embraces that movement will find itself with thousands more members."

"I understand what you are saying, Hans, but deep down I think most people would still say it's wrong, no matter how you frame it," said Werner. "When I think about two men having sex it makes my stomach turn, how could you engage in such a thing?"

"Werner, do you think love is wrong? Don't you think people should be able to love who they like? What difference does it make to you or anyone else what consenting adults do in their own room?"

"I guess I don't, but it goes against nature and nearly all religions speak of it as an evil, how do you explain that?"

"Werner, there are countless animals that are gay, we are just another, and when you talk about religion didn't Jesus talk about love and compassion? People are not prejudiced by nature, they don't discriminate against people simply because they felt a natural urge to, you like everyone else was taught to from an early age."

"All this might be true, and I take your point about religion saying we should look for the best in people, but how can your vision of the future ever come true? We are living in a country that believes in racial science, hell that's the reason we are both in here!"

"I am not saying that it will change, people's minds don't change overnight, but eventually, eventually, Werner, people will realise they are just being taught to hate for no reason and we will eventually get to a point where we all acknowledge our prejudices and move on and work together."

"Hans, I think you are dreaming, this is a pleasant fiction but being nasty to each other is as old a feeling as rage. We are just programmed to be this way, it's our nature to pick on others."

"It can happen, Werner, look at yourself, look at how you have changed in such a short period. Things will get better and people will start to wake up to their Government manipulation one day, you will see."

"This is all academic, Hans, we are going to die in this place and your dreams of a better world will die with them. We are nothing in here, we are less than the cockroaches we eat."

"Werner, isn't it just possible that one day people like me will have the right to live with whomever they want and be free to love whomever they want, just as you are allowed to do?"

"Only when the darkness that covers Germany passes will we see that day, Hans, and that day is a far cry from where we are now. Come on, let's get some sleep; you need to rest if you are to get your strength back and I need to think of some way we are going to escape from this place."

* * *

The next day Hans and Werner woke to a knocking on the cell door. As they awoke, they saw a slim, bony man enter the room. He was wearing a white science lab coat over a three-piece suit and had thick black round glasses that just about covered the majority of his face, apart from the wrinkles.

"You two, get up and stand up straight for the Professor," shouted one of the three guards that entered the cell.

The guards brought three wooden chairs in and then left.

"Please, I am sorry to abruptly wake you but do take a seat. My good friend Hans here already knows me, is that not so, Hans? But allow me to introduce myself to you, Mr Ritter. I am Professor Bonn."

"Yes, I know who you are, you allowed them to do that to me," said Hans.

"Hans, you're shaking. Please try to keep clam," whispered Werner.

"Come now, Hans, you had everything to live for and you threw it all away and for what? So you could indulge in your sick mind. If anyone is a monster it is you. I merely tried to help you, I merely tried to cure you of your disease. If you had completed your programme you could be walking free in Köln now; instead, you are in here with a Jew. Now let's not hear any more about your condition. I have not come to talk to you; frankly why you are still alive is a mystery to me anyway. I am here to talk to Mr. Ritter" said Professor Bonn.

"Me, what do you want from me, Professor?" said Werner.

"I was contacted by a senior member of the party regarding your placement at our centre, someone wants to see you. I was told that he would very much like to visit the centre and had heard about your case, which he had found of some interest. When he does come to the centre, I would like you to be on your best behaviour; this facility is to be given new funding next year and the last thing I want to do is show him a load of moaning half-dead skeletons;

so when he speaks to you, answer politely and to the point. He will not want his time wasted by the likes of you. Do we understand each other?"

"I understand what you are asking, Professor, but do you think he will want to speak to a former party member?" said Werner.

"I have no clue why this person would want to talk to you, all I know is his visit will run smoothly," said Professor Bonn.

"What about me, Professor? What am I supposed to do whilst this important person comes to visit Werner, just lay in this corner and die quietly?" said Hans.

"If only! You, Hans, will do whatever I decide, or you will be going back to Wing C for further enhanced interrogation. You would probably like that, wouldn't you? God, even being in the same room as you two repulses me! Guards! I am ready to leave," said Professor Bonn.

"Professor, what would you like us to do with the two prisoners?" asked the guard as he entered the room.

"Well, he gets here in two days so clean Mr Ritter up and make him look presentable," said Professor Bonn.

"And what about the other one, the girl?" said the guard.

"He has gone through enough, book him in for tomorrow morning and give him his freedom."

"With pleasure, Professor," said the guard.

When the Professor and the guards left, Werner and Hans started to talk quickly.

"What was all that about, Hans? What did they do to you?"

"It's not important, Werner, what is important is that man is the devil incarnate."

"I don't understand though, Hans, how did you end up in here anyway? You always seemed so settled. Surely you must have been hiding that you were gay for years, so how did they know? How did they find out?"

"It's a long story, Werner, I'm not sure I am in the mood for telling it."

"Please, Hans, I want to understand, I want to know how it is you are in here with me."

"Well, it's difficult to say, even to myself. I guess it all started with my love for Michael. You see, me and Michael have, or I should say had, a relationship for years that we shared in secret. The only person who knew was Penelope and honestly, she was fine with it. She was so supportive," said Hans.

"So, what happened?" Where are they both now? Isn't there something Penelope could do; I mean you guys have power and influence."

"Not anymore, Werner; anyway, I can't count on Penelope anymore. You see she was the one who put me in here."

"What? Why would she do that? I thought you just said she was supportive and knew you were gay?"

"Werner, the party found out, it was a clear-cut case of her or me. She chose herself and for that how can I be mad at her? She did what she needed to survive."

"You forgive her?! After all they have done to you in here? How can you be so calm about her? I would be mad as hell!"

"Werner, she was a true friend to me, she put my happiness before hers in many ways. She lied for me; she lived a cold life because she wanted me to be happy. Oh, it hurt me the way she denounced me but what could she do? I know in my heart she had no other option."

"You are a better man than me, that's all I can say."

"The look on her face is something that will live with me for the rest of my days. My god, speaking to you like this makes me think of the bar, that feels like a lifetime ago, doesn't it," said Hans.

"It sure does, who could have thought fate would deal us these cards," said Werner.

"Do you remember that time we were in the bar and Helmet got so drunk from that drinking competition?"

"Oh, you mean with the Austrians?" said Werner.

"Yeah, you remember they were walking around the bar acting like the big men until Helmet challenged them to a beer competition," said Hans.

"The poor guys didn't know what hit them, did they?"

"You remember the barmaid, I can't even remember her name now, but she switched their beers for the 9% ones and Helmet's to the 3% beers," said Hans.

"I completely forgot about that, well to be fair to the Austrian he must have put away about nine mugs of that stuff," said Werner.

"Yeah, until he grabbed his buddy's cap and threw up in it and passed out."

"Hahaha, that was a great night, wasn't it! And with the winnings, remember, Helmet ordered a free round for the house. We were like superstars for a night, man how we celebrated."

"Yeah, they were some great days."

"It's a shame we cannot celebrate like that now, you're so lucky you are going free tomorrow!" said Werner. "You must be excited, Hans, what will you do when you get out of here?"

"Werner, do you think either of us is getting out of here? We are condemned men! Do you think they would have allowed me to fail their sadistic programme and then allow me to walk free? You must be mad; there is only one place I am going tomorrow and that is in the ground."

"You think they are going to kill you? I don't believe it, why would they torture you and then put you in here for weeks, just to take you out the back and shoot you? It makes no sense, no sense at all. We are logical people, we do things efficiently so that we do not waste resources, and putting you in here has no wisdom behind their actions."

"When it comes to animals, natural resources, and human beings, then yes you are correct, but you have to remember that they do not see us as human beings. We are to them sub-human, a lower form. We are lower than animals to them, we are just something to be toyed with until they decide we are finally ready to be put out of our misery."

"I know, I have studied the party's literature, and as I told you I was all about promoting the values of the party until I came here, but I think we should never lose hope, Hans. No matter what they do to us we need to stay positive and optimistic otherwise they have already won. We need to one day escape this place so that we can find another that isn't dark and full of evil."

"Hope? Hope is a dangerous thing, Werner; hope can break a man for believing in it. I have seen hope destroy a man from the inside. I had hope, hope when I thought that if I followed the rules I would be set free. That girl who they brought before me, she had hope. Hope that if she did what those animals wanted she would be treated differently to all the other women in here; instead she was subjected to rape and humiliation. That is where your hope gets you in here, Werner! I am a realist, I know my time is up and you better get used to yours being, too. This man, whoever he is, who is interested in your case, what do you think they will do with you when he has gone? I will tell you what they will do, they will take away your new clothes, stop your new food rations and within a day you will end up in the same place as me."

"I don't believe you, Hans, I cannot believe that we will die in here alone. I don't believe I won't see Jenny again, I can't believe it. I will never lose faith in hope because if I do then what do I have?" said Werner.

"Jacob, where do you think he is now then? Walking the streets of Köln, enjoying a beer? No, he is most probably dead! You are a Jew, Werner, and I am a gay man, and we are living in a country that hates us both; the quicker you get used to this the quicker you will be able to accept the inevitability of our lives coming to an end."

"You believe what you want but I still believe God will provide for me. He will show me the way just as he did for Moses when he freed my people from the Egyptians. Maybe this is a test, like Abraham when he was told to sacrifice his only son; maybe God is asking us Jews to be tested before we will again return to the kingdom of heaven."

"You can do your God bothering as much as you like, Werner; if it helps you then go for it. But I will say goodnight and if you are going to speak to your God then say a prayer for me because tomorrow I won't be coming back," said Hans.

* * *

The next morning the doors swung open with an almighty crash. Two guards Werner had never seen before walked in, both as ugly looking as the other. Their faces were curled up into tight balls, angry and bitter. One had a scar across the side of his left cheek – must have been in a fight, Werner thought to himself.

"Hans, do not worry I am sure you will be just going through the process procedure," said Werner.

"Werner, if my only crime is to be put to death for believing in having the ability to love another person then I am guilty," said Hans.

"That's right, you are guilty, you dirty stinking rat, and now you will get all the freedom you ever wanted. I wonder if there is a gay heaven. What do you think? I bet you think there is one for you Jews, so will your friend be joining you in yours? I bet your books teach that being a gay is just as sinful. You see, even your friend thinks you are going to Hell," said the guard with the scar.

"That... that isn't true. I know this man, he is a good man," said Werner.

"Yeah, but you cannot say, can you! You cannot tell your so-called friend that he will be saved because you know that your book teaches you it is wrong," said the guard.

Werner couldn't bring himself to look Hans in the eyes.

"Hans, don't listen to him, you will be ok. I did as you asked last night and prayed for you to be ok and I believe God will answer my prayers this time," said Werner.

"Werner, you have been a good friend. If it had not have been for yours and Jacob's care I would have died already," said Hans.

The guards started to laugh.

"You don't feel any emotion! That is why despite all that has been done to me, I do not hate you. I pity you because your heart is black! You could never love as I have loved," said Hans.

"That's enough of your attitude, I didn't come in here asking for your opinion. Let's go!" said the guard.

Warner watched as the guards grabbed Hans by his shoulders, one with his right hand around the back of his neck and the other pulling him by the chest.

"Take care, Werner and remember no matter how much they try to break your spirit, no matter what you have done in the past, remember they cannot take away the love we have locked in our hearts. It has been my honour in knowing you, my friend," shouted Hans.

Another older guard came in the cell after Hans was taken away. He had thick silver hair with deep blue eyes.

"Right, you, let's get you into these new clothes and make sure you wash all over. You can use your old clothes as a towel to dry off. Professor Bonn wants you looking respectable before your visitor gets here," said the old guard.

"He is coming today?" said Werner.

"Yes, he will be here in about 30 minutes, that's why we needed to get rid of the gay before he got here, otherwise he might have stayed in here with you forever," said the guard.

The next thirty minutes drew out, with nothing but his thoughts Werner willed his mystery guest to be prompt.

The door swung open and there was a young, tall, strong-looking man. He was dressed in a full military outfit, its gold eagle shinning as the light bounced off it.

"Hello Werner, do you remember who I am?" asked the man.

Squinting his eyes, Werner found it hard to adjust his eyesight. He had to really stare at the man's face.

"Here, let me take my hat off so you can get a good look at me, that might help," said the man.

The man removed his military hat by its peak, running his hand along the rim of its black visor before removing it.

"Do you remember now?" asked the man.

"Peter, Peter is that you?" asked Werner.

"Yes, it's me, Werner, so you really are in here. I couldn't believe it at first when I read it in the ledger, but here you are as plain as day. I must say you have looked better. Guards! Bring us two chairs, a table, some food, and some coffee. Oh, and an ashtray, I take it you still smoke?" said Peter.

"I do. Peter, what are you doing here?" asked Werner.

"All in good time, Werner, all in good time. Let us talk freely once those boys have followed my orders and we are alone; you never know who is listening," said Peter.

Both men stood facing each other in an uncomfortable silence. Werner examined Peter's uniform – he had a few more stars on his jacket sleeves and Peter's shoes were shiny, as was his watch's leather strap and the holster that held his standard issued Luger in place.

"Thank you, men, now leave us to speak. I need to interrogate the prisoner on my own if I am to find out the information we need to track down the suspects. Now, Werner, take a seat, the guards will be waiting outside the door so don't even dream of making any funny moves. Take a seat and let us talk together as men," said Peter.

The guards left the room leaving just Werner and Peter standing in front of the two chairs and a table full of food.

"Werner, take a seat and have something to eat, would you. God, you look like a walking skeleton in those baggy old clothes," said Peter.

Werner sat and began to stuff food into his face, first a succulent piece of ham, then a lump of bread and finally some olives. Peter patiently smoked a cigarette, waiting for him to finish. He dried his mouth on his jacket and sleeve and put down the bread he was working his way through.

"So, what is it you want, Peter?" said Werner.

"What I want, Werner, is to help you. You don't belong in here with all these dirty filthy vermin. I know you, you are no Jew, and you are a good man, a man who loves the party and someone who shouldn't have been treated this way."

"Peter, it's ok, I have accepted my heritage and I am proud of it. I do not need your pity or your food. I am at peace with my God and I have come to realise that all I used to believe in was just mindless violence and perverted science. I thank you for your visit, but if you have come to see me just to see if I am still a believer in the party's values, then I am sorry but you won't be happy with the outcome. I am a Jew like my family before me and I won't be pressured into even denying it."

"I see you still have a passion for public speaking and listening to your own voice, I guess that's one thing that they haven't taken from you in here. I am here to help you, Werner, but you need to help yourself. It's true, I still think the Jews are the reason why so much of the world is in a desperate position. They loan and make money off the backs of German workers then charge extortionate amounts of interest. I mean, you are different, you look like a German, but the typical Jew, the typical Jew doesn't even look like a human being, he has a hooked nose and a rat-faced chin. If we had not taken action then we would be living under a communist totalitarian system under the orders of the godfather of German Jews, Herr Marx. Is that what you want for Germany?"

"Peter, I have heard all this before, hell I used to preach it at party meetings. I read the up-to-date letters of instruction from the party, I know what the party line is and I am telling you that now I know this is wrong, flat wrong! When I first came here people knew I had been in the party before, they knew and they still didn't attack me. Every night before I went to sleep, I would think that someone would cut my throat; after all, I had condemned thousands of their brothers to death with my speeches. I may not have put the bullet in them myself, but violence towards the Jews was provoked through people like me, people who were the wheels in a machine that was designed to inflict suffering and pain upon thousands. I am telling you now, Peter, that for this I cannot forgive myself, it is my burden to carry and I will not add to it by agreeing with you and your simple-minded dogma."

"I am sorry to hear this, Werner, I thought if I came here and talked to you myself that I could sort this mistake out, that if I knew you were still a believer in the party that I could help you and maybe even have you moved from this place. You know you are scheduled to be resettled in less than a week. I know you have heard rumours about what lays ahead for the inmates of this camp in Poland, but I can tell you that whatever you have imagined isn't half as hellish as the reality that awaits you."

"I am sorry to disappoint you but nothing you say is going to make me change my new life. Since being here I have lost friends, lost loved ones, and been subject to the guard's sadistic pleasures, I have even been tortured in the name of the party and none of this has broken me; in fact, it has just made my bond with God stronger. I think if you have no more to say then you should just go and leave me to rot in this cell because if you are awaiting a conversion then you will be waiting till the end of time."

"Werner, can you not see that I am here to try to help you?"

"I don't need your help and I have never asked you for it. I am no longer the leader's poodle, I no longer look the other way when men are being discriminated against and I certainly do not buy into all that party bullshit you have spewing out of your mouth."

Peter looked shocked, his face went from anger to admiration to a blank confused look within seconds.

"Werner, if this is how you feel then so be it, maybe there isn't anything I can do for you."

"I don't think there is, Peter, I see you are now a senior party official and I am a convicted Jew. What did you expect to happen, for us to go drinking together like the good old days? If you wanted that you should have come earlier – I had two of our old drinking buddies in here with me."

"Werner, you are delusional and making no sense at all. Maybe you have received too many blows to the head and that is why you are talking such gibberish. Look, all I want you to know is that I am going to help get you out of here."

"Why would you help me? You just told me you hate all Jews, I am a Jew! A Jew you promised you would rid Germany of!"

"Werner, calm down, if you start shouting any louder the guards will come in and we will not be able to talk anymore; here, have a cigarette and relax. Now, what I am going to do is this; I am going to tell Professor Bonn that I am taking you to be transferred to another resettlement centre in Berlin but what I am going to do is put you in the back of my car and drive you to the border."

"You are going to help me escape? Why? Why endanger yourself? If anyone else finds out about this, you will end up in here with me!"

"I am not doing it for you, I am doing it because of a promise I once made to your father. You remember when we used to get so drunk that we would get the tram to his place and carry on drinking at the late-night bar in his village?"

"Yes of course I remember those times, I haven't thought about them for quite some time, but I can still remember them," said Werner.

"Well, once when you had fallen asleep on the piano at the bar, and there was a fight, a fight in which I would have almost certainly been stabbed had it not been for your father's bravery. You see, I was taking the piss out of one of the soldiers that had come to the tavern from out of town. At first, it was harmless banter, but then after about five minutes of back-and-forth tempers got strained and before I knew it I was looking at the sharp end of a hunting knife. Before the soldier could stick me with it, your father smashed his stein over the soldier's knife wielding hand, sending him and the knife shattering to the floor. Once on the floor, your father landed a direct boot into the soldier's face and knocked him clean unconscious. I swore that night that I owed your father my life and that I would do my best to help protect him from any harm the way he had done for me. Do you know what your father said to me? He said he needed nothing, but his boy was always getting himself into trouble and if I want to do something for him then I should take care of you," said Peter.

Werner's eyes started to swell with tears.

"Do not get upset, Werner, I know all about what happened between you and your father, I read the files and I'm not here to rake up old graves. We may see things differently, you and I, but I know you loved your father just as much as I did and it is for that reason that I ask you to let me help you get out of here. Once you are at the border you are on your own and I will consider my debt repaid. So, Werner, what I need to know is do we have a deal?" said Peter.

# CHAPTER 11

"Come along, children, we are going to be late," said Werner.

"Granddad, do we have to go, I want to stay in and watch TV," said David.

As Werner looked around his apartment, he could see two small heads sat hidden behind the round circular dining table Maggie had bought him for his last birthday.

"I can see you both, you know; Nadia, it's not hard to see your curly hair from here, and David, your sneakers are sticking out from behind the sofa," said Werner. "We have talked about this, it's good to get on the streets once in a while."

"But I don't see why we have to go; we've been on three already. I don't like all the shouting; can I just stay here and watch the TV? Teenage Mutant Ninja Turtles is on next," said David.

"You have time for that rubbish anytime. Whether people shout is irrelevant, what is truly worrying is when people do not talk. That is the reason we must go today, that is the reason we must raise our voices," said Werner.

"I don't want to go! I don't want to walk; I am happy here in your flat! Can't we just go with Daddy? He is coming anyway so why can't we just drop you off on the way and then we can just go with him," said David.

"My boy, you are too clever for your own good sometimes, your father knows how important these things are to me and that's why he will be coming with me and so will you! It is our duty, you see, it's our duty to remind people that we care about others and that we want others to have the same rights and freedom we enjoy," said Werner.

There was a knock at the door.

In walked a well-dressed man, wearing brown brogue shoes, and a blue three-piece suit, with a white shirt and blue dotted tie.

"Hi, Dad, sorry I'm late, it was a hell of a day at the office. Looks like you have the kids ready. Hi guys, did you miss Papa? Now who is looking forward to seeing some rainbows?" said Peter.

"Not me, Dad, I don't know why Granddad makes us go with him all the time, David was just saying to him that we didn't want to go," said Nadia.

"Oh, come now, Nadia, you and your brother know it makes your grandfather happy to have you alongside him, isn't that right, Dad? Anyway, you think it's just you; I remember when Dad dragged me to all kinds of marches when I was young, you think at the time that you are going to something boring but I can tell you that these memories stay with you forever. I can still remember the day your granddad and grandma took me to the million-man march, and we went to see Dr King speak about civil rights. It was a beautiful day, wasn't it, Dad? And do you remember Mum stuck that badge on my shirt, what did it say now?" said Peter.

"It said 'hug me, I'm catholic' if I recall," said Werner.

"Yeah, that's right, Dad. You see, kids, no flies on your granddad, yep it said hug me I'm a catholic and you know what? I got the most candy I ever had that day from people who were also on that march," said Peter.

"Do you think if we wear badges like yours people will also give us candy, Papa?" said Nadia.

"They just might, Nadia, they just might, but you must remember that you don't go to these marches for the candy – that is just an advantage of going. What's important is why you went and what you are supporting," said Peter.

"Was Grandma Helen beautiful, Dad? asked Nadia.

"Mum? Well, you will have to ask Granddad about that, but I am sure his opinion is just as biased as mine," said Peter.

"She was one of the most beautiful women I have ever met. You know where your father gets his good heart, that's from your grandmother, and it's also where you get your beautiful green eyes, Nadia," said Werner.

"Granddad, can you tell us about Grandma?" asked Nadia.

"Oh, I don't think we have time for that, Nadia, not right now," said Werner.

"Please, Granddad, please, we never get to hear about Grandma Helen," said David and Nadia.

"Oh, go on, Dad, just for five minutes; we have time," said Peter.

"Well ok, let's take a seat. David, you and Nadia come and sit with me on the sofa. Peter, you can take the armchair – I just had the leather upholstered so let me know what you think," said Werner.

"It looks very nice, Dad; I have to say they did a good job. Not sure about this painting though, where did you get that?" said Peter.

"Mary dropped by and gave me it. Horrid, isn't it, I didn't have the heart to tell her, so I just let her hang it up. It was the easiest way of getting rid of her. I mean, what would I want with some painting with two faces and a keyboard splashed all over it? I can't even work out what it's supposed to mean, can you?" said Werner.

"Honestly, Dad, I have no idea. I don't think anyone does these days, they just put them up to try to look interesting. The yuppies at work buy them all," said Peter.

"Yuppies?" asked Werner.

"Never mind, Dad, come on, the kids are waiting, tell them about Mum," said Peter.

"Come on, Granddad, come on, Grandad," shouted David and Nadia.

"Ok, your grandma Helen, well where do I start? You were right, Nadia, she was the most beautiful, amazing woman. She always had such a kind smile; I think it was this that made me first fall in love with her," said Werner. "She died just before you were born, David, it's such a pity she didn't get a chance to meet you both, she would have been so proud."

"It is, Dad, I know she would have loved you two, especially you, Nadia, you have hair just like Mum did," said Peter.

"Hey, who's telling this story! Now, where was I, oh yes. Well, we first met in London," said Werner.

"London, we never knew you lived there, Grandpa," said David.

"Well, I did, son, I did and that's where I met your grandma Helen. You see, we were both in England after the Second World War. Those of us who fled Europe all tried to make our way to the UK to escape the horrors of the war," said Werner.

"Alright, Dad, let's not go into too much detail; they are only kids," said Peter.

"Yes, yes, I know, Peter. Don't worry, I know where to draw the line, I'm not senile, you know," said Werner. "Well you see, kids, originally I am from Germany and your grandma Helen, well she was from a country called Belarus, in Eastern Europe. It's part of the Soviet Union now but before it was its own country and I guess still kind of is."

"Wow, where is that, Grandpa?" asked Nadia.

"Here, Peter, hand me that atlas from below the TV table. Look, kids, I will show you," said Werner.

Werner flicked through the world atlas till he came across the pages on Minsk.

"See, your Grandma Helen, she was from Minsk, that's the capital, one day maybe your dad will take you there." Werner winked to Peter.

"And me, well I am from here, Koln in Germany. Oh, you should see it, kids, it's such an amazing city and you, Nadia, you would love the winter markets and the sweets they sell," said Werner.

As his finger slid over the atlas map of Europe, Werner found it had a mind of its own and kept moving from Germany, across until it finally stopped on the city of Oswiecim. "And you see, kids, this is near where your grandma was, and her first family was sent, years ago," Werner said with a sigh.

"First family? But, Grandad, how could Grandma Helen have two families, that's not allowed?" said Nadia.

"That's true, Nadia, you can't have two husbands, but you see this was before Grandma Helen met me and it was before her first family was taken from her. You see, she was only a young woman when she was sent to this camp," said Werner.

"Camp, do you mean like summer camp I went to last year?" said David.

"No, David, this is a different kind of camp, a camp where unspeakable horrors took place," said Werner.

"Dad, please not too much," said Peter.

"I know, I know, I won't go into detail," said Werner.

"Anyway, you see me, and your grandma Helen met in London, in a refugee centre to be precise – we were both looking for our families. You see, many of us were refugees from Europe and we came to England to start new lives and gain passage to America. That's how I ended up in New York City," said Werner.

"Did you find your family, Grandpa?" asked Nadia.

"Unfortunately not, Nadia, I was never able to track down any of my relatives; even to this day I have no idea where they went and what happened to all my cousins and family," said Werner.

"What about Grandma Helen, did she find anyone?" asked David.

"Well, we found out what happened to her first husband and two kids Emma and Leon. You see, they all died inside the camps I told you about," said Werner.

"Dead? Was Grandma Helen upset?" asked Nadia.

"You know that's a good question, Nadia, she was, she was upset till the day she died. We grownups call it depression; you remember, don't you, Peter, there were days your mother couldn't even leave the bed," said Werner.

Right then Werner looked over to Peter – he was drying his eyes with his blue crossed handkerchief.

"I remember, Dad; she was strong, kids, no doubt about it, but you see even grownups need to have some time alone when they are feeling sad," said Peter.

"You see, kids, it was the refugee centre in London that brought us together. I would see Grandma Helen every day running her finger down the list of names of people who had been found, she was like me, just constantly looking," said Werner.

"Who were you looking for, Granddad?" said Nadia.

"Me? I was looking for a lady named Jenny and her father who was a Rabbi," said Werner.

"Wow, he must have been an important man, Grandad," said David.

"He was, David, he was important in more ways than you will ever know; if it wasn't for him, none of us would be here," said Werner.

"What else can you tell us about Grandma, Grandad?" asked Nadia.

"Well, I can tell you the 23rd of March and December 11th were important dates to our grandma Helen, these were the dates of her children's birthdays, you see," said Werner.

"So that is why you always light candles then; you know, Dad, I don't think I even knew that," said Peter.

"I do it out of respect for your mother, Peter, you look just like her, you look more like her than me, that's for sure," said Werner.

"Well, we should thank god for that, shouldn't we, kids!" Peter joked.

"Come on now, I think we have talked enough; we are going to miss the start at this rate. Get your coats on and let's be going, I have some sweets in my jacket somewhere for you," said Werner.

"Now what do you say to your granddad?" said Peter.

"Thanks, Granddad, I love you," said Nadia.

"I love you too, Granddad," said David.

"Now come on, let's get our coats on and get moving otherwise we are going to miss the start and you know how much you like to see the fire jugglers," said Werner.

* * *

"WE'RE HERE, WE'RE QUEER GET USED TO IT. WE'RE HERE, WE'RE QUEER, GET USED TO IT. WE'RE HERE, WE'RE QUEER, GET USED TO IT. WE'RE HERE, WE'RE QUEER, GET USED TO IT."

The streets were full of colours and crowds. Werner had positioned himself and the rest of his family at the back of the procession, as he didn't like to be in the centre. There was just too much noise and too many people darting around the place.

Peter always looked a bit on edge at the marches; he had a tight hold on Nadia and David and would be constantly scanning the crowd to make sure people didn't get too close to them.

A man danced next to Peter in a cowboy outfit, complete with a rhinestone cowboy hat; some wore suits and had come straight from the office; others waved rainbow flags and many more shouted whilst pumping their fists in the air.

"Dad, I have to hand it to you, I can't see that many old age pensioners dragging around their adult son and his children – you couldn't make it up," said Peter.

"Well, we have been coming here for as long as I can remember. Look, that's where the hotdog vendor gave you those free hotdogs when you fell and hurt your knee that year, do you remember, Peter?' said Werner.

"1972, Dad, midtown sure has changed a lot since then hey."

"You remember, he kept giving you them for free until you stopped crying and couldn't eat anymore."

"Grandad, can we have a hotdog?" said Nadia.

"How about some candyfloss instead?" said a man dressed as a peacock.

"Wow, that's an amazing outfit, did you make it yourself?" said Peter.

"He did and I made mine too, we are the peacock twins, we like nothing better than a bit of peacocking," said another man dressed also like a peacock, but in quite different psychedelic colours.

"They are wonderful," said Werner.

"Oh, thank you, thank you all; here, little girl, have some," said the man dressed as a peacock.

On hearing the man, Nadia grabbed a big bag of candyfloss from the stash he was carrying. He smiled from ear to ear and she hugged the man.

"You see, Peter, that's why we come and that's why we have to insist we all come, it's not about groups, it's about standing up for what's right, it's about building a community and a country where everyone is welcome and everyone treats each other as family," said Werner.

"Daddy, why are those men holding signs?" asked David.

"They are holding protest signs, darling, that's what we are all doing here, protesting," said Peter.

"What are they protesting about? Are they mad with someone for something?" asked David.

"Well, they are protesting because they want to be treated like everyone else, they want to get married and be treated like anyone else who wanted to marry someone," said Peter.

"And they are not allowed to do that now? That's sad," said David.

"That's right, darling, they belong to a community discriminated against, so they have all come to protest to try to improve things," said Peter.

"Are we part of that community?" asked Nadia through a mouth full of candyfloss.

"Well that's a good question, dear; I am not gay, and neither is your granddad, but we can still be supporters and advocates for equal rights," said Peter.

"But then why do we have to come to these marches?" asked David.

"Let me take it from here, Peter. Nadia, David, come close and listen to me very carefully. If you want to know why we come to these marches you have to know your family history. You see when I was a young man I grew up in Germany. You know from your history lessons what happened in Europe to the Jewish people like us, don't you?" said Werner.

"Yes, they were all persecuted and killed," said David.

"That's correct and that is what is taught in the history books, but the truth is they were killed by people's willingness to look the other way. You see, when the bad people first started their campaign against the Jews, people didn't care, they saw the Nazi party give people jobs and they heard speeches that filled them with hope that their country would become great again. We Germans have always been a proud nation – look at the place today: it is the workhorse of Europe, because we are a hardworking, inventive nation who can come back from anything," said Werner.

"Back then I was once the same, I turned the other way when I saw injustice, I would not say anything when I saw a man get beaten in the street because I didn't want to get the same. I would make no effort to look after my fellow man's health because I thought, well, I am not one of them so why should I care about them. You see, we humans are a selfish bunch, we only really care about an issue when it affects us individually and that is why we are here today because we must change this, we must be the ones who fight toward freedom, human rights, and equality for others so that we can all live our lives in peace and freedom. That is why I took your father to as many civil rights marches during the sixties so that people of colour could have the same rights as us, and that is why we must come today so that gay people can also have those rights. We must never stop fighting for those who are discriminated and marginalized," said Werner.

"But, Granddad, those people over there are not in the march, they are shouting at us," said Nadia.

Werner turned his head to see what Nadia was describing; he could see a wooden cross and several signs coming from a small crowd of about thirty people. They were being held back by policemen, who were there to control the participants should things get out of hand. The signs read like a homophobic textbook. One stated that Jesus did not condone gay marriage, the other said that all gay people were going to Hell, another noted that marriage was an institution for a man and a woman, nothing else.

"Yes, dear, I can see the man you are talking about and it is sad he feels he needs to give his voice to a course that denies others the same rights he didn't have forty years ago. You see, that is a prime example of how quickly we forget our own backgrounds. As I told you before, I was once a person who ignored others' suffering. I would say, oh it's not me or my family affected so why should I care; but you see, things in my life changed dramatically during the war and I promised myself that I would not become just another person looking the other way. I would do what little I could to improve others' lives the way God would like us to do," said Werner.

"But those men are holding signs saying God hates gay people. Are they talking about the same God we pray to?" said David.

"It makes no difference which God someone prays to or not. What matters is your own moral persuasion and what you feel in your heart. You see, in life we often see things and we know straight away whether it's right or wrong, whether we should act or not, and by turning away and just ignoring the injustice, well then we are just as guilty as the people committing the unjust act," said Werner.

"Dad, you are overdoing it again. I told you before, all this goes over their heads, you should wait till they are older to tell them all this," said Peter.

"I am making a point and it's a good thing that people like me still do! Your generation would see us all working every hour God sends, just to buy some of those overpriced basketball sneakers. I tell you things might have been bad in my day, but I can't remember people stabbing each other in the back, stepping over anyone, just to make more money than they actually need. People were better off in the 1950s, they might not have had much but they certainly cared more about each other. Look at the politics in this country – anyone who says they are a socialist here is labelled a nutcase, simply for believing that people are more important than money! This country, honestly, it's like they think capitalism and the free market are the same thing!" said Werner.

"See, Dad, you've totally confused them now. Come on, kids, let's take the next subway exit, you can spend the money Granddad gave you. David, would you like an ice-cream?" asked Peter.

"YEAH, ICE-CREAM!" shouted Nadia and David.

"Oh, fine, use the kids to stop me from speaking my mind, typical!" said Werner.

The streets of New York were teeming with life that day, colours were coming from the crowd, the sun was setting through the buildings and just as the darkness of nightfall was creeping through the avenues, Werner felt Nadia's hand grasp his tightly. Gently she pulled him towards her so that her head could reach his ear.

"I love you, Grandpa," said Nadia.

Werner slightly squeezed Nadia's hand and gave her an assuring nod.

\* \* \*

"So, you still like the new house, Dad? I know it's not the Upper East Side, but you have such a great garden, the kids really do love it here," said Peter.

"I didn't think I would ever move, especially not to New Rochelle, but then again if you had asked me when I was a boy if I would end up in America, I would have told you, you were crazy. Life is a funny thing, Peter, one never knows where one will end up," said Werner.

"That's so true, Dad, when I look at the kids turning into teenagers it makes me wonder where the years have gone," said Peter.

"Here, Dad, let me help you with your jacket. When are you going to get rid of this thing anyway, you must have had it like ten years now," said Peter.

"Look, that is an original Gore-tex jacket, you know. It has breathable material," said Werner.

"I know, Dad, you have been telling me since 1985! Come on, let's get it off and then I can show you that thing I was telling you about on the computer. It's all the rage now, you know, they are calling it the internet and I told you they have this amazing site about World War Two," said Peter.

"I don't know, Peter, you know the saying, let sleeping dogs lie, and sometimes I think it is better to not go digging up the past," said Werner.

"But, Dad, it's for people like you, people who suffered during the war and lived to tell the tale. Think about it, you could be helping others by sharing your experiences," said Peter.

"I seriously doubt that anyone will be interested in anything I have to say," said Werner.

"Come on, Dad; please, just give it a go. What's the worst that can happen? Who knows where some quick enquires could lead to, maybe we could find out more about Mom's side of the family?"

"There will not be any information on your mother's family, that I can tell you. But if you are going to nag me all day then let's get this over with. Come on then, what do I do?"

After about 30 minutes of Peter hammering away at Werner's computer keyboard, he finally announced that Werner's post was created. It was on a site used mainly by people who had survived the Holocaust and wanted to share their stories. Werner was shocked to see so many people his age actively using the site. There were pictures of holding camps similar to the one Werner himself had been in. As he scrolled through the pictures the memories of his captivity came flooding back, then suddenly a picture stood out and made him freeze as if he had seen a ghost. It was Professor Bonn, standing next to a group of malnourished men, their bodies bent from hard labour and the faces lifeless.

"That fucking bastard! How could he do it, where was his humanity! I should have killed him when I had the chance!" shouted Werner.

"Dad, what are you talking about? Did you know him?"

"You don't know what people are capable of, Peter, when they are pushed into a situation where it is you or them. We enjoy the good life over here, but back then I saw people stab each other for an extra potato; I tell you, we humans are the worst of all God's creatures, we are capable of sinking to levels rats wouldn't go near."

"What did he do, Dad? Do you want to talk about it?"

"You must have heard about those Nazi doctors who conducted experiments on people during the war? Well, he was one of them; they all had fancy titles, Professor of Eugenics that kind of thing but they were all butchers. They killed people as if they were chimps in the lab. They were the incarnation of evil. You see, I can forgive the guards, some were sadistic and cruel, but basically, they were grunts who were often just following orders. Some, well one I got to know very well, didn't even want to be doing what they did; but the doctors and professors, those people I cannot forgive because they were educated men, who should have known better, but they believed in warped science, a science that promoted the division of human beings based on race as if there were ever a link between that and intelligence."

"I wonder who posted it, Dad; here, click on that little icon, it will tell you more about it."

As Werner followed Peter's instructions, he could see that the picture had been posted by Albert Oppenheimer, who was now also living in Tel Aviv, Israel. The picture's title was: 'Does anyone remember this man?' and the comments left below came from Jewish people all over the world; most were insults, but others noted that they had heard about Professor Bonn through other prisoners, prisoners who had endured his experimentations, and lived to tell of their experiences.

"This might be a bad idea, Peter, but I think I am going to email this Albert," said Werner.

# CHAPTER

## 12

RING, RING, RING, RING

"Hello, is that Albert?" asked Werner.

"Yes, is this Werner?" asked Albert.

"It is, oh it's so nice to hear from you in person, I was so glad when you sent me that message back from the website," said Werner.

"It really was nice to hear from you. So tell me, Werner, you said you knew the man in the photo?"

"Yes, it's Professor Bonn, he worked at the centre. How was it that you ended up with the photo?"

"Well, you see I was working as a health worker at the centre, well I say worked, but it was forced labour like everyone else, you know how it was. I was one of the last people to leave that place, and when the Russians came to liberate us, I just grabbed what was left in the desks of the offices. I remember just thinking, I need evidence, I need something to make sure people didn't forget about what happened here," said Albert.

"I'm so glad you did. Do you have any more photos? You see there were a few people in there that I knew, and I would like to know what happened to them."

"I have a whole box of them, I also have a few letters. I've tried to find most people and tried to match names, but honestly, it's a tough job. I've been at it for over forty years, it's only with the internet that I have in recent years been able to reach so many people."

"I would love to see them, it's just such a shame we are so far apart. You know, if it were not for those people and a couple of strokes of luck I wouldn't even be here."

"I bet you have a fascinating story, Werner; I would love to hear it. You know, this might sound a bit crazy but why don't you come here? You could stay with me and my wife Connie, we have a spare room."

"Oh no, I couldn't, Albert, it would be too much of an inconvenience and Israel is way too far to travel for an old man like me."

"Honestly, Werner, it's no trouble at all, and Connie, well, she's from Morocco so she loves entertaining, hospitality is a way of life for Moroccans, you know."

"I don't know, Albert, it's a lovely idea but are you sure it wouldn't inconvenience you?"

"I won't take no for an answer, it's settled. Bring those lovely grandkids you were telling me about if you want. You could make a holiday out of it. Tel Aviv is beautiful in summer, and you have to visit Jerusalem!"

"The holy city! I tell you what, Albert, let me speak to my son Peter and come back to you on that one. I have always wanted to go to Jerusalem," said Werner.

"You do that, Werner, and you get yourself over, we need to do this, we need to keep the past alive. I look forward to hearing from you again soon, my friend. Bye-bye for now," said Albert.

* * *

As Peter came through the wooden framed house, he walked through the sliding doors out to the garden patio.

"Hi Dad, I see the tomatoes are coming through," said Peter.

"They are indeed, Albert gave me some tips on how he grows his in Israel," said Werner.

"Oh, here we go again, Albert this and Albert that. You guys are going to have to get married one of these days," Peter said sarcastically.

"Sarcasm is the lowest form of wit, Peter, you know that."

"So how are things going with Albert, Dad? Are you guys still talking?" said Peter.

"Like you wouldn't believe, son, we chat almost every day now. It's actually great, I look forward to his calls. You know, he is originally from Ukraine, and he only ended up in the centre I was in because he was on business at the time in Germany. Imagine that, you go away on a business trip and as fate would have it, you end up in that awful place."

"Have you told him all about Hans and Jacob?"

"Yes, he knows all about them, we even talked about the bar we used to all visit. It's nice, you know, to swap these stories, it helps my mind remember old things tucked away in there."

"And what about Jenny, have you discussed her at all?"

"Why would you ask that? We never talk about her."

"You know, before it would bother me, Dad, you talking with such passion about another woman that wasn't Mum, but honestly now I think it would do you good to get it all off your chest."

"The truth is, Peter, I know you're right, but if I am honest with myself, I can't really remember what she looked like. I have this memory of her having thick black hair and this beautiful smile, but then I think to myself is this a real memory or one I have made up over the years from feelings, you know what I mean?"

"I get you, Dad, it's like one of those memories from childhood that you can't really remember whether they were real or not."

"Exactly. You know I loved your mother, I loved her with all my heart, it's just I never really got to know what happened to Jenny and I think that's why I still to this day think about her and what might have been."

"You need to go to see Albert, Dad, one way or another it will help, and what's the worst that could happen? You will go there, have some sun on the beach, swap stories, and have a few drinks. It sounds ok to me."

"I don't know, I really just don't know, what if it opens up old wounds?"

"It could, Dad, it could, but do you want to go through life knowing that you might have got answers, but you didn't take the chance to get them?"

"You're right, son, I should go. Where do you get all this wisdom from?"

"Chip off the old block, Dad," said Peter as he winked to his dad.

Sitting down in his dressing gown with his coffee Werner switched on his computer. It had been a few days since he had heard from Albert and he was a little worried that something might have happened. Thoughts of a violent attack or a road accident streamed through his mind, though he knew that this was probably not the case. Albert was probably just busy but why then hadn't he got in touch?

* * *

RING RING, RING RING

"Hello," said Peter.

"Peter, it's your dad, listen to this, I just got an email from Albert. Do you have five minutes? I want to read part of it to you."

"Sure, Dad, hang on a second. Nadia, watch out for that stove whilst I talk to Grandad," shouted Peter into the distance down the phone.

"No problem, Dad" Werner heard Nadia shout back through the phone.

"Go on then, Dad," said Peter.

"Ok so here it goes...." said Werner who preceded to read the email:

*Dear Werner,*

*Sorry for the loss of communication, as you can imagine it is rather manic around here during Yom Kippur, the people stay indoors; we go to the synagogue, starve ourselves and then as any good faster knows, stuff ourselves with great food and celebrate the passing.*

*It was a great time, I must say, the couple down the street had a little party to mark the passing of the festival. We had all the people from the neighbourhood turn up, all of us brought a cooked meal and some drinks. Then we went to the beach to celebrate into the night, this I liked. It's always nice to hear the sea, to see the children playing Matkot, it really does make me appreciate what is special in life.*

*I have been meaning to tell you I met a woman who was also from your region in Germany; she had just moved into our area and lives a few streets down from my house. She has such an interesting life story; you know how us old men are – we need to know everything about someone the moment we meet them!*

*Anyway, I digress, but it was interesting she had moved from Koln during the war to a rehabilitation centre, then to London where she had lived for 20 years before moving to Israel.*

*She was a little uptight at first, well you know how the English can be, anyway she was such a lovely woman, even in her old age I could tell she was a looker when she was younger, she also had a brilliant sense of humour, another thing I am sure she inherited from the Brits. I mean, no offence, but you Germans are not known for your funny bones now, are you.*

*Anyway, I wanted to ask you if you might have known any Jennys whilst you were at the centre? You see, she behaved very strangely, we were laughing and joking. I as you can imagine was telling longwinded stories and Connie was nagging me to get to the point when suddenly I mentioned I had a friend in New York named Werner Ritter who was also originally from Koln. Well it was crazy, she turned a pale white, went silent and very sheepish. Then she quietly said to Connie and me that she had to leave, put down her glass, and walked off down the beach. It was so bizarre.*

"Look, Peter, I don't have time to go into details, but I have made a decision. I am going to Israel tomorrow and I need you to come around and keep an eye on the house whilst I am away," said Werner.

"Israel, hang on a second, Dad, I know I said you should go but don't you think you should think this over a bit more, you usually plan for weeks!"

"Peter, listen to me, I cannot discuss everything right now, there is an El Al Airlines flight leaving tomorrow at 5pm, so do this for me, you understand? I don't have time to discuss everything, I just need you to be a good son right now and do as I ask!"

"Ok, ok Dad, you know I am here for you, just don't get too worked up about it all."

"Peter, I am fine, in fact right now I feel more alive than I have in years, just do as I ask, and I will be back home before you know it."

"Can I at least ask where you are going and how long you will be staying?"

"I will be staying with Albert and Connie in Tel Aviv, I can write the address down and leave it at my house for you, I will also leave their telephone number but I don't want you to get in touch unless there is an emergency. As for how long I will be staying, I am unsure. It could be a few days, it could be a week or so, I will call you and let you know once I know more."

"OK, Dad."

"You are a good boy, Peter and I love you for it, I will call you soon."

\* \* \*

Standing in Ben Gurion airport the first thing that struck Werner was the number of soldiers and people dressed in military light green uniforms wrapped in blue. As he slowly moved forward, he could see a young woman with bleach-blonde hair beckoning him forward.

"Ritter? Is that a German name?" said the young woman.

"Yes, it is," said Werner.

"I see and what were you father's and grandfather's names?" said the young woman.

"My father and grandfather?" asked Werner.

"Yes, and when did you leave Germany and move to America, sir?" said the young woman.

"I don't understand why it is important?" asked Werner.

"Sir, it would be helpful to us if you could just answer the questions; it's just airport security protocol," said the young woman.

"I don't really see what my parents' names have to do with security," said Werner. "I moved to the United Kingdom after the war and then eventually relocated to America, where I have lived all my life, is that good enough?"

"I see, and where in Israel will you be staying and be going?"

"I will be staying with my friend and his wife, and I will most probably just be visiting Tel Aviv and Jerusalem."

"I see. Write down their names and addresses on the entrance card and also your grandfather and father's names please."

Werner did as she asked.

"Ok, and will you be visiting East Jerusalem or anywhere in the Palestinian territories?" said the young woman.

"No, I won't, but I don't see what business it would be of yours anyway."

"Sir, we mean no offence; our questions are simply for security purposes; these are dangerous times for our nation, and it is my job to make sure I adhere to the strictest rules so that anybody meaning us any harm does not get in. You never know who can be trusted these days."

Werner stepped back from the counter and looked at the young lady addressing him. She was a young girl who must only have been in her twenties, wearing a green army military uniform, she looked like she was of eastern European descent.

"Look, young lady, I am a Jewish person who has the right to visit Israel, the land of my people; you can keep your questions and shove them! If you had been through what I had, you wouldn't be wasting an old man's time with such ridiculous questions."

"I'm sorry, sir, I didn't mean to offend; here we take very seriously the struggle our elders went through for us. I am just made to ask the same questions to everyone for security purposes; I know it can seem a bit much."

"Security hey, well, young lady I would like to tell you one of my favourite quotes, in that case, it's by Benjamin Franklin, I am sure you know who he is. He said: 'Any society that would give up a little liberty to gain a little security will deserve neither and lose both'. You have a think about that," said Werner.

"Here is your passport, sir, have a pleasant stay in Israel."

Driving from the airport Werner was mesmerised by the beauty of Israel, the trees that grow from the desert, the barren land of sand, and most of all the people. All different types, Arab, Jew, orthodox Jew, Europeans, Christians, it seemed like everyone from the world was heading to Jerusalem.

"There you go, sir, that will be 150 Shekels," said the taxi driver.

"Thank you and here, keep the change," said Werner.

"Thank you very much, sir, have a great stay in Tel Aviv, I hope you enjoy our country."

"I hope so too, my friend, I hope so too," said Werner.

Walking to the steps, the old white stone steps to Albert's door, Werner felt an uncomfortable feeling. As he took a moment to look over the street, he could see kids playing football against the large waste bins and a warm breeze on his face from the sea. He knew there was no turning back, not when he had come this far, and so, with a large gulp he knocked at the front door and waited for an answer.

The door was opened by an elderly lady with olive skin and an infectious smile that seemed to beckon Werner in.

"Oh my heavens, Werner, is that you?" asked Connie.

"It is, you must be Connie?" said Werner.

"I am indeed, come give me a hug."

Connie grabbed Werner tightly around the shoulders, her dress twinkling in the sun. She was wearing a traditional Moroccan outfit, made up of a long flowing skirt with a distinctly Arab looking pattern that flowed from half the skirt down around the rim, a traditional gold sash around her waist and open style top made up of a floral pattern. How beautiful, Werner thought.

"Albert, Albert, come and see who it is!" shouted Connie.

From out of nowhere a large man wearing cream cargo pants and a yellow polo shirt that was almost open completely apart from a few buttons, old grey chest hair bursting through where what should have been the top button. Albert grabbed Werner and gave him a huge hug, which almost knocked the wind from his lungs. Although the two men had never met, their embrace felt like two brothers who hadn't seen each other for years.

"Oh my, is that you, Werner? Please come on in," said Albert.

They all moved to the dining room of Albert and Connie's small apartment. It was a small place but one that Werner could immediately tell held a lot of love inside. There were pictures everywhere, most of the two of them on holiday. Some on the beach in Tel Aviv, others by Big Ben in London, and some that looked like with Connie's family in Marrakesh, but Werner couldn't be sure.

"Let me leave you boys to talk whilst I make up the spare bedroom, Werner. I must say this is a pleasant surprise; we have been longing for you to visit. I do hope you have brought some pictures of Nadia and David with you; Albert knows how much I like hearing about how they are getting on in school," said Connie.

"I have a couple in my wallet, here have a look," said Werner.

"Oh, aren't they both beautiful and that Nadia, boy will she be a looker when she becomes a woman. You know Peter will have to fight the boys off," said Connie.

"She is pretty, isn't she," said Werner.

"Now, Werner, tell me, why the rush? I thought you were going to come in November or next March? It's not that I and Connie don't want you here, we are just a little shocked that you came all this way unannounced and with no mention of it in your last email. That is another thing I wanted to ask you about, it was very cryptic – so do you know the woman I met?" said Albert.

"That, Albert, is why I am here, but please let's wait till Connie comes back. I want her to hear the whole story too, she must know as I don't want to keep you both in the dark any longer."

* * *

The group searched Albert's neighbourhood looking for Jenny. Connie went to Jenny's house but she wasn't there; a number of Connie's friends had seen her in the supermarket and on the street walking home, but this was before Werner had arrived in Tel Aviv. It was like she had vanished from the face of the earth.

After a week of searching, Werner was starting to lose hope, and both Albert and Connie could see it. He knew that he couldn't stay forever, there was only so much hospitality he could expect. It was time to make a decision, he thought, time to make plans to go back to his old life, and time to forget this pipe dream of ever seeing his mysterious Jenny again.

"Come on, Werner, keep your chin up, my friend, we will find her," said Albert.

"It's ok, Albert, I think we both know that I am not going to see Jenny again if indeed it was her in the first place," said Werner.

"What are you saying? That I invented her, that I made her up from the start? Why would I? I didn't even know about her before you came here and told me about her," said Albert.

"I am not saying that, I am merely saying that we are never going to find her. Look, I think I should just leave soon anyway, you and Connie have been great and I will never forget your support and hospitality, but I think we all need to face facts that even if the woman you met is the same Jenny I was married to in a previous life, she clearly isn't here anymore. I am going for a walk down the beachfront, I need some air," said Werner.

"Wait, I will come with you, let me just get my jacket," said Albert.

"No, I would rather you didn't. I just want to go by myself, to clear my head and think," said Werner.

Walking down the beach in Tel Aviv, Werner watched as the youngsters drank and smoked joints on the beach; there were faces from all over Europe on that beach he thought and people all talking in Hebrew, English, and other European languages, they all looked so happy and so content sat under their beach umbrellas and laid out on their sun loungers.

Seeing them all without a care in the world, Werner couldn't help but reflect upon his life, and his people. To have come from the ashes of Europe to being so free, it really was astonishing. The metal bars, guard runs, and barbed wire fences just seemed like a distant memory, one that he knew the Jewish people should never forget, but in a way, he wished they would for the future generation's sake. As he watched the young teenagers smoke cannabis, drink beers, and hang out at the many deli sandwich shops, he could feel himself thinking 'good on them', enjoying life the way it was supposed to be enjoyed. That, he thought, was what life was all about, enjoying the moments and remembering the ones that count. Just then he noticed the time – he had been walking for a good hour and knew he needed a rest. His legs had started to ache.

Werner noticed a young Ethiopian-looking waiter working in a cafe close to the beachfront. It seemed a good place to rest his bones and so he headed on over to grab a seat.

"What can I get for you, sir?" the man asked in Hebrew.

"I'm sorry, but my Hebrew is not very good, do you speak English?" said Werner.

"Ah, you are American, my apologies; of course, sir, now what can I get you?" said the waiter.

"I will have a coffee please, with milk and one sugar, oh, and also water; I think I will need it to get back home," said Werner.

"It looks like you've been out walking all day, hey, well good for you, it's always good to get a little exercise, never did anyone any harm, that's for sure. In fact, I dare say walking saved my life, well that and the government of Israel. Now, let me get you those drinks."

As a feeling of sadness washed over him he felt a feeling he hadn't felt for many years, it was one of remembrance, of something familiar like there was a great presence; he couldn't figure it out, what was it he was feeling right now, was it sadness because there was still so much inequality in the world and so much fighting for rights to still be done; was it a good feeling that whatever the problems that at least he now had a homeland; what was it, he thought, what was he feeling. Then he realised it was none of those things – it was a joy, a beauty, something so overwhelming he nearly missed it. His eyes scanned the coffee shop and before they even fixed in one place, he knew it was her.

Sitting in the corner of the shop was a woman reading a book, her hair white as snow, and her dress as red as the Chinese flag. As Werner stared at her she slowly lifted her head and turned towards him. Their eyes met and with one glance Werner knew that it was her, it was Jenny, her eyes just as dark and beautiful as ever.

Werner got up and walked slowly towards her in a transfixed state. As he did, he noticed she had put her book down and had started to rise also. When he got to her table he was shaking, he didn't know what to say to her. She then took him in her arms and embraced him with all the love and warmth he had felt all those many decades ago. She turned to him and kissed him slowly on the lips and whispered, "I've been waiting for you, my love."

# THE END

www.ingramcontent.com/pod-product-compliance
Lightning Source LLC
Chambersburg PA
CBHW020818260626
47169CB00003B/719